DRAGON'S PAWN

BY
CAROL L. DENNIS

POPULAR LIBRARY

An Imprint of Warner Books, Inc.

A Warner Communications Company

POPULAR LIBRARY EDITION

Copyright © 1987 by Carol L. Dennis
All rights reserved.

Popular Library® and Questar® are registered trademarks of
Warner Books, Inc.

Cover art by Janny Wurts

Popular Library books are published by
Warner Books, Inc.
666 Fifth Avenue
New York, N.Y. 10103

(W) A Warner Communications Company

Printed in the United States of America

First Printing: January, 1987

10 9 8 7 6 5 4 3 2 1

PROLOGUE

*T*HE Keepers met in the vast Hall of the Gate. Twelve pairs of concerned eyes watched Andronan, their silver-haired leader, his long-fingered hands resting quietly on the table before him. The ancient mage said, "We must act now, before it is too late."

Nods of agreement came from the group. The irrepressible Rory asked, "And what is it you'd be havin' us do?" The leprechaun had never lost his thick Irish brogue, although he had left Earth for the planet Realm centuries earlier.

"It is dangerous to use the gate," Librisald said, raising an admonitory finger, dust motes drifting to the stone floor from his gray robe. The Keepers turned their heads, startled to hear dissent from this source. The frail librarian peered from beneath his shaggy brows. He had spent so many hours poring over books in the university library that it was difficult for him to focus on anything more than a foot in front of his face.

"That is why I have called you together," Andronan said, drawing their attention by the tone of his voice. From a pocket in his deep blue robes he drew a black velvet box. It fit easily in the palm of his hand. Nevertheless, on seeing it the Keepers became more alert.

"You will open the box now?" Krom asked. The group had been summoned so hastily that he still wore his trader's trail garb instead of the Keepers' traditional robes. "The situation is that dangerous?"

"This box has remained closed for six hundred years. The time of peril to all Realm is now!" answered Andronan. The very curls on Andronan's head seemed charged with energy as he gently lifted the lid. Within, a circlet of metal in the shape of a dragon lay quiescent. "Wyrd," Andronan said gently.

As the Keepers gathered around to watch, one green eye opened lazily. The talisman had awakened.

"You have need of me?" The words echoed in the minds of the Keepers. "Ah, yesss," the sibilant thought touched each one. "You do."

"Rory," Andronan said, "you must be our messenger to Earth."

"Me," the leprechaun spluttered, "and why should I be goin'?"

"Because of your close—" Andronan's eyes twinkled as he continued soberly, "—ties with our alternate world." The leprechaun had made clandestine trips to Earth to sample the whiskey of his native Ireland on several occasions. Rory's quick glance at the mage told him Andronan knew of his forbidden jaunts, and the leprechaun's protests subsided immediately. "A fire wizard will send you easily. Wyrd will provide your destination." And with these words, Andronan handed the dragon bracelet to Rory. As soon as the bracelet touched Rory's hand, he disappeared.

The ancient mage smiled at the astounded Keepers. "The search for a hero begins!"

CHAPTER
One

*T*HE blaze in the stone fireplace glimmered, dimly lighting the main room of Jarl's comfortable cabin. A shower of sparks fell on the hearth with a loud pop. Minou, his yellow coon cat, bounded across the room away from the grate. "What ails you, cat?" he muttered. He stopped typing and rubbed the golden stubble of his beard. His bleary eyes scanned the room and he reached for his whiskey glass automatically.

"You could be a wee bit more hospitable."

Jarl put down his drink. He focused, not without difficulty, on the place from which the voice came. The foot-high figure of a man dressed all in brown jumped on his word processor. The creature wore a white owl's feather in his cap. Jarl's huge hand dwarfed the small being as he lazily batted it to one side in an inebriated gesture of negation.

"Demon damnation, it's drunk you must be! Didn't you hear me speak, Jarl Koenig?" the angry voice shrieked the last words as the tiny man stood upright and shook his minuscule fist in impotent fury.

"Bu—but you're not here. You're only a—a figment of

my imagination, so there's no need to pay any attention to you."

"Figment, indeed!" The little man drew himself up to his full height and puffed out his cheeks. "If it wasn't for the sheer waste, I'd upend that glass on your addled mortal noggin," he concluded with a screech as he slapped out a spark which left a scorched patch on his leathern britches. "Should have known better than to trust a thrice-bedamned fire wizard to send me anywhere on a quest," he grumbled.

Jarl raised his hand to cover the amused grin he couldn't repress.

"Well, are you going to stand there staring, man? Or will you be pouring poor Rory a drink? Unless these old nostrils deceive me, I smell real Irish whiskey." He smacked his lips at the thought.

"Some people see pink elephants. I've dreamed up a nutso vision this time, one of the little people, no less. A brownie with a Gaelic accent." Jarl smiled ruefully at his folly.

"I'm a perfectly good luchorpan," the small figure corrected him irascibly.

"Ha! Now I know I'm drunk! Leprechauns dress in green."

"My father was from over the water, and I dress like him. Make no mistake, even after being gone almost two thousand years, I'm still as Irish as Paddy's pig." The leprechaun rubbed his small hands together. "I'm glad to see you're not totally hopeless. Now pour me my whiskey," he demanded.

"What do you mean, not totally hopeless?" asked Jarl somewhat belligerently, holding the bottle behind his back.

"You recognized the old word for leprechaun, so you're not as ignorant as I expected you to be."

"My grandmother was from County Cork, and during much of my misspent youth I heard the old tales. Ah, beautiful queens and heroic deeds," said Jarl. He paused to consider aloud. "I'm talking to a little man who can't be here. I must be crazy as well as drunk." Jarl focused on his hallucinatory visitor.

"It's crazy you'll be driving me with your foolish, misbelieving ways." As he spoke, the wee manling jumped down on the top of the oaken desk and beckoned the man closer. When Jarl bent his blond head, Rory reached out quickly and punched him in the nose.

"Ouch!" Jarl jerked, spilling whiskey from the bottle he still held behind his back.

"Now do you believe I'm real?" Rory asked with a merry chuckle as he tipped his cap. "And you've spilled more whiskey than I could drink, so stop this foolishness and pour me a sip."

Jarl reached for his glass, intending to take a drink. "You surely seem to be here. I never heard of a tactile hallucination of one of the little people, so maybe you do exist." He gently touched his throbbing nose.

"Toadstools spare me from a thick-headed lackwit! What will it take to convince you?" The leprechaun hopped up and down, venting his frustration. He reminded Jarl of Rumpelstiltskin.

"Oh, tomorrow when I wake up, no leprechaun. Then I'll know I dreamed this whole conversation."

"You certainly don't look like very promising material to me. Give me a drink, man. Talking to mortals is thirsty business."

Jarl picked up the top of the whiskey bottle. He filled the cap to the brim and solemnly held it out between his thumb and forefinger. His guest took the proffered refreshment with alacrity, tipped the cap, and drained it. Then, without saying a word, he offered it to his host. Jarl refilled it a second, and then a third time.

"Ah, that was a potation to remember." He exhaled happily and rubbed his red-bearded chin. "Now I'd best be getting to the real purpose of my visit."

"Real purpush?" Jarl had matched his visitor drink for drink.

"Boyo, there's a job you must be doing."

"Job? I've got one already. This computer program is due in three weeks and I'm only two-thirds finished." Jarl pointed to the printout. Small, sooty footprints decorated the first sheet.

"Humankind is in a bad way. If you won't accept the challenge, your world may well be doomed."

"Okay, I'll play. Tell me your story." The alcohol in Jarl's system made him expansively affable.

"To start at the beginning would take too long, but I'll give you some background so you can understand." Rory peered into Jarl's flushed face. "You are still capable of listening to me, aren't you?"

Jarl managed a careful and deliberate nod.

"Years ago the little people disappeared. Magical creatures went through a gate between two alternate universes because there were more men and fewer of us each century. Men became increasingly logical. Logic! Fine thing! Tell logic to bring joy to the heart or a laugh to the lips. It was a poor exchange, if you ask me."

"I thought Christianity drove you away."

"Priestly propaganda said so, but the real reason we left was the development of science. Magic and technology don't mix. Mortal man made a poor choice when he decided to accept science."

"Well, the world is more technologically oriented now than when you left, so why are you here making footprints on my papers?"

"That's a good question. Don't think I asked for this job. When my name came up before the Council—but that's neither here nor there. Don't rush me. Impatience was always a mortal failing." He eyed the whiskey bottle hopefully, but Jarl didn't seem to notice. "Through our magic we were able to transport ourselves to another place—I suppose your scientists would call it an alternate universe." He spoke with disdain. "Science! The very word dirties my mouth." He cocked his head to one side. "You wouldn't consider giving a poor thirsty fellow another wee drink, would you?"

Jarl slowly unscrewed the top of the bottle. The effort of coordinating his brain and hand was almost too difficult a task.

"Your mystics would probably call it another plane, but whatever you choose to name the place, Realm exists."

"Realm? What's that?"

"Has all the whiskey you've been sipping gone to your head? Realm, I said," Rory repeated in exasperation.

"If you've moved off Earth, what brings your return?"

"Because we lived here so long, there are affinities or bonds between us and you. And frankly, we're finding it difficult to live with the evil creatures the human race keeps creating."

"We're creating evil creatures?" Jarl shook his head to clear it. He knew the next day he would have the father of all hangovers, but this really was some hallucination he'd dreamed up this time. "How?"

"By creating them in your thoughts."

"You mean we're manufacturing them in our minds?"

"Exactly! Now you're getting the idea." Rory nodded his satisfaction.

"Mankind has always dreamed and created," Jarl said, rubbing his hand across his eyes in a tired gesture.

"Now too many of you read books and see movies with horrible monsters. If humans believe, even temporarily, in a blood-drenched wizard, he becomes real in our world. We normal magical folk don't like your monsters."

Jarl's laugh drew a frown from Rory. "Preposterous!" Jarl said.

"You may well laugh. Before you're through, mortal fool, you won't think what I've told you is so humorous."

Jarl recognized that the leprechaun was quite serious. "If we believe in fairies, they exist?" he murmured incredulously. "James Barrie used that idea in his story of Peter Pan, but adults don't believe it."

"You'd better start believing," the unsmiling Rory told him in a grave little voice. He seated himself on a stack of books on the desk corner.

"You're actually serious? In your world the products of human minds are real?"

"Indeed, they are."

"I'm sorry to hear it, but why are you telling me about it? I don't write wild fantasy stories."

"When the time is right, you'll know. The talisman will take you when you're needed." Rory grinned. He flickered with the firelight and disappeared. The confused and drunken man seated alone in the room blinked.

Jarl shook his head in a vain effort to clear it. "Minou, you've got to remind me not to stare at the fire too long. What an imagination I've got. I'm wasted on nonfiction. Maybe I should try my hand at some of this fantasy stuff after all." At this point he noticed the cat curled up sound asleep. He ended his monologue and went unsteadily to bed.

The next morning Jarl stretched sleepily as the golden tracery of sunlight shot through the branches of the trees that surrounded his cabin. The cottony feeling in his mouth and the anvil chorus playing full tilt in his throbbing head signaled a class-one hangover.

Carefully holding his head so it wouldn't fall off and shatter, he plodded stolidly into the bathroom. He turned on the shower and he tested the water with his hand.

Firmly clasped around his right wrist was a bracelet in the form of a dragon. "Lord, where was I last night? I can't remember buying this," he said sleepily. The multifaceted gold crystals that formed the eyes of the metallic creature drew his attention like a magnet.

"Now where the devil did I get this?" he pondered aloud. The bracelet refused to slip from his wrist; he could find no clasp to release.

Deciding he needed his shower, he took it, bracelet notwithstanding. The scales shed water. For a moment in the steamy stall he could have sworn the eyelids of the dragon drooped with languorous pleasure. He told himself the idea was ridiculous.

After dressing, he decided to forgo the doubtful pleasures of a breakfast his stomach might not be able to keep down. He noticed the whiskey bottle was almost empty. "No wonder I'm hung over this morning," he muttered. He tipped the scant remainder in his glass and tossed it back as if he were in need of the pick-me-up. Which he was.

His blurry eyes roamed the room. In mute testimony, small sooty footprints marched across the top sheet of paper on his desk.

CHAPTER
Two

J ARL slowly lowered himself into his chair, trying to orient the sight of the elfin footprints with a reality he could understand. The bracelet seemed warm, and tighter. It curled around his arm and he imagined he could feel a faint pulse from the metal body. The dragon's eyes were so green! He lifted the bracelet closer to his face so he could see the lifelike details. The whole thing was a work of art, especially the emerald chips that formed the eyes. As he watched, they seemed to grow larger and larger, holding his gaze in spite of his will.

He raised his shocked face to look at where he was. What happened to his comfortable armchair? He felt the rough wood of a fallen tree under him. The bracelet was once again an inanimate piece of metal, but Jarl had the strangest notion. He could have sworn the transformation caught the left eyelid of the dragon in midwink. He had to be in his home. There was no logical way he could have moved outside into the woods around his home. Could he be hallucinating? The fallen tree he sat on seemed rcal enough. He reached out his hand to touch the green grass that grew before him. It felt like grass. It looked like grass. He pulled a piece, placing it in his mouth. It tasted like grass, too. A bird flew across the clearing before him. It ruffled its bright green feathers and sang a few notes. Jarl thought he recognized the opening bars of "The Wearing of the Green." He could have been dreaming except there was none of the wispy feeling of unreality a dream produced when you looked at it in detail.

The forest of oak and ash trees spread away in all directions. The small glade in which he sat seemed to be the only open space for miles. Far overhead, lacy white clouds decorated a teal-blue sky in which nothing moved. Under other circumstances he would have enjoyed the quiet isolation of his position.

In the center of the open space he saw a raised mound covered with bracken. He rose rather gingerly and rubbed his sore behind. Thank heaven, he thought, his hangover had disappeared. Almost like magic, he decided wryly. The rough bark felt permanently etched into his carcass. His corded brown work pants had provided him little protection.

When he approached the mound, he noticed that some small animal had been digging into its side. The sunlight reflected from a shiny object that sparkled in the loose dirt. His hand parted the vegetation cautiously.

"That's funny. It looks like a handle," he murmured to himself. Grasping it firmly, he tested his strength as he pulled it fully into the light. It was a sword.

Vaguely he got the impression of great age, even though the weapon shined brightly and seemed as sharp as new. He raised the sword and swung it in the air experimentally. The jeweled hilt fit his hand perfectly and grew more familiar with each swing. Every swish called a different note from the air. The sounds almost formed a musical pattern. "Like music," he said aloud.

"Stop, thief!" a nasty little voice shouted.

Jarl looked in the direction of the sound and saw a strange creature. Its yellow catlike eyes glittered evilly, and its pointed nose resembled the beak of a bird. Spindly legs held it partially erect. Between them he saw a scrawny tail projecting. Its clawed, four-fingered hand pulled distractedly at the patches of long, ragged fur that stood out over its head. Two tufts of fur looked as if they might cover pointed ears.

"I wasn't going anywhere," Jarl answered the weird apparition. His voice was calm despite his surprise and uneasiness at being transported to the glade so rapidly.

"Steal from a spriggan's treasure mound, will you!" The voice grew louder and more booming with every word as the creature inflated itself into gigantic proportions.

Jarl shaded his eyes with one hand as he looked sunward, for the head of the spriggan now towered over the surrounding trees. This had to be a dream!

"I wasn't stealing anything. If folklore is anything to trust, isn't it the spriggans who take things that don't belong to them?" Jarl refused to be intimidated by the huge form.

"That's a lie! It's a mortal lie! Only a thieving human would say a thing like that!" The spriggan's tremendous arm shook in the air as his finger emphasized every angry word.

At this point Jarl was more astounded than frightened, and his answer angered the creature further.

"Call me a thief, do you?" It tee-heed grotesquely. "So, I'll steal something of yours!"

Suddenly Jarl was looking up into his own face.

"This is a lovely body that I've got now."

To Jarl's horror, the words were coming from the mouth of the man-shape the spriggan was inhabiting. Jarl decided to sit down but came to an abrupt halt when he realized his tail made sitting awkward. His tail? The wicked sprite had stolen Jarl's body.

Busy flexing its new muscles and bending its new legs, the Jarl-creature laughed. Jarl in the spriggan's shape struggled to wield the shining sword.

"Dullard, are you?" Jarl-creature said in the man's voice. "Turn my own treasure on me, would you?" it questioned dourly. With a wave of Jarl's hand, it conjured a whirlwind.

The whirlwind spun around Jarl's spriggan body and carried it away in a cloud of leaves and dusty sand.

Dusty sand? In a forest? Jarl thought as he opened the slitted eyes he had automatically closed to protect his sight. When he felt the wind abate, he dropped a foot into soft yellow sand. Blinking his eyes, he tried to adjust to the bright light. The trees had disappeared. Not even cactus grew in the arid region where Jarl found himself. He stood next to an outcrop of rocks that looked as if some giant had dropped his blocks and gone to play elsewhere. The hot, dry wind sucked the moisture from his body. The heat from the sand struck at him like a blow. Even the rocks denied him shade, for the sun was directly overhead.

"Shades of L. Frank Baum, I'm in a desert. All this crazy dream needs now is a yellow brick road."

"Spriggan, you are out of your place and time," a cool voice told Jarl.

"I'm no spriggan," he replied. Jarl looked for the source of the sounds he heard inside his head. He wanted to wake up. The body he inhabited was ill kept and sandy. The hot sand burned his feet.

"Not?"

"No, not!" Jarl told the invisible speaker in angry tones. His new voice sounded petulant. "Where are you?" he demanded.

"Right here," the voice chuckled. A fennec, or desert fox, daintily stepped from behind a rock. At least it looked like the pictures of fennecs Jarl had seen once in a nature magazine. It had the typical large pricked ears and foxy brush.

"Small one, is there any way out of this desert?" Jarl addressed his companion politely. Courtesy never hurt anyone. If he wasn't dreaming this wild adventure, he just might need all the friends he could make, he reasoned silently to himself. After all, it wasn't in every dream that you met a talking fennec. In fact, he'd never actually seen one, not even in a zoo on his world. His world? Where was he? He knew with certainty he was not on Earth. If this wasn't a dream, what was happening to him?

Green eyes sparkled mischievously into his as the fennec replied, "Who's calling who 'small one'? You're just my size, you know."

"Sorry." Jarl made his spriggan's voice sound suitably repentant. It would be folly to lose contact with the only living being he could see in this Sheol of heat, sun, sand, and rock.

"What do you want me to call you?"

"Call me—" the fennec paused as if considering, "—Mirza."

Jarl's first instinct was to give his name. The fennec's pause reminded him of the old superstition that said knowing a person's name granted power over the person.

As if sensing his dilemma, Mirza said, "I already know your name. Jarl Koenig, I need your aid."

"How can I help you?" Since he was obviously out of his mind, he might as well play along, he decided.

"You wear the Dragon's Wyrd, a powerful talisman. Use it to free me."

For the first time he noticed the silver chain that circled her neck. It was fastened to an oddly carved metal ring, that vanished into the stone of the entrance to the cave behind her. He looked down at his scrawny arm, noticing the bracelet curled tightly around it. "I'd do it if I could, but—"

The small dust devils that whirled over the sand in the distance coalesced into the form of a djinn. The djinn approached with malevolent rapidity, growing larger as it came. Jarl just stared.

"It figures. All the trappings of an *Arabian Nights* tale. My subconscious has a lot to answer for. The next time I decide to drink with a leprechaun, I'm sticking to lemonade," Jarl said ruefully, forgetting about the fennec at his side.

The djinn stood before them, his humanoid body clad in baggy harem pants. The six pointed horns on his head gleamed exactly like his mammoth yellow teeth, which were visible in his cavernous mouth. He laughed down at them.

"He is Caschcasch," the fennec whispered inside Jarl's skull.

The djinn's voice boomed, "Ho, ho, little shape shifter. So you plan to escape me?"

Jarl wondered if all the evil in this adventure was going to come in giant economy size. How did this genie know the spriggan had swapped forms with him?

The gigantic hand of the genie reached out, first finger extended. Jarl just had time to wonder what a djinn did with such long, curved fingernails when a bolt of magic flashed at him. In his haste to duck, he threw up his spriggan arm on which the dragon bracelet glittered. It acted like a magnet, attracting the bolt to itself. The bolt reversed its direction to blast the djinn who sent it. An earsplitting crack reverberated from the surrounding rocks.

CHAPTER
Three

"*N*EATLY done, Jarl," the fennec commented.

"What was?" he asked.

"Destroying the power of our oversized host and regaining your own form. You're a very handsome man."

Suddenly he was aware that the little beast was female. Her feminine remark had clinched the vague suspicions he harbored. Professional heroes got to rescue beautiful princesses, but he had saved a fox. Well, he supposed one had to start in the hero business somewhere. He could sense Mirza's amusement. She "spoke" directly into his mind. Did that mean she could read his thoughts?

"It takes great power to break a changeling spell. The dragon channeled power into your change and returned the excess to the djinn," she explained kindly. "It will be centuries before he regains his full powers. In the meantime we can return to Realm."

"Realm?" he questioned.

The small auburn-haired animal ignored his query. She

stepped lightly over the sand and commanded, "Pick me up and hold me."

As Jarl reached down to comply, he briefly considered the events of the last few minutes. Or was it hours? In this setting, time had no meaning. He suffered from concept overload. Nothing made much sense to him.

"The Keepers approve, Dragon's Pawn." She touched noses with him gently. "Let us go."

Shaken out of his reverie by her last remark and the cool moistness of her nose against his, he felt the clean warmth of her fur. Her nose reached out gently to nudge his chin. The gesture was strangely erotic. He received sensations like those of holding a beautiful woman in his arms, but he was becoming too shockproof to worry. He slipped his hand over the front of the fennec's chest to hold it more firmly, preparatory to walking out into the desert sands. He promptly received a bitten finger for his pains. Clearly there were definite rules for holding fennecs.

"Visualize where you want to go," she told him sharply, "back to the spriggan's mound." Seeing his incomprehension, she added, "Look at the dragon, Jarl."

The eyes of the mythological beast, which were golden at first, gradually turned to green. The color expanded until the whole universe shone emerald. Then there was a wrench and a moment of vertigo. Jarl and Mirza stood in the glade of the spriggan.

"Take the sword! Quickly!" Mirza told him. It lay where he dropped it when the wind whirled him away.

"It's not mine. The spriggan said it belonged to him."

"Nonsense! He stole it from a hero's tomb centuries ago. As Dragon's Pawn, you'll have need of it. Take it and we'll go." Here the fennec nodded in a northern direction, where a faint path through the trees began.

"Who's stealing my sword?" a familiar voice questioned.

At once Mirza leaped from Jarl's arms. "The Dragon's Pawn, you fool. Stand at your peril," she warned, teeth flashing.

The spriggan stopped in midhop. "My lady—a thousand pardons," it whined.

"No more tricks, or we'll turn another scale to gold by destroying you."

In an eye blink the spriggan disappeared into his hill, leaving a clear path for Jarl and his new friend. Jarl picked up the abandoned sword. "I thought scales weighed gold, Mirza," he said.

"Not that kind of scales. Dragon's scales," she told him patiently.

He glanced around the glade. "What dragon?"

"The one on your arm. You have only to look carefully to see the change." She sounded exasperated.

"If it's all the same to you, I'd just as soon skip looking at the bracelet. That's how I got myself into this m—" Prudence stopped him from completing his statement. "Realm," he corrected himself, remembering his conversation of the night before.

Mirza cast him a look over her shoulder, pink tongue lolling as if in a grin. Did she know what he had almost said?

The dragon wristband gleamed bronze, all except for its tail, which was now formed of two golden scales.

"Follow me," Mirza commanded. She led the way along the narrow path that wound through the silent forest of giant trees.

The dim green light filtered through the thick, leafy branches overhead. The brightest object Jarl could see was the ruddy glow of the fennec's lustrous red pelt. Jarl remembered a girl he had once dated with hair of the same shade. He found himself thinking what a beautiful woman the fox would make if the spriggan used his shape-shifting magic on her. After an hour of following at the steady pace which Mirza set with little apparent effort, Jarl ventured to speak.

"Where are we going?"

"North."

"Are you fennecs all so short-spoken?"

"Usually we prefer not to speak at all."

"Well, I'd like some answers and I'd like them now."

The fennec turned and sat in the middle of the path with her tail curled neatly around her paws. Her amusement was evident.

"Where are we?"

"On Realm, an alternate Earth. Realm is Earth as it might be had man followed magic instead of science."

"How was I brought here?"

"Curiosity is not a virtue here, Dragon's Pawn. Remember the cat in the adage and what curiosity did to it."

"But—" he began, and then glanced down at the bracelet on his wrist. A tingle passed along his arm. The eyes of the beast glittered with life, greenly beckoning. With a wrench Jarl recognized the vertigo which was becoming all too familiar. When his stomach settled, he saw the dragon had transported him again.

He stood at a fork in the path. There was no sign of the fennec. Momentarily stunned by his rapid transition, he looked blankly at his two choices. The left branch seemed inviting, broader and well traveled. The right path led deeper into the forest. He felt a slight movement on his arm, but he carefully refrained from looking at the bracelet. Being jerked hither and yon as if he had no will of his own annoyed Jarl. He was deliberately being deprived of information. He turned his face to the left, preparatory to taking the first step down the path. The metal around his wrist constricted painfully.

"All right," he grumbled, taking the pointed hint. He clasped the hilt of the sword firmly as he set forth. The sword was an extension of his arm. He realized that sooner or later he would need a scabbard. Traveling around with an unsheathed sword in hand asked for trouble. He felt he had all the problems he needed without any additions.

As he stepped confidently on the right-hand trail, abandoning what looked like a road to civilization, the other path disappeared.

The afternoon had advanced to dusk when Jarl and the fennec arrived in the spriggan's glade. Now the shadows the trees threw across the trail grew longer, like the reaching fingers of the night they presaged. Already the warmth of the afternoon was sliding into the cool of evening.

Jarl forced his footsteps to a faster pace. All roads eventually arrived somewhere; accordingly, the sooner he got to the end of this one, the faster he would find shelter for the night.

The vacant sensation in his midsection predicted correctly the hunger he expected. The distance between his backbone and his navel seemed like a mile. First he missed breakfast and now a nonexistent evening meal. He began to think of all the things he wished he had to eat.

An errant breeze frolicked across the air before him, carrying an odor redolent of spices.

"Apple pie!" Jarl's nostrils twitched at the scent, which overpowered the piny smell of this part of the forest. He was so hungry he thought he was imagining the scent of pie. Then he turned a sharp bend and saw a croft in a small glade beside the path.

The shutters on the small window to the left of the wood door were open. On the sill sat the pie Jarl had scented from the woods.

Flat stones were set with no small effort to make a walk to the door. Multicolored flowers crowded together on each side of him as he approached. Little mists of steam rose from the still-hot vents in the nicely browned top of the pie. His wallet was on his dresser at home, and the few coins he had in his pants pocket probably wouldn't be any good here. He raised his hand to knock when the door opened from within.

"Come in," the wizened granny said, her alert black eyes snapping.

In spite of himself, Jarl smiled. She was exactly what one might expect to find in a small out-of-the-way cottage like this. There was a storybook atmosphere heightened by the fire merrily crackling in the grate and the caldron bubbling over the flames. The contented tabby drowsing on the hearth completed the setting. The coziness of the room reached out and enfolded him. He felt immediately at home.

"Sit," his hostess commanded. She ladled fragrant stew from the pot over the fire. She set a full dish before him.

"You act as if you expected me," Jarl said after a brief thank-you. The stew was delicious.

"Eat first, then we shall talk." She put hunks of fresh bread and cheese on the table.

Then she retreated to the corner of the room and began to spin. The soft whirr-whirr of the wheel made a quiet accompaniment to the hearty meal Jarl ate. Before the huge bowl was empty, the silent old woman added a generous wedge of the pie to the food before him. She pointed to the caldron, indicating that he might have more stew if he wished.

When Jarl finally finished, he pushed the bench back from the table. "Thank you," he said to the little old woman, who now rocked with the cat on her lap.

"You're welcome," she said quietly, eyes intent on what she was doing in the flickering light.

"Can you tell me where the road past your cottage goes?" Jarl broke the companionable silence.

"In the morning"—the old woman smiled warmly at him—"you'll be able to see the hill behind the house. When you get to the top of that hill, you'll see your destination in the next valley."

Her cryptic words mildly annoyed Jarl. Nobody in Realm answered his questions. When someone was ready to shed a little light on his situation, like Mirza, the crazy wrist shackle that he refused to look at zapped him off somewhere.

"Have you no other questions for me?" She cocked her head like an inquisitive sparrow.

"You weren't surprised when I arrived at your door," he said.

"That's right." She raised her eyebrows and waited for his next words.

"Why?"

A cheery peal of laughter was his answer. "My dear boy, why do you suppose a little old lady lives alone in the woods? Don't you remember the fairy tales from your youth —or don't they tell them on Earth anymore?"

For the present Jarl overlooked her knowing where he came from. "You mean you're a—a—" He floundered. He couldn't bring himself to say the word.

"Witch?" she concluded for him. "What a lovely compliment! You may consider me to be a wise woman instead of a witch if that makes you feel any more comfortable."

"How can I return to Earth?" If she knew where he came from, presumably she also knew how he could get home again.

"I'm not wise enough to answer that for you. A little way into the future I can see, but past that—" She shook her head ruefully. "Too much depends on the choices you make."

"Spriggans, djinns, talking fennecs . . . I can't make any sense out of what's happening to me," he told her. He ran his hand over the flat of the exposed blade of the sword he held balanced across his knees.

The old woman took note of the sword for the first time. "I have a gift for you," she said.

"A gift?" Jarl repeated, showing his incomprehension.

"Open the box in the corner." She gestured. "The scabbard is yours."

Jarl took the scabbard from the box. "Thanks," he said, sheathing the sword for the first time since he had taken it from the spriggan's mound. The belt fit him perfectly, but he unbuckled it when he found wearing it made sitting difficult. He laid it on the bench beside him and waited for what his hostess had to tell him.

"Now, let's see," the old woman muttered softly to herself. "Have we all the ingredients? Hero, magic talisman, weapon, fair maiden, and villains in plenty. . . ." Suddenly raising her voice, she said, "Ah, I know what's missing! You need to know the prophecy!"

"What prophecy?" Jarl burst out. "And what about that fair-maiden bit—"

"Shush now. How does it go . . ." She rocked silently for a time.

"How can you know a prophecy about me?" he questioned, hoping to speed her mental processes. He impatiently waited for her to continue.

She began to recite:

> "Balance good with evil's stain
> Lest dark wizard's powers reign.
> Every hap shall come aright
> When Dragon's Pawn is Keeper's Knight.
> Let in tiny sparks of day,
> Free those who are wizard's prey,
> Web of universe shine bright,
> Turn the Darkness into Light."

"But, but—" Jarl stammered, not helped at all by the rhyme.

"You're the Dragon's Pawn, Jarl," she told him seriously. "A riddle-prophecy does no one any good unless he solves it himself." Then taking pity on his bewilderment, she added, "I can only tell you this. The shortest way through is often the longest way around."

"I don't think I like being anyone's pawn," he began. "That's not exactly what I'd call a big help," he told her, forgetting for a moment that she was no ordinary woman.

"When you do the right thing, you'll know," she promised.

"How?"

"By watching the dragon." She pointed to his wristband.

"Every time I look at the darn thing, I get zapped from one place to another," he complained.

"The talisman will act on its own if you don't give it direction. Concentrate on what you need and see if the dragon can't provide it," she suggested.

"Can it take me home?"

"Not immediately; you have been summoned for a purpose."

"Will it tell me when I do the right things to get home?"

"You need only to look. You earn the dragon's scales through correct decisions and virtuous acts. There are three golden scales now. They mark three correct decisions on your part."

"What decisions?"

"Gaining the sword, rescuing Mirza by vanquishing the djinn, and choosing the way to my cottage. They were all correct choices. Each one changed a scale to gold."

"So I keep choosing, and bit by bit, if I'm lucky, the dragon turns to gold. Then what happens?" he asked. He had a curious feeling. It was almost as if he were a contestant in some kind of game show. Things just didn't seem real. They couldn't be—could they?

"Then you'll be Dragon's Pawn no longer," she concluded on a note of satisfaction.

"And—"

"Then you'll not need me to tell you the answer to the riddle. You'll know yourself."

Later, as Jarl settled himself on the comfortable pallet in the loft above the cottage, he tried to make sense of what had happened to him. He still had more questions than answers, but tomorrow was time enough to find out about the powers of his bracelet. He gave his wrist an absentminded pat. A sense of warmth and approval came from what so short a time ago had seemed only a piece of inanimate metal.

CHAPTER
Four

J*ARL* woke to the smell of frying bacon. "She must be a
witch, all right," he muttered to himself. Running his
hand over the golden stubble on his chin, he decided he
could let his beard grow. Electricity was one of the scientific
comforts that he had left behind him, along with his razor.

"The smell of bacon is one of the few things that can get
me up in a hurry in the morning," he called down to his
unseen hostess. He stretched luxuriously before throwing the
quilt aside and springing to his feet. He picked up his cow-
boy boots, smiling to himself at the incongruity of a hero in
a fairy-tale realm wearing a Texan's hallmark. This was the
only place where things were bigger—and stranger—than
the Lone Star State. As he started to walk to the ladder that
led to the lower floor, the bracelet gave a warning twitch.

"What the—" Jarl said, wondering why the dragon was
active for no reason he could understand. Well, perhaps that
wasn't correct. What was the coiled talisman trying to tell
him? He glanced down without thinking, as if the sight of
the dragon could give him the answer to his question. And
somehow it did. He returned to his pallet on the floor of the

loft and neatly folded the quilt over the top of the crude mattress. He looked at the bracelet and said, "Okay now?"

He descended with no further movement from the dragon. Who ever heard of a tidy talisman? He had taken it for granted that the shape on his arm belonged to a masculine creature. If he was going to start doing things like making his bed neatly every morning in approved Boy Scout fashion, he might begin to believe his bracelet was female. At the conclusion of his thoughts, he jumped involuntarily as the tail of the dragon gave him a sharp slap on the wrist. It felt like the rubber bands he and his friends had snapped each other with when they were children.

He stood dumbfounded in the middle of the cottage floor downstairs. The dragon's movement hadn't bothered him. Perhaps he was finally getting used to this place. After all, last night's witch seemed to be a kindly old granny in the morning's light. The old lady chuckled. He looked at her with one eyebrow raised in inquiry.

"How else is the dragon to get into communication with you? Oh, Jarl?" she laughed. "The problems you face. May you always surmount them as you have this morning," she added in a more serious vein. "Come eat," she urged.

He obeyed quickly, for the table had dishes that appealed both to his eyes and his nose. Eggs, bacon, crusty bread, fresh butter, and tall glasses of cider to wash it all down sat on the table. He alternated honey and pink jam on his bread slices, unable to decide which he preferred.

"Would you like to join me? I'm having a hot cup of tea," she said.

"I usually drink coffee for breakfast, but I'll try a cup." The bracelet twitched uneasily. "Please," he finished.

The witch's amusement showed in her smile, which she made no attempt to hide. "Poor man, bitten by the fennec he befriended. Then chastised by his talisman," she said in a tone that told him she didn't really pity him at all.

"How the dev—" He corrected himself at once: "—dickens did you know about that?"

"Secrets of the trade, my boy. Secrets of the trade."

He looked into his cup and noticed that his tea was pink. "Pink tea?" he asked. He had never tasted anything like it before.

"Coralberry. You liked the jam I made from it," she told him with satisfaction.

"It was delicious."

"There are many plants here that no longer survive on Earth." She rose from the table and bustled over to a small box on the mantel above the fireplace. "Here, keep this in your pocket." With these words she handed him a sprig of vivid green. It had a clean, fresh scent that he did not recognize.

"What's this?"

"Moley," she answered.

"Holy moley!" he said half jokingly.

"Yes, indeed, it wards off enchantments and sweetens the air."

"Thanks," he told her, peering at it closely. "The last fellow on Earth who used this was Odysseus," he mused.

"Right!" she told him delightedly as she cleared the table. "It is always scarce, and unicorns cannot resist it. Fortunately, it was so rare that men didn't discover it and use it to hunt the unicorns to extinction."

He gulped. "Are there unicorns here?"

"Naturally," she punned, seeing his lips curve at her little joke.

"Will I see any?" He stopped himself abruptly. He was asking questions like an ignorant teenager instead of a full-grown man. He didn't like feeling childish.

"Perhaps sooner than you think," she told him cryptically. Then, changing the subject, she said, "Now it's time for you to chop a little kindling for me. The logs are out behind the cottage. Split enough to fill the woodbox over there in the corner."

"I'll be glad to," Jarl answered, feeling it was the least he could do. He really liked his weird hostess. He wondered if her witchly powers told her things like that. He willingly chopped away at the mammoth pile of logs with the ax he found stuck in the chopping block. Women weren't so different here after all. No man would have let a good ax stand out in the weather. He split the wood neatly and piled it in the box inside the house. When he turned to put the last pile in the diminutive wheelbarrow, he saw a unicorn come out of the woods.

He stood there gawking at the beautiful animal, afraid to move. One of the pieces of wood fell from the top of his sagging load and hit him sharply on the toe, breaking the spell.

"Ouch!" he said, carefully placing the wood down so he could wheel it in and add it to the pile. He was sure his movement would frighten the creature away. He remembered enough of his mythology to know how shy unicorns were. To his surprise, the unicorn approached until it was only a few feet away.

Moving slowly, he wiped his hands on his pants. He thought the unicorn scented the moley in his jacket pocket. Reaching out to stroke the glossy neck, he settled the long silvery mane all on one side. Then he saw a frayed rope around the beast's neck. He severed it with his pocket knife, saying, "There you are, beautiful."

"Thank you," the unicorn thought inside Jarl's head.

The thought reminded him of the telepathic conversations with Mirza. He missed the little devil. She had made a good companion. The unicorn nudged him gently. Her horn was quite short, nothing like the length he expected from old tapestry renditions and pictures of unicorns that survived on Earth.

"I'm a female," she thought. "There is no necessity for me to have a long horn. Only males need to use them in the mock battles at mating time," she told him, answering the question he hadn't even voiced.

Jarl felt a little nervous. Did everybody here know his name—or were they all reading his mind? He didn't care much for that idea.

"It's Wyrd," she said gently.

"Yeah. It sure is weird," he told her, surprised when a

feminine giggle tickled his mind. A giggling unicorn? This whole experience had to be real. In his wildest dreams he couldn't have envisioned a mirthful unicorn—but here she was.

"Jarl, the name of your bracelet is Wyrd. Not weird-strange. Wyrd-fateful," she explained.

Light dawned. "Oh, I understand. W-Y-R-D," he spelled. He did not see anything incongruous in spelling a word to prove to a unicorn he knew what she meant.

"You felt no desire to capture me?"

"Unicorns need to be free, I'm sure," he answered.

The unicorn eyed his bracelet. "Don't be afraid," he told her. "It would not hurt you." He tried to reassure her. If it was within his power, the dragon talisman would be her protector, not a feared thing.

He felt her soft laughter within his mind. "Silly man," she said, "you have done well. Another scale has turned to gold."

When Jarl looked at his bracelet, he saw it was true. He thought the female creatures of Realm were very attractive. The unicorn nudged him, inviting him to continue petting her, which he did. He continued thinking. The witch was a charming person, in spite of her age. Erotic visions flashed through his mind as he pondered what the young women of Realm might be like. A dainty unicorn hoof came down on his foot, and she pulled away from him with flared nostrils. The unicorn acted just like a jealous woman. It amused Jarl when he realized this; it was his turn to enjoy humor. Usually around here the laughter was at him. It was a welcome change.

"Jarl," the old woman called, "I have something for you. Are you finished?"

Her words broke the spell that bound Jarl and the unicorn together. "Good-bye," she thought. She trotted majestically back into the forest while he raised his hand in farewell.

The witch appeared around the corner just in time to see the creature enter the belt of forest that surrounded the clearing.

"That girl," the wise woman told him, "is getting to be a real little minx."

"You mean the unicorn?"

"Who else?"

"Does she come here often?"

"Often enough to be a real nuisance sometimes." Her smile told him she was not seriously disturbed by the unicorn's visits.

Still bemused by his meeting, Jarl asked, "You know her well, then?"

"Known her family for years. She gets more like her father every day." She chuckled. "One of these times she's going to get her tail feathers singed, pushing her magic in here where it's not needed. She'll learn. She'll learn," she went on, almost as if she had forgotten Jarl's presence. Then with a jerk she brought herself back to the present. "Well, are you going to finish the job you started or not?"

"Yes," he said awkwardly. He tried to recapture his sense of normalcy. On Earth he hadn't believed in the fantastic beasts of fairyland, but seeing the unicorn had made a great impression on him. He wondered if he would see it again. Then he completed stacking the kindling. "I'm finished," he said.

"Well done," she told him shortly. "I've something you'll be needing before long." From behind her back she took a bridle. Jarl noted the fine workmanship. It weighed almost nothing in his hands.

"It's light, but it's strong," the witch told him.

"The gift is a nice idea, but I have no horse to put it on."

"The hero always rides a horse," she said. Then she took pity on his incomprehension. "You'll have one soon, or I'll turn in my crystal ball." She picked up a leathern pouch from the ground. "Here is your lunch—and dinner, if you should need it," she said, giving it to him. "Your time here is over. Now go." She gestured toward the path that ran along the clearing and vanished over the hill behind the house.

"Thank you for everything," he told her sincerely. Moved

by an impulse he didn't understand, he bent over and kissed the old woman's cheek in good-bye.

Shocked by his impulse, he stood still. If his kiss offended the witch, she might make him hop through the rest of his life with a green skin.

CHAPTER
Five

"*G*O along with you," the old woman said in a flustered voice. He saw the kiss pleased her.

As he walked along the path to the top of the hill, he thought, I've just kissed a self-confessed witch. This is one crazy adventure.

A chestnut mare stepped from behind a dense clump of bushes in front of him just as he reached the top of the hill. "It was very good policy to kiss the old dame good-bye." The horse's thought reached Jarl's mind.

He stood and stared, the bridle hanging limply in his hand.

"Well," the voice echoed in his head, "are you going to stand there all day like a ninny, or are you going to put it on me?"

He bridled the mare and ran his hand down the chestnut neck. It reminded him of the unicorn's. He led her over to a convenient rock and, using it as a mounting block, got astride the mare's bare back. While he gathered the reins, she turned around to face the cottage far below them. The old wise woman was a tiny figure in the distance. They saw her remove her apron and wave it at them before she reentered her cottage. As soon as she disappeared inside, the mare turned and began moving.

Her walk became a trot, and her trot a gallop. It was like riding the wind, and yet Jarl wished she could travel even faster. He felt a sense of urgency in the very air that rushed by them. A blackbird rose from the limb of a lightning-blasted tree on the edge of a swamp. He felt the muscles of his mount redouble their effort, increasing their pace. He gave up all thought of guiding the mare and concentrated on staying astride. He promised himself that he would never again be unappreciative of a saddle. He missed the solid feel of stirrups under his boots. They left the woods and swamp far behind them. The mare seemed tireless. It was well past noon before her pace began to slacken. They traveled down a broad valley between a range of ever-taller mountains. She finally veered from the almost invisible trail she had followed to ascend an old, well-defined path.

Giant boulders strewed the side of the mountain, a reminder of some ancient catastrophe of monumental proportions. The mare slowed, and he could feel how the exertion had weakened her. For the first time since mounting, he applied pressure to the reins. She stopped obediently at his command. He dismounted and prepared to sit on a nearby rock while she rested.

"Not here," the mare told him, speaking to him for the second time that day. "Up. There's water," she added as an inducement, waiting for him to remount.

"Far?" he questioned.

"Not too far; only a small distance."

"Then I'll walk," he told her, removing the bridle from her head. She might want to nibble the sparse grass as they traveled at the much slower pace his walking caused.

"This way," she urged as they rounded an especially large boulder.

A huge flat area held what remained of an old building. It had been fairly large, but not one stone was standing on another. Only in the exact center of the cleared space was there something remaining. A mosaic in the shape of a pentagram encircled a small well that had escaped the general destruction. Jarl followed the mare into the tiled space around the well. He felt the lessening of the constriction of his bracelet, which had gradually been growing tighter. The sun sank lower on the rim of the mountains.

"We will rest here," the mare told him. "It is safe."

"What do you mean safe?" Jarl asked, somewhat out of breath. In Realm even the animals understood more of the situation than he did. On Earth some of his best friends were four-footed. In fact, he preferred animals to people. He accepted them as companions with no urge to dominate the relationship. The fiercest watchdogs sensed his amity. No animal had ever bitten him—except that dratted fennec, he thought half fondly. He wondered where the fennec was now.

"You miss Mirza?" the horse inquired.

"Do you know her?" he asked eagerly. Maybe the creatures had a bush telegraph in Realm. They all knew who he was. Perhaps they were all familiars of the witch.

The horse gave a very feminine chuckle. He stared at her in horror. She sounded just like the unicorn! Her acid comments were just like those of his foxy friend. His mind raced over his adventures, kaleidoscoping them into a whole picture instead of separate, unrelated fragments. Awareness in his eyes, he asked, "Are you a, a, uh—shape shifter?" he concluded delicately. He did not want to use the prefix 'were.' Werewolf, no. Were-fennec—maybe, he thought.

Approval emanated from his equine companion. "Intelligent as well as kind," she commented. She neither admitted nor denied her ability to change form at will.

He narrowed his thoughts to the time with Mirza. When the djinn had appeared, what had he said? It was something like, "So, little shape shifter, you plan to escape." Jarl's features lit with his discovery. "He didn't mean me; he meant you! That silver chain around your neck bound you to the rock. Silver kept you from changing shape to free yourself. That was why you needed me to rescue you, wasn't it?"

"Correct." The mare nodded.

As the sun finally disappeared entirely, Jarl could see the faint green glow which seeped from the rocks. The glow illuminated the pentagram upon which they stood. The air, which had been distinctly chilly, with a sharp nip to the wind, stilled. It became comfortably warm within the aura of the green light.

"Well, why don't you change back into a fox so you can get more comfortable?" he asked. He wanted to see how she managed the change. "There's not very much room inside the pentagram," he explained.

"There will be enough. You will have to wait awhile before I satisfy your curiosity," the mare told him. The coquettish shake of her head was reminiscent of a young girl.

"Why?" he asked. He felt more at home now that he knew he could recognize her in more than one shape. How he remained ignorant so long puzzled him.

"Because within the pentagram I cannot change."

"Why not?"

"Because it is a—" She paused, obviously searching for an explanation he would understand.

He felt inexplicably stupid as he waited for her to speak.

"—a magic field itself," she continued. "It protects us from any evil in the vicinity. It's the reason I ran so hard to get us here before night."

"Well, I appreciate your efforts, but what kind of evil do you mean? I haven't been here long enough to make anyone angry with me."

"The Dragon's Pawn has enemies because he is what he is, not because he has done anything to deserve them. When Good meets Evil, there is always total war, all-out confrontation, whether Good wishes it or not."

"I hope I'm one of the good guys," he said lightly, trying to dispel a sense of impending trouble. It wasn't coming from the bracelet this time. The hair on the back of his neck had risen like the hackles on a good watchdog as she spoke.

"Tomorrow, if you wish, when we leave I will conjure you a white hat," she offered teasingly.

"No, I'm quite all right as I am." Conjure, he thought. She must be a witch herself. Perhaps she's the sister of the old wise woman. They surely know each other.

The mare nudged him playfully. "I'm not that old," she said flirtatiously. She blew through her nostrils and nudged him again. It was somewhat disconcerting. He wasn't expecting the second gesture. He almost fell outside of the pentagram. Only her quick warning caused him to twist himself and remain inside the greenish glow that spelled safety.

"I'm sorry," she apologized. "Gone—or hurt—if you'd fallen outside," she said hesitantly.

"This is no time for horseplay, evidently," he said. He put his hand on her neck to show her he didn't mind.

"It's no joking matter. Seeing the future isn't one of my talents, but I know there will be trouble in plenty before we reach Realmgate safely." She turned to the well. Jarl saw it had mysteriously filled while they talked. It now was so full his companion could drink from it easily.

"How will I feed you?" Jarl asked. His hunger had reminded him of the amount of food a horse could eat. There was no vegetation within the pentagram, and outside was unsafe.

"Open the pouch and see what's inside," she said confidently.

He untied the bag from his belt. He felt lopsided for a moment with the sword unbalanced by the weight of the witch's food sack. He opened it and reached inside. One apple followed another. He bit into one, holding the bag under his arm and offering the other apple to the horse. She ate it, core and all. She removed the core of his apple from his hand and ate it, too.

"There are some advantages to your shape I hadn't thought of," he teased her gently.

"Try the bag again," she advised.

This time there were two sandwiches within.

"No roast beef for me," she told him. "You eat them."

"What will you eat? A horse can't make a meal on an apple and two cores."

"Put down the bag with the top open," she commanded.

Jarl placed it on the ground. He watched, astounded, as she began to pull wisps of hay from the bag during the whole time he devoured the two sandwiches.

"There must be a whole bale of hay in that bag, but I don't believe it."

"You should. My gr—" She stopped abruptly. "The old wise woman isn't a witch for nothing. The bag has a very potent spell on it. It will feed us whatever is best for us at the time. Want to try for a little dessert?"

He reached within and found a large apple tart for himself and a measure of oats for the mare. "Darned if that isn't a handy gadget." Magic was beginning to seem normal to him. He didn't try to rationalize how such things as shape shifting and food materializations were done. He only knew that in Realm they worked. Somehow he began to think that life back home—where he naturally desired to return—would seem a little mundane. He did want to return, didn't he? He throttled his doubt instantly.

The bag obligingly fluffed up with hay like a pillow, so he curled up on the stones to rest. The mare stood sentinel over him, watching the blackness outside the circle grow deeper and deeper. The man slept on, unaware of what was happening a scant yard or so from his place of refuge.

The darkness grew until it blotted out the moon and the stars; still the mare kept vigil. A disembodied voice began to speak, but the mare gave no sign she heard.

"Give the Dragon's Pawn to us."

"Us—us—us," echoed small sibilant voices after their master's.

"You cannot win," the Unseen continued.

"Not win—not win—not win," the tiny voices mocked mindlessly.

Only the mare's flicking ears showed she heard, but she refused to answer.

The one-sided conversation continued. The voices promised the direst revenge for noncompliance and the sweetest rewards of which the evil presence could think. "Power, wealth, knowledge!" the Unseen ended its oration.

Still the horse said nothing in answer. The blackness was a pall close around the pentagram. The only light was the greenish glow emanating from the stones within the shape and from the well. The light streamed upward into the starlit sky which the mare knew existed far above the local gathering of evil power. She was tiring. The glow grew fainter. It took great effort to summon the power of the well. Every faculty she had concentrated on coaxing and controlling the power to protect Jarl and herself.

Jarl awoke with a start. As his eyes slowly adjusted to the pale green glow which faded as he watched, he remembered the events that preceded their arrival in this place. For a second the green phosphorescence paled to almost nothing, and the mare gasped, "Jarl! Concentrate on the Dragon's Wyrd! Summon its power or we die!"

CHAPTER
Six

*H*E felt the pulsing evil awaiting greedily without. He wondered why he didn't feel more afraid. Perhaps it was the total unreality of the situation.... No, unreality was not the word. The whole situation was different from anything he had ever encountered. His mind told him that what was happening couldn't be real, but some much more basic part of him fed him information that he knew instinctively was true. He sensed that the unseen creatures waited hungrily for the chance to attack and destroy them utterly. He looked into the eyes of the dragon on his wrist. They glowed richly amber. Slowly the green light which surrounded them turned to gold. The golden light spread, wider, ever wider, farther and farther, driving back the blackness until it finally paled, allowing stars to shine through dimly.

"You'll be sorry, my lady. There will be other meetings, other places. I promise you shall be most sorry." The voice sank to the lowest of whispers and the echoes whined, "Sorry—sorry—sorry."

Jarl felt a ripple of distaste flow through him. The sound

of the whining voice still grated on his nerves. "What in the name of all that's holy was that?" he asked in an awed tone. He shook his shoulders to rid himself of the unpleasant crawling sensation those small "sorrying" voices had raised within him.

"In the name of all that's unholy," the mare corrected. "That was a major minion of the dark wizard."

"Who is this wizard? What's his name?"

"Even if I knew it, I would not say it. Do you not have a saying about speaking of the devil?"

"Speak of the devil and there he is," Jarl repeated the old maxim.

"Yes, that's what I mean. Names have power. Anytime you think of evil, its power grows. If you actually say the name of a wizard, you may summon his attention. The attention of the Dark Lord is something none of us needs just now."

"What do we do next?"

"We need to get to Realmgate."

"How about if I just get on your back, look at Wyrd here, and have him zap us there?" In his enthusiasm, he was sure he could solve their problem easily. He remembered the surge of power he had called from the talisman he wore. It made him feel confident of success.

"Even magic has its limits. We must save the dragon's might for really dangerous situations and as a backup for the magic which I can summon."

"Why didn't you ask for help sooner? If I hadn't awakened—"

"Before this day is over we may well use the powers that you have in reserve. Don't worry. You'll get your chance to battle all too soon now that the Shadowlord has some idea where we are."

"Look at you! You're too exhausted to walk, much less trot or gallop, carrying me. I can't ride with you in such a shape," he protested. "Couldn't I change myself into something and carry you for a while?"

"With me as big as a horse?" she quipped. Her soft laughter had more than a touch of a whinny in it.

Her exhaustion showed, and she was more female than anything else, Jarl thought compassionately. *And she got that way while I slept like a child through all that danger.*

"Don't berate yourself, Jarl," she thought gently. "There is still magic here, of a kind. For me," she added, seeing his curious look around him. "If you would help," she requested.

"Surely, what shall I do?"

His hand went to his sword automatically, she noted. It was a good sign. Her chosen one was hero material, although he probably didn't realize it. "Gather some water in your hands and carry it over there behind those rocks." She gestured with her head to show him the direction which was easy to see because the sun was rising.

Behind the rocks was the remains of what had once been a good-sized pool. Rocks now filled most of it. A small corner showed blue, the deep color indicating an almost bottomless depth.

"Put the water in the pool," she commanded. "Hurry, before you spill it all. It is precious; do not waste it on bare ground," she told him as his amazement slowed his reactions.

When the water left his hands, it flowed smoothly into the blue pool, which slowly changed to green before his eyes. The mare stepped into the water from a little shelf that Jarl had not noticed. When he peered into the emerald liquid, he faintly saw a series of wide, shallow steps leading down into the depths. His horse immersed herself completely.

"Hey! What are you doing?" he called, leaning over the pool anxiously.

"I'm quite all right now," she told him happily. "The goddess has allowed the power of the water to refresh me. I'm as good as I ever was," she told him. She scrambled out of the water and heaved herself onto the dry bank.

The water gradually returned to its original hue as he watched. "I could use a dip myself. Have we time?"

"Yes," she answered. She stood in the sun, letting the breeze dry her mane and tail. "Go ahead," she invited. "The water is quite ordinary now."

Jarl stood, undecided. He didn't mind bathing in front of a horse. Nevertheless, he wasn't too sure just what shape Mirza really inhabited when she was normal. Skinny-dipping in mixed company wasn't his usual habit.

"I'll wait over by the well on the other side of the rock," she told him. "The bag will still have hay in it, and I'll begin breakfast while I wait for you," she said understandingly.

He would have felt better if he had not caught the undertone of amusement her thoughts carried. The longer he conversed with her, the more meaning he got from her thoughts. At first all he understood were the words themselves. Lately he found he read the tones of her thoughts as well as he could tell emotions from the faces of people who spoke aloud. He already knew her better than anyone else he had known for so short a time. He laid his clothes on the bank and slipped into the blue water.

"Yee-ow!" he gasped, finding the water icy cold. He felt, rather than heard, her chuckle. "Mirza, you little devil, you knew darn well this water is freezing!"

"A little cold water never hurt anyone. You're wide awake. That's an added benefit of bathing in a mountain pool."

He spluttered, arose to the surface, and climbed out. He toweled off with his shirt, knowing it would soon dry in the sun. He hated to put on his pants, which were full of horsehair from the previous day's travel. He beat at them and horsehair flew.

"Mirza, is there any way to get a saddle?"

"So you don't like riding bareback?"

"I don't mind feeling a little stiff, but the real problem is the dirt and hair I've ground into my pants. I beat them on a rock, so they're cleaner than they were. As soon as I ride awhile, I'll have as much hair on my breeches as you have on your back. Wouldn't a saddle feel better to you, too?"

"A saddle you want, a saddle we'll get. I know just the place," she assured him.

As they walked slowly down the trail from the refuge, Jarl began to think about the comfort of a saddle. He wasn't sure he really wanted one after all. There was a pleasant feeling of being one with Mirza as he sat on her broad back. Using a saddle would make her seem more of an animal and less of a companion.

"Er—ah, Mirza," he began.

"It's too late to change your mind, Jarl. We're too close to the ogre's keep to back out now. If you want a saddle, you'll have to fight for it."

"Ogre's keep?" he repeated, hoping it was just a name for a local landmark.

"Yes," she told him sweetly. "Ogre's keep, complete with resident ogre. His name's Mog. Defeat him in single combat, and the saddle is yours."

"Hold it right there. I'm a peaceable person. I don't actually want a saddle anyway. I especially don't want one I have to win from an ogre. They're supposed to be pretty ugly customers," he told Mirza seriously.

"Ugly!" A gigantic voice roared out in almost unintelligible syllables. "Who dares call Mog, the handsomest ogre in all Realm, ugly?"

A huge brown shape that Jarl had mistaken for a small hillock reared up and turned. Jarl was face to knee with the owner of the saddle Mirza expected him to win. In armed combat, he reminded himself. He wondered if he could force her to turn tail and run away so rapidly the ogre couldn't catch them.

"My hero," she thought. Jarl noted he could tell when she was being sarcastic as she charged forward into battle of her own accord.

Jarl had no choice. His sword sprang to his hand, and he whirled it through the air. He hoped the speed of his mount and the dexterity of his attack would work. Not very bright, ogres moved ponderously. His only chance lay in riding in, slashing, and escaping the downward blow of the tree-sized club Mog was raising.

To Jarl, even though Mirza was galloping rapidly, it felt as if things were happening in slow motion. On closer inspection, Jarl could understand why he had mistaken the ogre for a small hill. Size only partly caused his error. Moss and lichen grew in the folds of Mog's soiled brown tunic. The buckle of the belt which girdled the monster's titanic paunch was green with age. Jarl wondered how long creatures of this sort lived. The gigantic gnarled fist grasping the club and the moss-gray beard and hairy thatch upon the ogre's head, coupled with his fangs, indicated not only age, but great wickedness. As Mog roared, Jarl saw the stumps of his browned teeth were interspersed with gaps which looked as if the ogre had been chewing megalithic boulders.

Mirza danced sideways as the club thudded harmlessly into the ground on the space she had occupied seconds before. The blow left an indentation as long as Jarl was tall. As she ran behind Mog, Jarl stood on her back. He reached up as high as possible and brought the sword across the back of the tremendous knee. Jarl felt a satisfying crunch as the sword bit deep into cartilage and ligaments. Mog shouted in mingled pain, rage, and surprise. Jarl nearly fell off Mirza's back when the ogre lurched. The ogre kept himself semi-erect with the help of his club, which he pulled back in agony. The club grazed Jarl's shoulder more by accident than design.

The puzzled look on Mog's face as he felt his knee with his hairy hand gave way to anger as his piglike eyes searched for his enemy. He stumbled to a nearby ledge of rock, upon which he leaned. Mirza quickly carried Jarl to an elevation where Jarl was in a position to reach Mog's neck.

"Strike!" she commanded, shocking him into action. Only the snick of the ancient sword's passing through the vertebrae apprised Jarl of his success. Great gouts of blood poured from the severed trunk of the ogre, which twitched grotesquely. The head lay facedown in the dirt at the foot of the ledge. Jarl was glad. He didn't want to see the look on the dead face. He felt ill and relieved at the same time.

"It is never pleasant to kill a living creature, no matter how wicked," Mirza consoled him mentally.

"I didn't need any saddle he had," he said. "We could have simply avoided passing this way."

"Yes, that's true. Still, there were many others who fought Mog and lost. He preyed on everyone in his vicinity."

"So he stole an occasional cow or goat," he defended his former adversary.

"He lived on human flesh. He deserved to die," Mirza said mercilessly. "Look at your bracelet for proof."

Another scale gleamed gold. He didn't know what to say. No one told him, but the turning of the dragon's scales to gold on his bracelet must gain points of some kind. Maybe when he earned enough, he would be zapped back home. The area of golden scales was becoming slightly larger as the thin, gilded tide crept up the body of the dragon. Jarl hoped his antagonists weren't going to increase, too. Mog was about the biggest thing he'd ever seen—alive, that is.

CHAPTER
Seven

*H*IS mount stepped daintily around the pool of blood that was gradually soaking into the earth. In the side of the hill was a cave. She boldly stepped into it. The opening was so large Jarl didn't have to lower his head to pass through, although he remained on her back.

The remains of human bones strewn carelessly on the floor proved the truth of her words. A pile of objects Mog had stolen from his victims sat at the back of the cave.

Mirza snorted fastidiously. "Find a saddle and let's leave this place."

He couldn't tell whether her horse's shape influenced her distaste or if she herself was revolted by the ogre's den. The area reeked of an unnamable odor that brought to mind fear, gluttony, and corruption. Jarl scanned the pile, seeing jewelry, sacks of coins, and bits and pieces of clothing that caught Mog's eye and must have seemed worth saving to him.

Jarl hesitated to rummage, but Mirza urged him on, so he finally dislodged a burlap-wrapped package. Behind it, wedged on the side of an overturned bronze jar of magnificent proportions, was a leathern saddle. There was something about the saddle he could not clearly see in the dim light cast by the two torches Mog had left burning along the rough natural walls of the cave. When he pulled it closer, he saw an embossed design decorated the saddle.

He hoisted the saddle awkwardly to his shoulder and began to walk toward the entrance. Mirza advised, "Take a sack of those coins." She nosed a second pile of clothing beside the treasure stack. "Take this, too," she ordered, pawing the floor next to a heap of green cloth.

He picked up the bag of coins as commanded. When he went to look at the green cloth, he laughed. Holding it in front of him, he said, "What do you want with this? It's a dress."

"Don't be foolish! And don't argue, either. Just take it with you and we can go."

Burdened as he was with saddle, dress, and sack of gold, he was making slow progress when Mirza snapped, "Here. I'll help carry that."

After the saddle was on her back, they left the cave. Both took deep breaths of the fresh air. The stench in the cavern had been sickening. Jarl awkwardly made a ball of the green material. Mirza interrupted him, saying, "Don't do that! Hold it by the waist and double it over. You can carry it thrown over the pommel of the saddle." His horse sounded as if she intended to wear the dress. His chuckle did not go unremarked.

"If you plan to ride, I suggest you mount directly. These hills are host to some other creatures of the Shadowlord. Death always calls scavengers."

"Creatures of the Shadowlord?" he asked as she lost no time in trotting away from the ogre's cave.

"Yes," she answered tersely, keeping up the trot.

Her manner of speaking reminded him that she was really the fennec he had met earlier. He suspected that they were trotting to punish him for his laughter and inept handling of the dress. He remembered the pleasant feeling of contact with Mirza's living back and compared it to the sensations given by the dead leather. He wished he had not complained about a few horsehairs stuck to his pants.

"Mirza," he said, forcing a part of his mind to think about posting to save him the slap he got from the saddle every time he made a mistake.

"Yes?"

"This saddle is too heavy to bother keeping," he told her, longing for a resumption of her exhilarating gallop, which she had given up when he saddled her.

"The saddle isn't nearly as heavy as you are. If you've discovered a conscience about riding, you can always walk, you know."

She made her unreasonable offer in such reasonable tones that Jarl was sure she was still annoyed with him. She seemed to be becoming more and more womanlike. Was that why some women were called vixens?

Her abrupt cessation of movement almost cast him over her head. "Are you serious about wanting to spare me the burden of carrying you?"

"Yes." There was no denying his irritation. He hoped his short answer made his emotion plain to her.

"Look."

"Where?" They stood on a trail over a valley far below. He could see for miles, but he wasn't sure what she wanted him to focus his attention on.

"Down there. Below us. It's a group of traders."

"Do we want to buy something?" he asked, not understanding her.

"You have the sack, don't you?"

"Yes, but—"

"You can easily afford some supplies and a packhorse, or riding horse, if you wish."

"Is it what you want?" he inquired, strangely reluctant to think of riding another animal.

"Well, it's easier for me. You're a pretty hefty specimen, you know."

"Let's get moving. We've got to see a trader about a horse," he told her, half expecting her to bolt down the trail.

Mirza contrarily resumed a decorous trot that eventually brought them out of the hills and into the valley. They entered the camp of the trader at dusk. Teamsters were setting up beside the road in an open spot that looked as if it had been used this way many times. The guards drew their weapons, not sure if the newcomer threatened their master. Although they saw Jarl dismount, they continued watching him. All but the largest of the men sheathed their swords.

"Do you claim shelter and fire rights for the night?" the guard asked.

"Yes, and I would buy, if this is a trader's caravan."

"This is the outfit of Master Trader Krom," the guard said, more hospitable now he realized a prospective customer stood before him.

A heavyset man dressed in rich clothing joined the group around Jarl and Mirza. At his appearance the others faded away to attend to their allotted tasks. Krom radiated authority. Jarl could see who commanded here easily. Without a word being spoken, the master trader created order from disorder.

"And what can I do for you? It is not often I meet an honest man bent on business while traveling this stretch of road. It's too near the territory of Mog to appeal to any but hurried travelers."

Mirza pawed the ground restlessly.

"Ah," said Trader Krom, "would you like to sell the mare? She would bring a good price in Kingstown," he continued, walking around Mirza as he spoke.

"No, I'm afraid not," Jarl told him.

"Pity. I could give you an honest price and still turn a tidy penny on her at the court." The trader began to run his hand over Mirza, but suddenly stopped when she stepped on his foot. "Ah, that's the way it is," he said.

"I'd like to buy two horses from you. I have ridden my mount hard, and would prefer that she rest for a few days," Jarl said.

His last words went unnoticed. The guards started a fire.

The first bright flames illuminated the saddle, showing the embossing clearly.

"By the Bright Ones," the master trader breathed. "How came you by this?" He indicated the saddle.

"The ogre Mog is dead," Jarl said flatly. "This saddle was within his cave. Since I needed one, I helped myself."

The trader traced the designs with a gentle finger. "This is the saddle that Ordovan leather masters crafted for Prince Leon."

A number of guards had gathered around Mirza, Jarl, and the master trader since organizing the camp. Jarl could feel the hostility in the air around him.

"These guards are hillmen, owing their allegiance to King Caeryl. Prince Leon, his son, has been missing for weeks," Mirza whispered in Jarl's mind.

"Shall we bind him, master?" asked the burly leader of the guards.

"For what reason?" inquired the trader with a slight smile.

"He has our prince's saddle. Mayhap he can tell us of the lad's whereabouts."

"Didn't the king's seer say that the little prince's disappearance was the result of black magic?"

A dumb nod was the guard's answer. He waited for further information from his leader.

"Although this man has the saddle of the prince, I do not think he is in the pay of the Shadowlord." The guards shuffled uneasily at the name, some glancing over their shoulders into the darkness. "His"—he paused with a twinkle in his eye—"horse is not ensorcelled by any dark power."

"But, master," the guard protested, reluctant to give up his desire to question Jarl under duress.

"Enough! You may well ask yourself how the saddle came into the possession of—" He looked at Jarl expectantly.

"Jarl."

"And—" the trader asked, indicating the horse with his head.

"Mirza, I call her."

"Very well. How the saddle came into the possession of Jarl here."

"And just how did you get the saddle?" the guard asked Jarl.

"It was in Mog's cave in a pile of treasure the ogre stole from his victims."

"How did you happen to be there when the ogre died? He was under the protection of the Shadowlord, like most of the hellish creatures who have been appearing here in Realm."

"Aye," the other guards muttered, shifting uneasily. Mentioned for the second time that night was the name Shadowlord.

During this exchange, the master trader said no word, clearly wanting to know more details himself.

"Tell us," the guards demanded.

"Yes, now!" ordered a man whose slight build contrasted with the husky build of the other guards. "To meddle with the servants of evil often calls down woe."

Nods of agreement went around the circle.

"He attacked me and I—" Jarl took a slight breath before admitting, "—killed him."

"You?" the huge guard scoffed openly.

"Quiet, Snell," Trader Krom reprimanded. "He wears the ancient Sword of the Dragon."

A dozen pairs of eyes looked at Jarl's sword as the fire sprang up unexpectedly in a chill wind that eddied around the camp. For no reason Jarl could discern, a shiver passed over him, causing the hair on the back of his neck to stand on end. The bracelet on his wrist tightened, then released to a comfortable level as the temperature returned to normal.

"We offer you the hospitality of the camp," the trader said.

"Thank you. I accept."

Jarl unsaddled Mirza.

"Ah, that feels better," she told him mentally. "Don't worry, I'll be here in the morning," she promised, rolling in the grass at the edge of the clearing where the camp ended.

"Very well," Jarl acknowledged.

When he returned to the fire, the guards had prepared a simple meal. The trader ate the same fare as his men, Jarl noticed. That would help to account for the respect they showed him.

Jarl bargained for a rough but clean fur cloak-blanket in which he rolled up close by the fire. When morning arrived, he chose a likely looking pair of hill ponies from the trader's string. Jarl paid for them with a gold piece from the ogre's hoard. Mirza came and waited for the saddle without being called. This impressed the guards who were preparing their own mounts, but it didn't seem to surprise the trader. Telling her to rest, Jarl readied the sturdier of the two ponies for their northward journey.

CHAPTER
Eight

*J*ARL, astride the pony, rode beside Mirza at a steady gait. She set the pace at a rapid walk that did not quite break into a trot. Without words, he sensed they were traveling at a rate they could keep up all day if necessary. He wondered if there were further adventures awaiting him. She seemed familiar with the area. His talisman was quiet, so it was probably safe to enjoy the ride—if he could forget about returning home, that was.

His companion was silent, concentrating on the trail. He eyed the scenery, since directing his mount was not difficult. Squirrels inhabited the branches of the oak trees; birds occasionally flew across the trail; a deer bounded out of the forest, but scenting man, dashed back into the safety of the woods. Jarl decided he could have been at home, judging from what he saw as they rode.

"Were you really so content there?" Mirza questioned abruptly.

"Why, of course. It's my home."

"Then Realm holds nothing for you?"

"What could there possibly be here for me? I can't even

do card tricks, and this whole place is magic. The sword actually conquered the ogre, you know. Without it, I'd be pretty much at the mercy of anyone who attacked me."

Mirza snorted and picked up the pace. For the remainder of that day she said nothing to him. She led the way until they came to a small island in the middle of a broad river. She entered the water with no word to her companion, giving him no option but to follow. Even drawing up his legs didn't keep his feet out of the water.

Exasperated with her, he said, "Why are we going off the path now? Shouldn't we be searching for a safe place to spend the night?"

"There is none such near enough for us to reach. Tonight we shall have to depend on the properties of running water. Only a strong spell, aimed specifically at us, can do harm over the protection of the water."

"Why don't we keep moving until we come to a town or another of those star-wells?"

"The pentagram at the well is what remains of the Old Magic and is much stronger than any we command now. The Old Ones used up their powers defeating those who would have opened the Realmgate and this universe to beings of unadulterated evil. The Shadowlord is now courting the same beings. There are few places in Realm that are so proof against Evil."

"Wyrd stays wrapped around my wrist all day. Hasn't he rested enough to take us to Realmgate?" Jarl touched the dragon's head fondly, receiving in exchange a sense of approval and acceptance.

"You don't fully understand the danger we passed through at the star-well," she explained patiently. "The forces the dragon vanquished there were incredible."

"You said our opponent was a minor minion!"

"Even a minor minion of the Shadowlord can call forth evil of such potency that few in Realm could withstand its full force. I could not have battled alone to save us."

"Someone besides me was helping?"

"It is best that we not discuss that until we reach Realmgate, far to the north. Fellkeep, gate of the Shadowlord, is to the south. The farther north we go, the stronger our magic becomes, the weaker his. That is why I have hurried so. I would not dare to stop here if we were not leagues distant from his seat of wickedness."

"The force of magic abates with distance?"

She nodded. "It would take tremendous power to reach us here. That is why we are safe. If the Shadowlord was certain of who you are, he would have attacked in force at the merchant's camp. Killing Mog is not definitive proof that you are Dragon's Pawn. At Realmgate you will learn to use your talisman to the fullest, and when you awaken its total abilities, the Shadowlord will find you easily. He must not discover you until you are ready to harness Wyrd to your purpose."

This was the longest speech Mirza had said to him. Jarl pondered the incredible ideas it contained as Mirza led him ever deeper into the island. It didn't seem fair to have a talisman and then be warned against using it until he reached their allies at Realmgate. Most of the heroes in the books he read had hopped right in swinging, like Beowulf, and hacked their way to victory. Impatiently he wished he could do the same. Then a thought caused him to ask, "And after I fight the Shadowlord—what happens next?"

"That depends on whether you win or lose," she told him dryly.

"Lose! I'm supposed to be the hero!"

"Some heroes do lose, you know," she thought gently.

"But—"

"Don't think of losing. Think of winning. When you have vanquished our enemy, you may return to Earth—if you wish."

"What's this 'if I wish' stuff? That's why I'm going north. To get to the gate so I can return home."

"Is all so safe in your world that you would return so speedily?"

He had the feeling that she knew more about Earth than

she was admitting. When he considered the current tension on his planet, he knew she meant the remark ironically.

"Exactly," she interrupted his thoughts. "It depends on what type of dangers you prefer to live with."

They stood in a small cleared area almost dead center on the island. He unpacked the spare pony as Mirza, for once, condescended to tell him what lay ahead within the next day's travel. Out of the corner of his eye he saw her pick up the green dress. She disappeared into the densest underbrush that the island offered. Thankful for his camping experiences, he made a stone-encircled bed for the fire. Soon the fire cast cheery beams and welcome warmth into the somewhat chill air. He thought it was perceptibly colder than it had been at the spriggan's mound. As he considered what Mirza told him, he gained new respect for the powers of the witch who had been so hospitable. Perhaps her cottage was the outpost for the good guys.

"Correct," Mirza's thought reached him. "She is a Keeper."

"Keeper? Oh, I see. The good guys are Keepers, right?"

"Right," she thought.

Used to hearing her within his mind, he was startled when he actually heard her call from across the clearing.

"Jarl?"

The sound of her soft laughter brought him to his senses. He closed his mouth, realizing he was gawking like an idiot. Everything was happening too fast for him. He felt a flash of sympathy for the dull-witted ogre, with whom he had a bond at that moment. She was beautiful. In human form she yet retained portions of her former shapes. Her fennec-red hair flowed like the unicorn's mane. Her body was every bit as well-proportioned as it had been when she was a horse. Because she was human, she appealed to him even more strongly than she had ever done in the past. And she knew it.

"Is that your real body?" Jarl blurted like some callow youth at the mercy of his glands.

Her nod was a graceful gesture of agreement. He was

dumbstruck. At last he understood how Romeo must have felt the night he first saw Juliet. He didn't know how long he stood there looking at her.

Then she said, "The fire's going out," in a conversational tone.

"I'd better get more wood," he muttered gruffly, sure he had made a fool of himself.

He was returning with the second load of faggots when Wyrd almost amputated his wrist. He heard Mirza scream. He plunged through the underbrush and burst into the clearing just as a vast black dragon arose from the ground with Mirza in its talons. As rapidly as he drew his blade, he was still too late to reach the dragon. Wyrd tightened on his arm, a signal that this creature was the Shadowlord's. Jarl knew he had to do something, but he realized his inability to attack an airborne dragon. The beast was magical, so what better weapon could he use than magic itself? He wasn't a trained shape shifter, and he didn't know if Wyrd could transform him, but he was ready to try anything. Jarl didn't know much about commanding magical powers, but he had to learn sometime. This was an emergency! Jarl held the talisman before his eyes, ready to command the aid of Wyrd's power to transform himself into an even larger, fiercer, swifter dragon, or to hurl a bolt of death. The green eyes stirred to life under Jarl's summons. Then a thought, faint as a whisper, reached him from Mirza.

"Don't use the power of Wyrd. Go to Realmgate. Follow the trail north. The Shadowlord must not discover how close he came to you. . . ."

Her admonition faded into nothingness as a clap of thunder followed the total disappearance of dragon and woman. Jarl felt panic setting in. His first impulse was to saddle one of the ponies and start riding south. Further reflection told him they were already at their destination, moved by some magical transportation, snapped from here to there—wherever that might be. Wrapped in his cloak-blanket, Jarl spent a restless night drowsing and awakening, tossing and turning, waiting for the faint rays of morning sun to arrive over the horizon.

As is usual in such cases, Jarl dropped off to a sound sleep shortly before dawn and missed the sunrise. The scent of hot bread awakened him.

"About time," a familiar voice chided.

"Rory? Is that you?"

"Get the sleep out of your eyes and look, man. Of course it's me. Who did you expect, the witch herself?" He took a large bite out of the bread and honey he was holding in his hand.

"Where did you get that?" Jarl asked.

"Witch sent it." Rory chomped on, delivering his answer between bites. "Delicious." He swallowed. "Wash up and join me," he invited. "It's your breakfast I'm eating."

Jarl lost no time in washing. He hoped he would return fast enough to eat at least some of the witch's gift. For a little man, Rory had an amazing capacity for food. And whiskey, Jarl remembered belatedly.

Fortunately, there was still plenty for him to eat. The witch had sent a small jar of his favorite pink jelly. Jarl munched his way through a hunk of warm bread before asking, "What brings you here?"

"What else?" I'm a messenger boy sent hither and yon whenever you need information," Rory complained. "Why send a perfectly peaceful leprechaun into danger like this? At least the witch didn't materialize me half in the fire like that flame wizard who sent me the last time."

"Do you have a message for me, then? I suppose you know a black dragon snatched Mirza away last night."

"Yes, I know. You showed good sense for a mortal. You waited here for directions and didn't waste the power of your bracelet."

"Well, now I want to get started. How many days' journey south is Fellkeep?"

"You're not going to Fellkeep."

"Yes, I am!"

"Humans! You are a rattleskulled lot, as I've always said.

You plan to rush south into the full power of the Shadowlord with no way to harness your major weapon, Wyrd? You shouldn't be called Dragon's Pawn. You should be named Dragon's Dimwit, lackbrain," Rory berated.

"What am I supposed to do if I can't rescue Mirza now?"

"Sensible. Most sensible. You need to do another major deed, removing some evil, to repower your bracelet, and you also need to become the ally of a dragon."

"Doesn't Wyrd count?"

"If he did, would I tell you to befriend a dragon? Lackwit!" Rory stamped on the ground.

Jarl noted, and not for the first time, that the leprechaun had the temper to match his flaming hair and beard. "Great!" Jarl mocked. "If there are any dragons who aren't already recruited by the opposition." He paused. "And is my major deed already picked out for me, too?"

"We like to leave a hero a choice or two on his own. I was sent to deliver a message, and I did. Now it's time for me to go," Rory said, pocketing the empty jar the witch sent the coralberry jam in.

"Oh, no, you don't," Jarl yelped as he advanced to grab Rory.

"Look!" Rory shouted, pointing behind Jarl.

Naturally Jarl glanced over his shoulder. Rory's merry chuckle as he disappeared was the next sound Jarl heard. Nothing stood behind him at all. It was a typical leprechaun trick. The minute Jarl took his eyes from Rory, the leprechaun was free. "Probably still has the first pot of gold he ever found," Jarl muttered into the empty glade.

Gloomily Jarl loaded his belongings. He had a nice collection of articles: sword and scabbard, fur cloak, magic lunch pouch, two hill ponies, and a bag of ogre's gold. He would have traded it all with no hesitation for Mirza's return.

Leaving the island, which hadn't proved a protected enough spot in spite of Mirza's faith in running water, he wet his feet for the second time. It didn't improve his mood any. The bright sunshine might just as well have been drizzle or pouring rain for all the notice he took of it. When he came to a spot where the road allowed him to look ahead, he saw a broad valley below him. The small holdings were laid out in neat patterns. A rural village had grown at the place where another road crossed the one he traveled. He twitched the reins and started down.

When he reached town, there was a meeting taking place in the wide spot in front of the local inn.

A hulking rustic grabbed his horse's bridle. "Here be one!" he growled in stentorian tones. His huge hand on the bridle pulled the pony into a clear space in the middle of a group of villagers. Jarl didn't particularly like someone's taking charge of his mount, but he was thirsty for something besides water. The magic bag only supplied food. The water in Realm was so clear that any stream was a good source. If the beverages matched the houses and the dress of the populace, Jarl expected to find ale at the inn. So he dismounted and started toward the inn door.

"Where d'ye think yer goin'?" the gorilloid type who still held Jarl's mount asked. He moved in front of Jarl, pulling the horse.

Since the bracelet gave no sign, Jarl figured there was no reason for concern. Jarl glanced up into his questioner's face before replying politely, "I'm going to have a drink, if you'll excuse me." He was glad his sword rested in his scabbard. He felt this fellow was looking for a fight. He had no intention of ending his long ride with any broken bones.

"Plenty to drink—after ye agree, hero," the man said.

"Now, Cruncher, that's no way to recruit a champion. He wears a sword and rides a saddle fit for a prince. When he understands our plight, he'll be happy to assist us," a jovial man said from the door of the inn. "The Oak Tree Inn welcomes you, hero. Enter, enter," he encouraged Jarl. "Stable his horses, Cruncher."

"Yes, master. I'll take good care of them."

"Jack Cruncher is a good man, if a little clod-pated," the innkeeper said as he poured a thick mug full of brown ale.

Jarl took a long drink, finding it excellent. Others came and sat. A peach-cheeked maid began to serve them.

The late afternoon sun slanted in the doorway, lighting the dim interior of the room. Jarl drank his second mug of ale more slowly, savoring the flavor.

He told the maid who served him, "I'll stay the night."

"My mother herself will prepare your chamber, sir. I hope it will be to your liking."

"Isn't this the best inn in town?" Jarl teased, knowing that a place as small as this could only support one hostelry.

"Oh, yes, sir, but it's the dragon—" she began to explain when her father came over to the table.

"Go on, girl. Have you no work to do in the kitchen?" With a "Yes, father," and a bob to Jarl, she disappeared through the back door of the room.

"This dragon she spoke of—"

"He's the bane of the whole valley. Fafnir's his name. He lives in the crags to the east," the innkeeper said.

"Scarce a decent piece of livestock left in the whole valley," a grizzled old farmer put in, wiping his mouth on his sleeve.

"I lost two."

"And I four."

"All my flock but two," added another lugubriously.

"What do you expect? Your farm is nearest his cave."

Ready to deny any interest in the situation, Jarl stopped when he felt the tightening of his bracelet. Shrieks and screams from outside drew the men to the door. A dark form came between the awed watchers and the setting sun; it was the dragon, flying low. Fafnir strafed the village like a Messerschmitt. Two thatched roofs blazed. It was late before the bucket brigade which Jarl joined doused both fires. Bone-weary, Jarl tumbled into his bed after dinner. Tomorrow was soon enough to play the hero. He directed his sleepy mental question to Wyrd: "How am I going to kill this dragon and yet make a dragon my ally?"

The bracelet gleamed, inert in the moonlight that streamed through a slit in the shuttered window. The teeth of Wyrd were exposed in a toothy smile.

CHAPTER
Nine

*J*ARL wakened at dawn. He was not looking forward to this day. Fafnir. The very name sent shivers down his backbone. Well, the sword had killed an ogre. Perhaps it could kill a dragon, too.

Leaving Mirza's pony behind, he set off directly after his breakfast, assured by his well-wishers from the village that the dragon rarely attacked before noon. Jarl didn't find the thought particularly comforting. Perhaps it would make more sense to keep going north once he was out of town. It wasn't his problem. Then he chided himself for his moment of cowardice. He wanted to rescue Mirza, not be quick-toasted by a dragon.

Anyone with any sense would be asleep this early. Maybe he could kill the dragon before it awakened. One snick, and the job finished. If this dragon had a treasure hoard, he could give it to the villagers for reparations. The hillside grew too steep for riding. He didn't want to continue. He considered how much faster a horse could run than a man. Further thought told him that neither a man nor a horse could outrun a flying dragon. The day seemed colder. Or did the chill originate inside him? He knew a hero never showed his fear. He wondered how brave he looked. Either he was no hero, or a hero felt fear like any man. He took a deep breath to steady himself. Then he did one of the hardest things he had ever done. He dismounted, unbridled the pony, and left it to graze. It wouldn't go far with so much grass to eat. He put the saddle on a convenient boulder. If he didn't return, the pony was free; if he did, he could always resaddle.

He slogged higher and higher. The grass gave way to scree and rock. For each step he took forward, he slipped back a half step. Before he reached the mouth of the cave, he was quite out of breath. Perseverance won. Finally he stood peering into the large, black opening. He puffed a few times, catching his breath.

"Tsk, tsk, young man," a rumbly voice purred. "For a hero, you're badly out of shape."

Two green eyes appeared in the darkness. They were looking at him! So much for slaying a sleeping saurian, he thought, amazed at how being in Realm had changed him. He could contemplate slaying a dragon using alliteration. Perhaps the witch had put a spell on him. Actually, the eyes didn't unnerve him as much as their height from the cave's floor. Jarl looked up into them.

"Er." He paused. He swallowed, shoving his fear down deep inside. He would deal with it later. A tiny thought trickled through his fear. If you survive. "Er." How did one address a dragon? "Fafnir?"

"Brilliant deduction, dear boy. I shall be quite sorry to have to parbroil and eat you. Intelligent brains are so crunchy. You'll be a rare treat."

"Oh, but I'm not very smart. If I were, would I be here, where you can eat me? Definitely not. I'd be on my way out of this valley as fast as my horse could carry me if I had any sense."

"Hmmm." The eyes blinked. "I still appreciate your coming up here. You'll save me a flying trip to shop for a nice sheep or cow for lunch. I hate to eat out," the dragon mused aloud.

"That's why I'm here. I'm kind of new to heroic doings. I had to kill Mog, the ogre, with my magic sword. Wyrd here zapped a genie for me earlier." Jarl tried to sound confident. The dragon couldn't know Jarl felt wringing wet. Jarl took a deep breath while he awaited the dragon's reply.

"Just a moment. Come closer," Fafnir commanded.

"I'll admit I'm not brilliant, but I'm not a total clot, either. Why should I approach and give you a better chance to make things hot for me?" Jarl winced at his inadvertent pun. He decided he must be catching it from hearing the dragon.

"A joke! A joke!" The dragon smiled as he slithered into the light. His long neck snaked from the cave. He looked almost moth-eaten. His front claws fumbled among his scales and finally brought out a pair of spectacles which he perched on his nose. "Now, my boy, let me have a look at you." Fafnir lowered his head until one plate-sized eye was only inches away from Jarl.

The glasses slid down until they halted behind Fafnir's huge nostrils. Jarl looked at the imposing bulk of Fafnir and decided he was as good as dead anyway if the dragon decided to eat him. What had Jarl to lose? The matter was out of his hands. His sense of resignation to his fate ended the worst of his fear. Jarl reached up and gently pushed the dragon's glasses back into position.

"Thank you." His old eyes sighted the bracelet. "Oh, you're the Dragon's Pawn. That puts a different complexion on things. Are you agreeable to negotiation of our—er—difficulties?"

"You'll have to stop stealing livestock from the villagers. They'll all starve if you don't."

"I'll starve if I do," Fafnir said in an injured tone.

"There are plenty of woods around here. Why not eat the wild animals you can catch?"

"That's just the trouble. I never thought I'd have to admit it, but I've grown so old I can't catch anything but those stupid, tasteless, tame animals. Every time I go into a power dive, my glasses slip down and I can't see. I bruised my nose just the other day when I tried. I hit a tree." A tear the size of a grapefruit plopped wetly on Jarl's head, drenching him. He patted the dragon in commiseration before moving to a drier distance.

"I'm sorry to hear that, but the village livestock is *verboten*."

"*Sprechen Sie Deutsch?*" Fafnir quavered. "*Wunderbar!*"

"Only a few words. Not enough to hold a conversation with anyone," Jarl admitted.

"I haven't had anyone to speak German with for nine hundred years. I've been alone ever since my boy left," the dragon explained with a shrug. This unfurled his wings and caused such a draft that Jarl almost fell over. He sneezed.

"My dear boy, you mustn't stand about with a wet head. Whatever are you thinking of? You'll catch cold." Fafnir backed a few paces, snaked his head into his cave, and came out with a towel draped over his fangs. He offered it to Jarl. "Hrumph," he said.

Jarl undraped the towel. "Thank you."

"Use it to dry yourself. Can't have the Dragon's Pawn with a cold, you know."

"Getting back to the livestock situation," Jarl said, "am I correct in assuming you aren't raiding for the fun of it, but to survive?"

"Well, sometimes I celebrate a little with a quick pass over the village—"

"If I solve your food problem, you'll have to give that up, too, although for holidays we might work something out. You might start bonfires for the village." The dragon was a crusty old fellow with no real harm in him, and if lighting a fire or two pleased him and salved his pride, the villagers ought to let him do it gladly. It shouldn't be too hard to arrange, since he would leave their animals alone in the future.

"How can you solve my problem? I don't eat much anymore, but I still like two square meals a day and a little snack before bedtime—something warm for my tummy, you know."

"Wait here for me. I've got just the thing, but I left it

down with my saddle." Jarl found it easy to retrace his steps. He picked up the witch's bag and started the return journey. The trip upslope hadn't become any easier. He puffed his way to the cave ledge. "Fafnir," he called softly. He noticed the dragon's eyes were closed.

"I wasn't asleep. I just closed my eyes to rest them," the old saurian said in a crotchety manner.

"I never said you were. It's here on this ledge in the sun. It looks like a good place to—close your eyes to rest them," Jarl told him.

"Well, what have you for me? I love surprises."

Jarl handed Fafnir the pouch. "It's magic. If you open it, you'll find your breakfast in it." Jarl crossed his fingers. It had to work for the dragon. He watched. Fafnir's claws fumbled with the bag.

"Kippers! My favorite! I haven't had a breakfast like this in centuries. When I used to visit my cousin, the Loathly Worm, he always had kippers for me." Here Fafnir tipped the pouch into his mouth. Jarl looked on in awe as a barrel-ful of fish slipped down the dragon's throat. "Would you care for a few?" Fafnir offered hospitably.

"No, thanks," Jarl hurriedly refused. "I've already had my breakfast."

The dragon put the bag on the ground. He patted it several times with a gentle claw. "Charming magic," he commented.

"Do we have a deal? You stop raids and you may keep the bag."

Fafnir picked a stray kipper from between his teeth.

"Oh, and you'd better give me a dozen pieces of gold to pay for the damages the farmers have suffered."

Fafnir's head shot straight up into the air. "Gold? What makes you believe I've got any gold? Money! That's all you humans think of. It isn't worthy of you, my dear Pawn, if you'll pardon the informality." Fafnir delicately placed one claw on the bag.

"Oh, that's all right." Jarl looked Fafnir in the eye. "You mean you're a poor dragon?"

"Of course not!" The dragon turned his head and emitted a short belch that withered a bush growing on the hillside. Then he raised his nose and blew seven perfect smoke rings into the air.

"That's a neat trick."

"Oh, when I was younger, I could blow a dozen or so and then loop the loop through each one as they dissipated into the air," the dragon said modestly.

Jarl felt Fafnir was trying to take his mind from the idea of reparation payments. He returned to the subject. "Now about the gold—"

"Well, if you insist, I might be able to find the odd piece or two—"

"Twelve," Jarl reminded the dragon.

"Six," Fafnir bargained.

"Ten."

"Nine," Fafnir said firmly.

"Agreed. Nine pieces of gold to repay the farmers." Jarl felt relieved. For a moment he thought he had not been outrageous enough in his first demand to allow room to bargain.

"And you'll do me a small favor," the dragon added silkily.

"A favor?" Something in Fafnir's voice warned Jarl. What kind of a favor could a man do a dragon?

"A little something you can do for me," Fafnir spoke very casually.

Jarl took a deep breath. "Very well," he told Fafnir, hoping he wasn't going to regret making the promise. Befriend a dragon, indeed! "And in return you faithfully pledge no more raiding in the valley."

"I do," the dragon said, solemnly blowing a cloud of white smoke upward.

"What's the favor?" Jarl asked.

"My worthless son, Fafnoddle, is a disgrace to dragonry. We Fafnirs descended from the original in Norse mythology —you are from Earth, are you not? I thought I recognized your accent—Noddle's betrayed his lineage. I want you to go to his cave in the Black Mountains and take him with you on your quest."

"What quest?"

"My dear Pawn, all heroes go on quests. It's the nature of the job, you know. They rescue fair damsels, break enchantments, and kill monsters. You are planning on being a hero, aren't you?" Here Fafnir got very heated about his subject, and he belched a flame that narrowly missed his listener. A scorched-hair odor permeated the air.

Jarl ran his hand over his head nervously. It had been a close call. "It looks like it."

"Well, then take Noddle with you. Perhaps if he becomes involved in the adventurous life, he can still be a credit to the family."

"But what if he, er—"

"Out with it, Pawn. Out with it. Don't dillydally."

"Perhaps he is otherwise engaged, I meant."

"Nonsense!" Fafnir unfurled his wings and brought them back against his body with a crack that reminded Jarl of a Spanish señorita's use of her fan. He was ready, half expecting another burst of fire, but the rush of wind generated by Fafnir's wings almost blew him off the ledge. The dragon grabbed him by the scabbard belt as he was going over the edge. He felt a sickening sense of vertigo, followed by the stomach-wrenching scent of charred kippers, as the dragon opened his mouth and set him gently back on the ledge.

"As I was saying before you so rudely flew away," Fafnir continued, burnishing one of his large claws on his scaly chest, "as a hero you should be able to fight him in battle and bend him to your will." What looked to Jarl like a crocodile tear shimmered in the dragon's dinner-plate eye.

"Don't worry. I won't hurt him."

"Oh, I'm not worried about that! All you'll have to do is threaten him, and he'll agree. That's Noddle's chief weakness. He's a pacifist."

"How can you say he's a pacifist when he kills all the animals he needs to survive?"

Fafnir turned his head and sighed. Jarl was glad of the

courtesy. He had not enjoyed his flight off the ledge. "He's a vegetarian," Fafnir hissed in some distress. Seeing the look on Jarl's face, he added, "He's the first lettuce licker we've ever had in the family. That carrot-crunching son of mine is so cowardly he'll never be able to attract a mate. He may well be the last of the line. I'm glad his mother didn't live to see the day. A more vicious temper I've never encountered. In her heyday she would have laid waste to this whole valley in hours," he concluded admiringly, allowing himself a gap-toothed grin at the thought.

"Well, I'll try to get Noddle to join me." Privately Jarl wondered what help a pacifistic vegetarian would be in a fight, but he was wiser than to say so in front of the paci-fist's father.

"You're a hero! You'd better succeed!" At this point Faf-nir's tail reached out, snaked around Jarl, and removed him from harm's way. Fafnir emitted a gout of blue fire that melted a few of the pebbles where Jarl had been standing.

"Rather clever, don't you think?" Fafnir preened himself like a great bird, ignoring his captive's white face. "I can reason a priori and a posteriori," he commented, waving his tail, which still clutched Jarl, who wondered if heroes ever lost their breakfasts in situations such as his. "Sorry," his captor told him, releasing his hold at last.

"How shall I be able to find Noddle in the mountains?" Jarl said carefully, waiting as his stomach settled.

"Ask Wryd. He'll tell you. It's not out of your way." With these words, Fafnir lowered his head on the magic bag and closed his eyes.

"Good-bye," Jarl said, but his only answer was a rumbling snore. Dragons seemed a rude and unpredictable lot. This one was too old to be his ally. Jarl carefully pocketed the gold coins Fafnir had stacked nearby with his tail as they talked. He would return to the village, get directions to the Black Mountains, and then fulfill his promise to the old saurian.

CHAPTER
Ten

*T*HE citizens gathered at the inn watched silently as Jarl approached. A farmer spoke his mind bluntly.

"Horse must be faster than I thought," the old man said in a quavery voice.

"Probably didn't even go to the cave," another added, wiping his nose on his sleeve.

"Well, maybe the dragon was out," a third offered more charitably.

"Not a mark on him," growled Cruncher in a disappointed tone.

"Bet there's not a mark on the dragon, either," cackled the village wit.

"Fine hero he turned out to be."

Amis, the innkeeper's daughter, rushed out the inn door, hurried the last few steps to where Jarl was dismounting, and threw her arms around him. "You killed the dragon!" she gushed.

Jarl, not expecting such a buxom reception, almost disgraced himself by falling. At the last moment an instinct for self-preservation caused him to steady himself by putting his arms around her cozy figure. He did not bask in his hero's welcome long. Wyrd tightened on his arm immediately.

Shrieks from the villagers alerted Jarl to the source of the danger. Fafnir was lazily circling, preparing to make a dragon-point landing in the village square. His imposing bulk shadowed the open area, eclipsing the sun. He settled himself neatly, coiling his tail in a semicircle to take up the least space possible. His thoughtful gesture was neither necessary nor appreciated, because the fleeing populace cowered inside their homes as they frantically barred their doors.

Amis had such a stranglehold on Jarl that his major worry was enough oxygen to survive. "Hey, there. It's all right," Jarl told her, to no avail.

"Is this the way you keep your promise?" Fafnir roared, puffing agitated smoke rings in the air.

"I haven't broken mine," Jarl averred. "You're the one who's come without an invitation." His attempt at righteous annoyance was ineffective. Amis kept pushing him backward in her desire to get as far from the dragon as possible and still keep in the closest physical contact with Jarl.

"I'm not hurting a thing," Fafnir protested with an air of innocence that ill became his mammoth presence.

"You're scaring the villagers half to death. I thought we'd agreed that you would stay in the mountains," Jarl told him sternly. He pried Amis's hands from his neck and forced as much of her as he could behind him.

Cracks were appearing in doorways as people heard the conversation. Amis peeped wide-eyed from behind Jarl. Rumpf, her father, made the most of his opportunity and waddled from the inn, grabbed her, and hurried her inside his establishment.

"You've got to keep your side of the bargain!" Fafnir hissed.

Jarl shrugged resignedly. "All right. I'm going. Let me explain to innkeeper Rumpf here, and then I'll be on my way."

Jarl's horse moved restively each time the dragon spoke.

When Fafnir sidled closer, the hill pony bolted for the safety of the stable.

"Very well. No more dillydallying with local wenches!" Fafnir lowered his head until his huge eye was level with Jarl's. "Understood?" he hissed, then placed a taloned claw delicately over his mouth as a loud rumble and the stench of sulfurous, half-digested kippers followed.

"The sooner you leave, the sooner I'll be able to go," Jarl reminded him, trying not to breathe until the dragon was aloft.

With a final rip-roaring belch that Fafnir directed to the ground, he carefully raised his wings and floated upward like a huge balloon. Only a charred belch mark and the lingering scent of half-digested kippers proved Fafnir had paid the village a visit.

Jarl explained his bargain to the innkeeper, who kept a firm hold on his daughter. She seemed about to attack Jarl with further cries of "My hero!" Jarl hoped her father found a husband for her soon. Her unsolicited affection definitely unnerved him. Jarl gave the gold pieces to Rumpf, who promised to distribute them fairly. This earned him a cheer from the people who had crowded into the inn to hear what Jarl had to tell. When they realized that Fafnir promised not to set any more dwellings on fire, but instead would appear only when summoned to light bonfires for celebrations, the women and children gave a cheer.

Warmth around his wrist caused him to look at his bracelet. Another scale had turned to gold.

The grateful villagers gladly filled two saddlebags with provisions. Jarl thanked them before setting out for the Black Mountains. He was impatient to find Noddle, Fafnir's son. Rory had told him he needed to make an ally of a dragon. Against all logic, Jarl hoped he might be able to convince the vegetarian pacifist to join him. He glanced at Wyrd. Another scale turned to gold. He wondered if the old wise woman knew.

By riding until dusk, Jarl crossed the valley that day. He felt a sense of urgency. The Shadowlord was a powerful wizard with aspirations that went far beyond this alternate Earth. If magic were unleashed on Jarl's world, science would be powerless against it. Earth couldn't win if the leaders refused to acknowledge magic. Some scientists still insisted that although there might be other intelligence in the universe, it would never contact the Earth. He couldn't see scientists accepting the powers of the Shadowlord very easily. And the military . . .

Jarl made camp that night under the shelter of an overhanging rock. He felt relatively protected, but he missed Mirza. According to the directions given him by the villagers, it would take him another two days to reach the Black Mountains. If Fafnir knew what he was talking about, Wyrd would point the way to the dragon he sought. Jarl placed his hand gently over the bracelet. The action reassured him. He slept deeply, without dreams, in the eerie golden glow which surrounded him. A stray moonbeam gleamed briefly on Wyrd, silently talismaning a protective shield of magic about Jarl and his horses. The searching black shadows that swooped saw only bare rock where the dragon bracelet kept vigil.

The next day saw Jarl walking about as much as he rode because the highway became a dim trail, almost washed away in spots. Sometimes it wound around a mountain. The trail narrowed so that the saddlebags scraped the rocky wall while infinity dropped beside it. Jarl led the way and the ponies followed trustingly. An occasional rock was dislodged by their passing, but he could not hear it land, so far below was the earth. And the villagers called these foothills! At times both man and pony almost sat when the path dipped steeply. By the end of that day Jarl knew the hill ponies were a wise choice. Showier horses could not have been so loyal and surefooted as the shaggy animals he purchased from Trader Krom. He gave them an extra pat and a ration of oats from the saddlebags. The sparse grass wouldn't make a meal even if his ponies foraged all night. Jarl ate a piece of bread, a hunk of cheese, and an apple for his supper. Lighting a fire was beyond his strength.

As he slept, the Wyrd-glow warmed as well as protected. The dragon bracelet watched over his two companions soundlessly.

Jarl awoke refreshed. He searched beside the trail until he found the thin trickle of water that filled the basin his horses had drunk from the previous night. He refilled his water bottle, a gift from the innkeeper. The depredations of Fafnir had almost ruined his business, and so Rumpf had expressed his appreciation with the water bottle.

For a time the trail wound more or less levelly through the mountains. The rock gradually changed from a light shade to a gray so dark he understood why the mountains were called black. He couldn't identify the stone. On this the last day before he reached the heart of the range, he noticed the strata getting darker and darker. By late afternoon he was surrounded by pitch-black rock. A chill wind sprang up, making travel uncomfortable. Jarl walked, leading the ponies, until he came to a narrow defile which ended in a level patch of ground that looked like the remains of an amphitheater. Across the open space he saw what looked like an unroofed building that could shelter him and his ponies for the night. As he reached the end of the narrow passageway through the rock, Wyrd tightened. Jarl stopped immediately. He sensed this place was old, but no message of his senses warned him of evil. The ruins lay quiet, seemingly deserted by whoever —or whatever—had made them. He decided to step cautiously into the open just as a laser beam swept the path ahead of him where he would have been but for Wyrd's signal.

He pulled out his sword while his brain scrabbled to find a reasonable explanation for a futuristic weapon in so ancient a location. He dropped the pony's reins, hoping its training included standing when the reins fell to the ground. His eyes widened in surprise as his enemy stood before the opening, blocking his vision of the ruins.

One look at the humanoid, metal-encased alien before him told him what he faced: a monstrous robot warrior. A creature from human fiction, it had no natural place in this alternate universe. For the first time he had personal experience to prove Rory's story of human creations incarnate in Realm.

"Halt, human," the robot voice commanded.

"Robot, explain your presence in this world."

"I am the loyal servitor of the Almighty Metallic Leader. I will kill you."

Jarl wondered who programmed the robot. Its words sounded ludicrous. "Are you such a slave that you can't answer the question a human asks you?" Jarl taunted, trying to think of a way to save himself.

"I destroy all humans. You are human," the machine said tonelessly and raised its weapon.

Jarl had no choice but battle. He had more brains than to stand still and await his annihilation. He didn't want to risk the chance of a beam ricocheting off the unknown black rock of the defile and wounding or killing him or his ponies, leaving him afoot, perhaps wounded, alone and miles from nowhere.

His reaction was immediate and final. His sword swept up at the light lanced toward him. The blade of the sword caught the brilliant ray. The sword emitted a high keening that affected Jarl like the sound of fingernails on a blackboard. The jewels on the hilt glimmered with unearthly fire. His sword was drawing power from the laser—how, Jarl never knew. He advanced as the robot's weapon emptied itself of its charge. The metal warrior dropped it and raised its arms to grapple with its human adversary. One incandescent touch of the sword turned it to fine white ashes blowing on the wind, powdering the nearby black rocks before disappearing.

Jarl realized Wyrd had taken no part in the battle. The power of the sword was incredible. Its might differed from his talisman's, but its capability for destruction was awesome. No wonder Mirza wanted him to take the sword from the spriggan! Now it vibrated with life as he held it in his hand. The jewels had seemed beautiful before, but now they flashed coruscating fire which danced within their colorful interiors. Some great battle in the past must have used almost all of its power. The force of the laser had returned it to its former glory.

As he watched the gems, the faint thread of Mirza's voice seeped into his mind. He concentrated fiercely, but the message was a mere mental whisper.

"The Shadowlord is furious with you! There is little time to lose. You need not go to Realmgate after all. . . . Come!"

The urgency Jarl felt behind the words worried him. "Mirza! Mirza!" He tried mindspeech, but he knew it was useless. Even though the sword's enormous boosting ability amplified his attempt, he was not a good enough telepath to reach through the veils of evil which shrouded Mirza from him. The effort must have cost her a great deal. He barely understood her thoughts.

The dying sun perched atop the mountains which ringed the ruined amphitheater. Its rays turned the rock an ominous red, and Jarl rode his pony to the remains of the roofless building. The stillness of the vast area magnified the small sounds of Jarl's making camp. Any material used by the builders had long since moldered into its component elements. Jarl wondered who had built so well in such an inaccessible location. What possible purpose could there be for such structures as had once dominated this level miniplain deep within the mountains' fastness?

Wyrd clasped his arm lightly, so Jarl knew there was no present danger. It was safe—or at least as secure as any other place on Realm.

When the last rays of the sun disappeared beyond the rim of the farthest mountain, a pale phosphorescence lit the area. Tiny sparks advanced and retreated under the light of the strange stars, but Jarl did not see the dance. He was far too tired to know or care.

Wyrd watched for a time. Then on impulse—the first one he'd had in a millennium—his mind swiftly rearranged the atoms which composed his body. He had no wish to frighten the younglings, but the music they danced into the air reminded him of his youth, when his species was still bound within corporeal bodies. As his form danced, the young ones formed an awed circle around him. He beckoned to them by changing colors and adding delicate scents of plants long forgotten. Colors flashed, aromas wafted, and music tinkled in a dance whose figures filled the very air with the essence of joy.

Jarl slept. He didn't stir when Wyrd rematerialized a metallic body around his arm.

The next morning he awoke as dawn broke over the rim of the black, snowcapped peaks which surrounded the amphitheater like a jagged wall. After a meager meal, he and the hill pony circled the open space while he searched for the continuation of the path he had followed. He stood deep in the Black Mountains. Why had Wyrd offered no direction? Jarl raised the bracelet to eye height and thought distinctly and strongly: "Wyrd! I want to talk with you." He received the mental sensation of a lazy reply.

"Yesss, Dragon's Pawn?"

"You can talk to me telepathically?"

"Only a human would sstate the obviousss sso sstupidly."

"You've been on my wrist for days and never spoken to me. Presumably you understand the rules of this crazy place, and you made no effort to communicate with me." Jarl spoke aloud, giving his bracelet a disgusted look.

"Thought sendings are dangerous when evil lurks to listen. You respond well to pressure."

Jarl noticed that Wyrd was managing his *s*'s better as he continued to talk, although a faint hiss appeared from time to time in Jarl's mind. Jarl had the distinct feeling that the dragon was making a joke, but he didn't think much of Wyrd's sense of humor. "Would you mind telling me how to find Fafnoddle, since Fafnir promised you would aid me once we reached these mountains?"

"Of course." As Wyrd thought the words, his diminutive head negligently moved so his nose pointed to a fallen rock. "Sstraight ahead."

Jarl rode to the indicated boulder. By standing in the stirrups, he could see over it. Years before, it had dropped from the rim above it. Without Wyrd's suggestion, Jarl knew he might not have found the continuation of the path. "Thanks," he murmured aloud, but he received no reply. "How far is it?" His bracelet kept silence, as if it were no more than an ordinary piece of metal. He tried several more questions, but his talisman ignored him. "All right. No more conversation," Jarl said, giving up his attempt to get more information. He settled himself comfortably in the saddle and patted his mount. "Just me and my trusty cayuse," he drawled, tugging on the lead rope of the other pony that followed.

Several times he dismounted to lead his pony around rockfalls that partially blocked their way. No bird broke the blue of the sky. The chill air bore no scent. The mountains were lonely sentinels. Jarl felt his living presence made him an alien intruder into the vastness of the natural fortress around him. He stubbornly refused to speak to Wyrd—the dragon probably wouldn't answer anyway, he reasoned to himself.

"Sstop, Pawn," Wyrd hissed within Jarl's mind.

"Why?" Jarl asked as he pulled on the reins to halt the obedient pony. "I don't see anything to stop for—unless you want me to go rock collecting."

"There." Wyrd's head pointed upward to a ledge.

The increasing nervousness of his mount should have alerted Jarl to the proximity of the dragon. He was exasperated with himself. He really would have to stop depending on other people—or creatures—if he intended to rescue Mirza from the power of the Shadowlord.

He scrutinized the boulder-strewn side of the mountain before him. "Wyrd, I don't see the opening."

The bracelet remained silent. Jarl dismounted and soothed his skittish horses with handfuls of oats from the saddlebags. Food was going to be a problem if he didn't make contact with Fafnoddle soon. He looped the reins over a convenient rock. He gazed at the landscape around him. Did a boulder hide the mouth of the dragon's cave? There were a great many rocks to check, so he decided to begin. As he worked his way around the first rock, he heard the crash of glass.

A giant opening in the side of the mountain appeared as if by magic. An irritated roar and billows of smoke erupted from it.

Jarl had found the dragon.

CHAPTER
Eleven

A S soon as the smoke cleared, Jarl wiped his watering eyes and climbed to the ledge outside of the cave.

"Is anybody home?" he called. He wished he felt comfortable beginning a conversation with a dragon.

"No!" hissed a voice from inside.

"Fafnoddle, are you in there?"

"No!"

"I'm coming in." Jarl took a deep breath and stepped forward.

"In that case, be careful. There's some very nasty stuff crawling over the floor."

Once inside, Jarl looked around in wonder. The roof of the cave emitted a gentle golden glow. Along both sides of the gigantic cavern enormous stone beds of flowers and greenery flourished. The place was a gardener's paradise.

"Well, seeing as you've come uninvited, don't just stand there. Help me!" a petulant voice hissed.

Jarl looked past the banks of greenery to the rear of the cave. On a natural shelf perched a bronze dragon. His tail twitched ominously, reminding Jarl of Minou, his cat, when she was angry. The dragon's wings were furled because the back of the cave was too narrow for flying. A poisonous orange glow came from a puddle of viscous material that spread questing pseudopods even as Jarl watched.

"Hurry!"

"What do you want me to do?"

"Take a pinch of that herb on your left and throw it into the mess on the floor."

"You mean the moley?"

"Yes. Hurry!" A thin line of neon trickled upward toward the saurian. "Be careful. Don't let it touch you," the dragon warned.

The puddle appeared sentient, because it began to send out thin feelers in Jarl's direction as he approached. Jarl took the generous handful of moley that he gathered and tossed it into the puddle while Fafnoddle muttered words in a strange language. At least Jarl thought they were words. They were, unless the dragon was gargling. The puddle turned brown, then black, shrinking upon itself until it winked out of existence. An ululating shriek echoed shrilly from the walls.

"What was that?" Jarl asked, shaking his head to clear the last traces of the unpleasant sound from his ears.

"Another experiment gone wrong." The dragon sighed, hopping down to turn the pages of an ancient book propped on a rock. One long claw ran across the page as the dragon read out loud to himself. He seemed to have completely forgotten his visitor.

Fafnoddle was absentminded as well as being a pacifist and an evident vegetarian, Jarl noticed. Jarl perched on a stone to wait. Finally the dragon turned and noticed him.

"Oh, are you still here?"

"Did you think I'd come just to rescue you from your predicament?" Jarl smiled. He could understand what bothered Fafnir. There was nothing intimidating about this dragon. In spite of his tremendous size, he was too scholarly to frighten anyone. He reminded Jarl of some of his college professors. No wonder the old fire breather wanted his son to change. From a dragonly point of view, Fafnoddle was a travesty of dragonhood.

"Well, not really. If you wait long enough, something usually turns up," answered Fafnoddle.

"So I noticed," Jarl said, remembering the thin line of fluid climbing the rock where Fafnoddle sat earlier.

Fafnoddle clearly remembered, too. "I suppose you're expecting a reward—dragon's treasure and all that?" Fafnoddle lowered his head until it was level with Jarl's. He tilted it inquisitively.

"No, I'm not."

"That's a relief." Fafnoddle blinked owlishly. "Most humans would, you know."

"I don't want any dragon gold."

"Just as well. I don't have a red cent. All the money I collected during my youth I spent for my garden and magic lessons."

"I see. You're not materialistic like most dragons."

Fafnoddle shook his head disparagingly. "I haven't an avaricious bone in my body," he mourned. "I'm a great disappointment to my father."

"Speaking of your father—Fafnir sent me."

The dragon's head shot up in surprise. "You know my father? You met him and lived to tell the tale?"

Jarl nodded.

"He must be mellowing in his old age, then. Time was when he simply ate all the humans who crossed his path." The dragon's head speared down to eye level. "You didn't hurt him, did you?"

The rapidity of the dragon's movement reminded Jarl of a rattlesnake's strike. For the first time he felt a twinge of awe. A young dragon was quite a different proposition from an old one. "I wish you'd stop that. It makes my head swim," Jarl complained before answering the dragon's question. "I didn't ruffle a single scale. Fafnir sent me to you."

"What for?"

"Don't be so suspicious."

"My father . . . I only wish you could have heard all those

lectures about the glory of the family, the Fafnir honor, the joys of treasure hoarding. . . ." He absentmindedly scratched a magical symbol on the floor with his index talon. Impressed, Jarl noted that the mark was incised in inch deep into the rocky floor. Fafnoddle shook his head sadly. "I'm afraid I'm a big disappointment to my family."

Jarl looked at the length of the dragon and imagined his wingspan. Anything this beast did would be giant economy sized. "Your father would like you to accompany me," Jarl repeated patiently.

"Knowing my father, he probably wants me to shake the fertilizer off my scales and go out and bathe myself in blood." Fafnoddle shivered, sending tiny ripples of brown dust to the floor.

Jarl noted a strong barnyard smell even as his vivid imagination painted a picture of a rapacious dragon attacking humanity. He sincerely hoped he would never earn the enmity of a dragon. "Not exactly. I'm going on a—quest. Fafnir though it would be an interesting experience for you to go with me."

"What do you expect of me? I'd better warn you, I'm a dragon of strong convictions. I'm a pacifist. I abhor violence. I certainly don't have either the time or inclination to fly around the country doing dragonly deeds of derring-do." Fafnoddle stopped. "That was quite clever of me," he complimented himself. "Dragonly deeds of derring-do," he repeated theatrically, in case Jarl had missed his verbal tour de force.

"Very alliterative, but let's return to the subject at hand. I'd like you to be my companion."

"I hate to be repetitive, but why should I? Past experience tells me my wily sire has something up his scales."

"He has your welfare at heart, I'm sure. And a leprechaun told me I'd need a dragon ally," Jarl added honestly.

Fafnoddle slowly lowered his head until it rested on the floor. Jarl found this movement more disturbing than the quick lowering. There was a certain inevitability that produced a zero at the bone when a dragon's head came to rest within inches of an all-too-mortal human body. Be careful what you ask for, Jarl thought. You might get it.

Wise golden eyes studied Jarl silently. "Well, you look all right—for a human," Fafnoddle amended.

"There is a beautiful woman—" Jarl began.

"Isn't there always?" the dragon interrupted.

"—named Mirza," Jarl continued, ignoring the remark.

"Mirza?" Fafnoddle's head shot up, narrowly missing a stalactite in his surprise.

"Do you know her?"

"She's highly thought of in Realm. Everyone knows her."

"I'm going to free her."

The dragon's eyes widened. "Who would dare to lock her up?"

"The Shadowlord. She's at his castle. I had a message that said I should come to her."

"The Shadowlord, you say? That upstart. The last I heard he settled at Fellkeep in the south. Miserable location. Nothing but marsh and sea."

"Well, over the years he's gained power. He's recruiting non-Realm creatures created by the human minds of Earth."

"Earth? Bless my scales, I haven't heard that place mentioned in years. When the Keepers' Council rejected Shadow, he swore he'd become their master, but nobody actually believed that he meant what he said. And how could it be possible? The Keepers range the alternate universes at will. They have powers beyond belief at their command."

"Somehow or other, something is fouling up their plans. From what I've seen, the Keepers have quite a battle on their hands."

"If he's dared to capture Mirza, he's become bold indeed," the dragon inadvertently punned. "Her mother was very good to me when I was a dragonette. I'll have to go along and see what I can do."

"Good. I can use your help." Jarl wondered how old Mirza was.

Fafnoddle eyed the bracelet on Jarl's wrist. "Hmmm. I see you must be the current Dragon's Knight."

"Not Knight. Pawn," Jarl corrected him. "That's why I need your assistance."

"That's true. If you were Dragon's Knight, you wouldn't need me. You and Wyrd would be an unbeatable combination. Since you're only a Pawn as yet, I'll come." Fafnoddle paused and glanced around at his garden. "I must make a few preparations."

Jarl watched as the dragon slithered over to turn a golden knob. Fafnoddle peered under some plants. Small droplets of water were forming on the underside of golden piping.

"That should do it." The dragon picked a glowing globe and popped it into his mouth. "Would you care for some fruit?" His taloned claw delicately picked another and offered it to Jarl. It was slightly larger than an orange.

"Thanks." Jarl bit into his, and the taste surprised him. "It's steak!" he said, taking another bite.

"No, it's fruit, created to taste like steak. Even under these special lights, it's hard to grow. I'll set my watering system on steady drip. I've studied for years to become a master mage, but once a new variety is growing, the plants respond best to ordinary care."

Ordinary care? Jarl glanced at the steady golden glow being emitted from the high ceiling. He noted the pipes of precious metal and the oddly colored fluid that produced so prolific and wonderful a crop. What would Fafnoddle consider extraordinary? Like any gardener, the dragon pinched here and discarded a leaf there. He tilted his head and seemed to be listening.

"What are you doing?" Jarl strained to hear, but could discern no sound.

"Listening to make sure the plants are growing well." Fafnoddle noticed Jarl's look and said apologetically, "You have to be very careful with transplanted sunshine. There's so much of it in the desert region of Realm, no one cares if I move a little of it here. It's not really very complicated magic."

"Maybe not for you, but I'm impressed. My grandmother

was quite a gardener, and she would have gone berserk over your setup."

The dragon fluffed his scales with pleasure at the compliment and then shivered. "Please don't use such harsh terms. Berserk. The very thought of a berserker swashbuckling around, lopping off heads with indiscriminate abandon, petrifies me. Rescuing one young witch shouldn't be very dangerous—should it?" He looked at Jarl for reassurance.

"We can handle it together," Jarl told him, hoping he wasn't uttering the largest lie of his life.

"Well, I'm ready."

Jarl preceded him to the mouth of the cave and slipped his way down to his mount. All was well until Fafnoddle jumped off the ledge and landed directly in front of the startled and outraged ponies. At once Jarl found himself the chief performer in a bucking-horse act appropriate for any rodeo.

The dragon backed off a few paces and curled up, bracing his head on his looped tail. "Bravo!" he hissed.

Jarl couldn't take the time to decide if the commendation belonged to him or his horse. The word seemed to encourage his pony to more frenzied exertion. Jarl was unabashedly holding on to the high carved cantle with one hand and the pommel of the saddle with the other.

The amused snorts coming from the dragon were not helping make Jarl's ride any easier. Each time the dragon emitted a sound, the horse bucked higher in the air. His one thought was to rid himself of his rider and leave the vicinity of the dragon, which his instincts told him was a hereditary enemy. His dam hadn't reared any weak-witted foals!

Finally sheer exhaustion stopped the pony's rebellion. He stood, shaken, eyes rolling, obedient to the pull of the reins because he had no strength remaining to disobey. His lathered sides heaved and his heart galloped.

"That was some show," the dragon told Jarl admiringly.

"I'm glad you enjoyed it." Jarl was quite as shaken as his mount by the unexpected exertion. Seeing how large the dragon was when he spread his wings to land before the pony made Jarl appreciate his horse's reservations about having a dragon as a traveling companion. "We aren't going to be able to travel together unless my horse accepts you." Jarl dismounted and urged his mount down the path.

"It's a good thing I've given up smoking. That would have disturbed the poor beast. Don't worry. I'll take care of it." He waved a scaly forelimb and the horse quieted at once.

"How did you do that?"

"A little magic. He doesn't see me as I really am now. He's also forgotten ever seeing me in my true form."

"What does he see when he looks at you?" Jarl's curiosity forced him to ask. Fafnoddle still looked like a dragon to him. In fact, Fafnoddle looked magnificent in the sunlight. Each separate tooth gleamed whitely like an extravagant toothpaste advertisement. Jarl could easily imagine such a creature carrying off a sacrificial maiden for a luncheon date. No one would ever guess he was a vegetarian by looking at him.

"Oh, he thinks I'm a hummingbird," Fafnoddle said modestly.

"That will help. We've still got a problem to solve."

"My spell will last. He'll see me as a hummingbird for as long as I will it," the dragon said huffily.

"That's not the trouble. I can see that walking isn't your strong suit, Noddle." Without thinking, Jarl used the shortened version of the dragon's name.

"Do I call you Pawn?" the dragon hissed in an injured tone.

"I'm sorry if I hurt your feelings," Jarl said quickly. The thought of an enraged saurian set his teeth on edge. "It's just that Fafnoddle seems such a mouthful."

"Call me Faf, then, if you must shorten my name. Noddle makes me sound a bit of a fool, you know."

"A fool is the last thing I'd think of calling you."

"Well, I haven't involved myself in human affairs for several hundred years, and I wouldn't want any humans to think I was lacking in brains. Normally I wouldn't hurt anything, but if I lose my temper, I'm apt to let off steam like anyone else," he said.

Jarl hid a smile. "Faf it is, then. And I'm Jarl."

"Very well, Jarl."

"Now, back to the business at hand. Could you actually transform yourself into something that could travel with me more comfortably?"

"Probably, but I'd rather save my magic in case we really need it later during this adventure. Magic is a resource that requires conservation. If I use my powers too often, my scales tarnish."

"Oh, I see. Well, then, could you fly ahead of me and meet me later?"

"Surely. Let me show you the hidden path. It starts at the top of this mountain."

Jarl blanched. The mountainside was almost straight up, and he already had some experience in climbing it to reach Fafnoddle's lair. "I might be able to make it, but the ponies can't."

"Hmmm." The dragon stretched his wings as he thought. Then he walked to the horse, spread his wings, puffed a hot breath under himself, and rose, clutching the horse in his talons.

Dragon and horse disappeared above and Jarl stared. What was Faf doing? In a few minutes the dragon returned, dipping low in a controlled power glide, to scoop Jarl up in his claws and ascend once more into the air. Jarl's stomach almost emptied itself in surprise, but luckily the trip was short. With his feet firmly on the plateau at the top of the peak, Jarl's stomach flopped into its accustomed location. His mount grazed on a small patch of grass beside the mountain lake. He seemed skittish. Jarl didn't blame him. Did the animal believe a hummingbird had carried him? The pony paid no attention to the dragon, so the spell must be holding.

"What about my pack pony?" Jarl asked.

"He'll only be in the way. If you'll permit me, I'll send

him over the mountains into a meadow. You can pick him up later, if you decide you want him."

Jarl nodded his agreement. "Just bring me the saddlebags," he requested.

The dragon disappeared downward. In a moment he returned. He dropped the saddlebags beside Jarl.

"Thanks," Jarl said, loading them on his mount. "How does a lake come to be here at the top of a mountain?"

"A little hocus-pocus. In the north there's a vast lake brimming with water. I merely helped myself to enough to fill this basin."

No matter what the dragon said, it looked like a great deal more than hocus-pocus to Jarl. He mounted and rode around the water to the break in the plateau. He could see the remains of a road that lead gently downward. Who leveled the top of the mountain? Then he saw the pentagram incised in the smooth stone at the side of the lake.

Faf gestured negligently. "Old Ones. Real magic workers. They were here and gone long before my ancestors emigrated from Earth."

When Jarl and Faf reached the downward slope, the dragon said, "I'll see you at the bottom." He unfurled his wings, caught an updraft, and sailed like a surrealistic kite until he began some fancy flying.

Jarl was almost certain the act was for his benefit. One graceful maneuver followed another. "He's showing off just like a little kid," Jarl murmured to himself. "It's some show."

His bracelet, which up to this time had kept complete silence, allowed a faint hint of gentle agreement to insinuate itself into Jarl's mind. Jarl smiled. Another scale had turned to gold.

CHAPTER
Twelve

*T*HE sturdy-footed pony picked his way carefully down to the point where the little hummingbird he could see awaited them.

In this manner a hop, skip, and jump system of travel evolved. Faf would name a place ahead some little distance and amuse himself cavorting in the air until Jarl was almost there. Then the dragon would swoop and land, awaiting his partner in the adventure. He absented himself when Jarl made camp. He left his friend to the joys of a carnivorous meal which turned his vegetarian stomach. Sometimes human beings were too ferocious to believe. He didn't mind Jarl's catching the fish—they were ugly when removed from the water. How could Jarl bring himself to snare and eat those cute rabbits? Faf shuddered when he thought about it as he soared. After dinner Faf returned and settled his tail carefully in the midst of the coals of Jarl's fire.

As he explained the first time he did it, "Sorry, but I can't abide a cold tail. A dragon could catch pneumonia sitting about all night with his tail chilled."

Several days later Jarl arrived at the bank of a broad river.

He needed to cross it to make his next rendezvous with Faf-noddle. The road was overgrown. No one had passed this way for a long time. Jarl supposed it was because of its proximity to Fellkeep. The Shadowlord made an unpleasant neighbor. Jarl remembered the desolate look of the abandoned cottages he passed. So far, he hadn't met a soul.

While he studied the water to see if he could detect a place to ford the river, he heard splashing and wicked squeals of glee. He waited, prudently keeping concealed until he knew what creatures were coming down the river. A flat raft came in view. A dull brown lizardlike animal poled it. Or was it an animal? Surely that was suffering he saw when it raised its eyes to meet his. It sensed where he was, although he knew he was out of the line of sight of anything on the water. Then he noticed the heavy ropes that bound the creature to the raft.

The other beings on the raft were vaguely human in general outline, but their pale, misshaped faces and ugly bodies were travesties of human form. At three feet, they were almost a full foot shorter than the lizard-person, but they were so hunched over they appeared shorter. One urged the lizard to greater effort by scratching it with catlike claws. It kicked the lizard. When Jarl saw its goat's feet, he knew what it was. His grandmother had told him tales of the korred, a truly nasty species of dark elf.

The current was strong. In spite of the efforts of the lizard, the raft swung close to shore where low-growing creepers trailed over the korred. Although the sounds they made were strange, Jarl could understand what they said. Jarl wondered how this could be until he remembered Wyrd. It was important for him to know what was happening, so Wyrd made him fluent in the creature's speech.

"Push, wyvern, or we shall not bother to take you home!" the korred rasped with a scratch on the lizard's hide that left four streams of blood seeping.

The wyvern was doing all the work involved in rafting wherever they were going. Not one korred attempted to assist the wyvern, although several offered taunts and further claw marks. At closer range Jarl saw the creature's tattered back. The hot sun beat down as the rope bonds rubbed across the cuts with every movement of the pole. Jarl dismounted silently and drew his sword. The raft was almost ready to touch the bank. As it passed Jarl's hiding place, he swept his sword over the ropes, which parted easily under its keen blade.

In a flash the wyvern disappeared in the water. Jarl used his foot to give the raft a healthy shove into the main current. He followed on the bank, watching the antics of the korred as they tried to regain control of their craft. He smiled as he thought of the rapids Faf warned him about that morning. He heard the angry screeches of the korred turn to howls of fear as the raft began its journey through the rock-strewn rapids. They were afraid of the water. Jarl hoped they couldn't swim.

He retraced his steps to his horse. The hill pony had not moved from the spot where he left it. Jarl was about to ride farther upstream searching for a shallow place when he felt a faint message begin to form in his mind.

"Help . . . me . . . Man-one, or . . . I perish."

There was something commanding about the weak sending he was receiving. A wyvern must be some type of magical being. He walked to the spot near where the wyvern disappeared.

"I hear you," he thought strongly, not certain if he could communicate in mindspeech.

"This water . . . is not home to me. My wounds call hungry ones . . . to feast. I must get out of the water . . . welcome though the cool kiss of moisture is to me. . . ."

The voice trailed off, but Jarl saw a pale green trifingered hand clasping the bank almost at his feet. He reached down and grasped it, drawing the wyvern onto the bank. It weighed surprisingly little. Chameleonlike, her color had changed to match the leaves around them. The most unexpected thing about his new friend was her sex. Although he saw nothing to suggest her femininity, he knew she was female.

"That is so. . . ."

Could everything—one, he mentally corrected himself—read his thoughts here in Realm?

"Only when you think strongly about me."

The wyvern's head drooped. Jarl caught her before she fell to the ground. The pony made no demur when he climbed into the saddle with the wyvern clutched in front of him.

Jarl didn't think it was a good idea to wait around. There was always a chance that those korred might return. Any friends of theirs were sure to spell trouble. They outnumbered him even if they gained no help. He couldn't protect both himself and the wyvern from attack.

Upstream the river narrowed and Jarl was able to cross. He headed inland, searching for the open space Faf had found in one of his aerial surveys. Faf scouted at least a day's journey ahead and told Jarl about it each evening. It gave him something useful to do while he waited for Jarl to catch up to him.

Jarl watched for the open space amid the oak trees where he was to make his evening camp. Faf mentioned a small stream that wound through the glade. Somehow Jarl sensed the wyvern would want to be near water.

The sight of several squirrels alerted him to the proximity of the oaks. "It must be around here somewhere," he muttered to himself.

"Ahead and to the left, Man-one," the wyvern's thought touched him briefly.

"How do you know?"

"There is power in the oak. Ahead you will find a giant tree. You may leave me at its base."

"You're so weak. . . ."

"There will be help for me. Do not worry, Man-one."

Jarl reluctantly agreed to the wyvern's wishes. He placed her carefully under the oak she indicated. Then he walked on, leading the horse, in the direction she pointed out to him.

It was only a short way to the open space Faf had mentioned. Jarl and Faf arrived at the same time. Jarl knew Faf was a vegetarian. Still, it was unnerving to wait below and see something so huge zeroing in on the same little clearing where you stood. Jarl still marveled that the pony should believe Faf was a hummingbird. Without the dragon's spell, the pony would bolt through the woods while Jarl fought for control.

"Sorry I'm a little late," Faf greeted him. "I brought you something for dinner. I didn't think you'd be able to catch anything in these woods."

Jarl caught the knapsack Faf dropped from between his claws. It held steak fruit and some bread.

"How did you get this? Do the steak plants grow in other places?"

"I made a lightning trip home today. My plants are fine."

"It's taken us days to get this far. Can you really fly that much faster on your own?"

"Let's just say we dragons have a few secrets up our scales," Faf said mysteriously.

Jarl could tell from Faf's manner that he had no intention of satisfying Jarl's curiosity. "You said you expected me to be unable to catch anything in these woods. Why?"

"This is one of the last safe places near Fellkeep. It's a dryad colony. Each dryad protects her tree and the creatures that live in it. In large numbers dryads are capable of relatively strong magic. Creatures inimical to life and peaceful pursuits are not welcome here. I used to come here as a dragonette because most dragons can't enter here."

"When things got too tough at home?"

"You might say that. I feel that someone else is sheltering in this grove beside us. Do you know anything about him?"

"Her," Jarl corrected. "It's a wyvern."

"A wyvern! How did she get here? I've never seen one of them so far north. They used to live in the marsh near Fell-keep."

"I brought her."

"They don't think much of anything masculine. How did you meet her?"

Jarl told him what happened.

"That makes sense. The korred are usually only minor annoyances. I suppose if the Shadowlord is all the things you say, they're in league with him. They've never been kind in their dealings with humans. They lump anyone who looks human together and hate them all equally. Most dragons have nothing to do with them. We don't like prejudice. Many perfectly adequate beings don't have scales," he said, somewhat weakening his protestations of tolerance.

Jarl offered to share his steak-fruit with the dragon, but he claimed he was full. There was enough fruit in the bag for several more meals.

"Thanks for the fruit. The wild game is sparse lately."

"I imagine the Shadowlord and his allies misuse the animals for their pleasure."

"They hunt in these woods?"

"Not exactly. I want you to wear this special moley and carry this," Faf said, reaching in the knapsack and taking out an odoriferous lump.

"Whew! What a stench!"

"Never mind the smell. You must keep this with you at all times. I'm not sure how much protection Wyrd can give you from the mockers."

"Mockers?"

"The Shadowlord's creatures can call a human to them in spite of their desire to stay away. They can call other creatures, too, more's the pity. Some of them don't know enough to wear garlic or carry moley as a safety charm."

"I'll carry the moley, but the smell of the garlic would draw attention to me."

"Some of my grimoires say mockers feed on the life essence of living creatures. It is rare to find the desiccated husks of the mocker-called. On those occasions, every bone in their bodies is the same—broken." Faf proffered the garlic again.

Jarl shook his head. "Not for me, Faf. Wyrd ought to be some protection."

"Very well. I tried," Faf said before he dug a hole with one talon and buried the small lump.

"What do these mockers look like?"

"No one has ever seen them. On the way home I stopped off at a friend's cottage to learn the latest news. If the Shadowlord gains control of Realmgate, he can invade any world he chooses. When I heard about the mockers, I thought you might need a little extra protection. Some magicians theorize they are demons called from another plane of existence. They only operate in the dark. With any luck, I hope never to see one." Faf's scales rippled.

Jarl added the second piece of moley to the one the witch had given him.

"Oh, you already had a piece."

"You never can tell when an extra bit of moley will come in handy—and now I have a spare." Jarl wrapped himself in his cloak, more for a sense of comfort than because he needed the warmth.

The dragon sprawled out in a half circle around the fire with Jarl on the opened side. Faf positioned the tip of his tail in the glowing embers. "Ah," Jarl heard him murmur, "all the comforts of home."

The next morning Jarl felt a flurry of leaves on his face. He opened his eyes, but he saw no one. Puzzled, he rubbed them and looked again. Then he heard a giggle.

"Here," a soft feminine voice called.

"Where?" Jarl asked, checking to see if someone was behind Faf.

"Here, mortal! In the tree above you."

Jarl dutifully peered into the branches over his head. Careful searching showed him the form of a young girl. She stood in a crotch many feet in the air.

"Be careful! You might fall."

"Pooh. Not me!"

"If I were your father, I'd tan your hide, young lady. You'll break every bone in your body if you fall."

Faf's chuckle reminded Jarl that he and the girl were not

alone in the glade. Jarl turned to glare at his friend. "And a big help you are! Wouldn't you worry if that was a young dragon up there on that limb?"

"Not particularly."

Jarl's expression spoke for him. Faf hastened to explain himself.

"Dragonettes are born knowing how to fly."

"All right, all right. So I picked a poor example, but you know what I mean. You're still amused. What's so funny? I'd like to be in on the joke."

"That—er—young girl is a dryad."

"Dryad or not, isn't she a little young to be climbing so high?"

"What a nice compliment," the dryad commented, having materialized at the foot of the tree.

"Hello, Windflower."

"Good morning to you, Faf. What brings you to my woods? I haven't seen you for four or five hundred seasons."

Then Jarl remembered his mythology. A dryad was as old as her oak. This tree would need half a dozen men to encircle it. As usual in Realm, looks were deceiving.

"Jarl Dragon's Pawn and I are going to rescue Mirza from the Shadowlord."

"I will send word to my sisters. Mirza has always been kind. We did not know she was imprisoned. If ever Oak can aid you, you have only to ask."

"Thank you," Faf and Jarl said in unison.

"How are you involved in this rescue, Faf? The last I heard, you were secretly studying magic far from your father."

"I'm still studying. This is a vacation for me. I thought a little exposure to magic in the real world might prove edifying."

"You must be very watchful. There is a degree of protection for Jarl because he is the Dragon's Pawn, but his protection probably doesn't extend to you, Noddy dear."

Now it was Jarl's turn to smile. The dragon's scales on his neck and head shifted slightly, showing their well-burnished edges in the light of the morning sun. Jarl realized he was seeing a rare sight. Faf was blushing.

"Hrumph!" Faf choked back a warm reply. "I'll be careful."

"The Shadowlord is evil beyond knowing. We have set up wards in each oak glade to protect the innocent. Trapped, taken, or destroyed before they can reach our sanctuaries is their usual fate."

"Jarl's talisman grows in strength every day as Jarl grows in wisdom. When the testing time comes, he will succeed." Faf's golden eyes gleamed with surety as he spoke.

"I almost forgot my original reason for coming here," Windflower said, looking over her shoulder with one hand and leg melding into the oak. "Seabreeze sends her thanks."

Jarl wondered who Seabreeze was, but the dryad's next words answered his question.

"She left this morning for the wyverns' cave by the Marshy Sea. The Shadowlord's accomplices are damming the great river in an attempt to dry up the marsh. He wants to destroy the wyverns because they command sea magic. I see Wyrd's scales gain gold as you help the wyverns. Goodbye." With her last word she disappeared into the tree.

"Are all dryads as beautiful and abrupt as that?"

"I've known a good many. They're just like anyone. Each is an individual. Windflower is a Keeper and the ruler of the Oaken Circle. The press of her duties at this dangerous time makes her a little abstracted." The dragon stretched like a cat and pounded his tail upon the ground. "Kinks. I'd better get airborne and let the sun limber me up. Keep going due south. Wait for me at the top of the first hill you come to this afternoon. If you look sharp and there's no mist, you may be able to see Fell Forest. We're in the land of King Caeryl already."

Jarl watched his friend shoot into the air. Wyrd fitted his wrist closely as he mounted, prepared to face whatever the day might bring. Wyrd wasn't uncomfortable, but Jarl felt warned that the price of life was constant vigilance.

CHAPTER
Thirteen

*T*HE day passed uneventfully until the lengthening shadows of the misshapen trees which lined the path reached across the slender open space Jarl traveled. The path wound steadily upward. Jarl thought he would reach the meeting place by late afternoon. It was lonely traveling by himself, but having the dragon reconnoiter each day's journey before he made it was helpful.

Jarl's hand felt cold; Wyrd gradually tightened in warning. As soon as Jarl became alert to the possibilities of peril, Wyrd loosened the pressure. Jarl's eyes scanned the vegetation on both sides of the path. In some places vines straggled from treetop to treetop, forming a canopy over the trail. From time to time a huge tree branch overreached the narrow ribbon of road. Jarl entered one such dark patch just as his horse bolted. The first lunge of the horse was his only warning. As he clung to the saddle, he leaned forward and the rope noose aimed for his head trailed over his back harmlessly.

The brigands hidden beside the path had no chance to stop him now that his horse had gained its stride. Jarl urged it on, knowing that he needed a relatively clear spot to face his enemies. Sounds of pursuit were strengthened by the arrow that whizzed by him. He planned to stop his mount when he got to a place where he could swing his sword. If luck was with him, it would be a large enough area for Faf to land. The tiny circling dot in the sky was almost sure to be his companion—he hoped.

"Catch him! Don't let him get away!"

The words rang in Jarl's ears. His horse faltered. The trail was so overgrown he couldn't see the sky. His only chance lay in escaping the never-ending green tunnel. He hesitated to leave the path. All he needed was to find himself lost in territory his searchers knew well. As if sensing his desperation, his horse put on one last burst of speed, temporarily outdistancing the rain of arrows that followed them. This last effort brought them to the top of the rise Faf mentioned earlier.

Jarl pulled on the reins and dismounted, giving his horse a hurried slap to move him out of harm's way. He drew his sword as the first of the robbers reached him. The jeweled hilt soaked up the rays of the sun, sparkling. The first robber's eyes widened when he saw the sword. His greed to claim Jarl's weapon caused him to underestimate Jarl's swordsmanship. His careless attack left his neck vulnerable. Like a striking adder, the sword separated the robber's head from his body. Jarl had no time to regret his actions. He was battling the second and third robbers consecutively. A fourth was trying to circle around him from behind. A fifth skulked, jackallike, at the fringe of the battle as he worked his way around to Jarl's horse with the valuable saddle.

So intent on reaving was this last bandit that he didn't pay attention to the huge shadow that swept the clearing. Faf's first burst of flame charred him neatly dead. The shock of the dragon's arrival gave Jarl the edge he needed. A lunge finished off one of his attackers. Faf darted across the open space and picked up the horrified robber who had been trying to position himself behind Jarl. For a while the air rang with the clang of swords in use. Jarl managed to get inside his opponent's guard. The only brigand remaining found himself firmly clutched in Faf's talons ten feet in the air.

"Bravo!" Faf hissed as he settled gently to the ground.

"I thought for a while that you weren't going to make the fight," Jarl gasped. "I could have used your help a little sooner."

"But you were doing so well—"

"I know. And you hate violence." Jarl panted slightly.

"Exactly. And what are we going to do with him?" Faf opened his giant claw which curled gently—for a dragon—around the surviving attacker, who hit the ground with a thump.

On seeing the plate-sized eye within a foot of his face, the brave robber fainted.

Jarl remembered his meeting with Faf's father. He couldn't help feeling some sympathy for the robber, who looked rather young to be a hardened criminal. "First we'll revive him. Then we'll find out why they attacked me," Jarl announced.

A little water from Jarl's canteen brought the youthful criminal around, but no sooner did he open his eyes than he fainted for the second time.

"What the—" Jarl ejaculated in puzzlement. He turned to see what had terrified the robber. Faf stood right behind Jarl. His head was poised over Jarl's shoulder. During his association with Faf, Jarl had become used to the dragon's looks and idiosyncrasies. He had forgotten how a normal human might react to so imposing a specimen of dragonry. When Jarl tactfully explained this to Faf, the dragon nodded and moved out of the robber's sight.

This time when the would-be robber revived, Jarl began to question him. "Who are you?"

"Will Fletcherson," the youth said, unobtrusively trying to see if the dragon was still present.

"Why did you attack me?"

"We needed food and a way to get back into the king's good graces."

"King?"

"King Caeryl. We were cast out of his kingdom for laziness and petty thievery. We thought it would be easy to steal for a living. We were wrong. These deserted lands belong to the Shadowlord. We lived hand to mouth, glad to find a patch of berries or an abandoned fruit orchard." A tear rolled down the boy's face, leaving a clear track in the dirt which covered it.

"Go on," Jarl commanded, impatient to have his questions answered. At least these men were not in the Shadowlord's pay.

"It was your saddle that decided us. We recognized it."

"Oh, you mean Prince Leon's saddle."

"Did you take it from him?" Will faced his captor with an angry look.

Impressed by Will's clear loyalty to the young prince, Jarl told him quietly, "No, I did not. It was in the treasure of Mog, the ogre."

"Ogres are mean. They spell trouble for any man. Did you outsmart him?

"No." Jarl glanced at Faf. He had learned to read the dragon's expressions from their daily conversations. When the amused nostrils of the dragon quivered, Jarl knew the cause. Now he was answering the prisoner's questions.

The curt monosyllable intrigued Will. "Then how did you come by it?"

"I killed him," Jarl said.

A look of admiration lit Will's face. "I knew we shouldn't have tried to rob you. I was kind of glad when you escaped my noose. We might never have chased you but for the saddle. Gilly, our leader, told us if we took the saddle and you to the king, he might forgive us. The prince was kidnapped just before we were exiled."

"The lad's learned his lesson. Mayhap we should make a slight detour and tell King Caeryl the probable whereabouts of his son."

Will turned and, recognizing the dragon, paled.

"Don't worry. He won't hurt you. He's my friend."

"Dragons aren't usually friendly," Will said, trying to look brave and failing.

Faf snorted, and Jarl said hurriedly. "Where's the best place to make camp?"

"Around those rocks is a sheltered area. It isn't safe to build a fire in the open. We met an old hermit who warned Gilly and the rest of us that strange things range this area in the dark."

"If you'll give me your parole, I'll trust you. Tomorrow we'll set out for the palace. I'll let you have credit for rescuing the saddle, and perhaps the king will readmit you to the kingdom."

"I promise," Will told Jarl with shining eyes.

Jarl noted his prisoner's changed demeanor. The youngest member of the band, he probably was just lazy, not a hardened criminal. Jarl set Will to gathering an evening's supply of wood.

"What were you saying about the prince? Do you know where he is?" Jarl asked Faf when they were alone.

"I have reason to believe he's at Fellkeep."

"How do you know?" Jarl kept an eye on Will as he spoke.

"I saw an ill-assorted group of creatures delivering a young man who was bound and gagged to raiders wearing the Shadowlord's cloaks.

"You saw and didn't try to rescue him?"

"How was I to know it was a prince? An updraft brought the name Leon to me, but I didn't hear any honorific attached. Besides, there were a great many of them and only one of me. If they were connected to the Shadowlord, some of them were probably magic workers. I'm still learning. I'd promised to meet you—and a good thing it was, too—and I dislike violence." After listening to Faf's catalog of excuses, Jarl said, "All right. I hear you."

They camped under a rocky overhang that held the fire's warmth and yet shielded the light from possible enemies. There was enough room for Faf, too. Will enjoyed the last of the steak fruit with Jarl and Faf. His eyes bugged when he saw the dragon bury his tail in the embers of the fire.

"Do you really think the king will forgive me? It will make my mother happy to have me back. Especially since I've decided to work for a living."

"I've never met the king, but I'll try," Jarl promised. He decided Will was a good enough lad, although not very strong-minded.

Jarl and Will fell asleep, but Faf only drowsed. There was something—something evil—in the air. Being a magical creature himself, he knew that Wyrd's protective aura was not fully effective. Ponder though he did, he could not understand what the problem might be.

"Faf! Are you awake?" Jarl whispered. He could see the up-and-down movement of the dragon's eyes that signified a nod. "What is it, Wyrd?" Jarl thought sleepily as the bracelet tightened on his arm.

"So, as I promised, we meet again, meddlesome one," a silky voice wafted through the darkness. "You have led me a merry chase. For days I have searched for you."

Jarl recognized the voice from his previous meeting. He heard it the night Mirza and he were protected by the pentagram of the well. He didn't answer. Faf's eyes narrowed to slits, but he, too, was silent.

"What—what is it?" Will's scared question broke the silence.

"It's a minion of the Shadowlord's. We've met before," Jarl answered grimly.

"The power of your talisman is weak. You are Pawn indeed."

"In deed, in deed, in deed," a tiny chorus answered.

"What do they want?" Will's voice broke on the last word.

"We were called. You called us to you."

"I never did!" Will's frightened voice shrilled.

"We know you didn't mean to, but you must have a summoning token if you're telling the truth," Faf said. "Search your pockets." Faf's tail poked the fire, encouragingly the embers to blaze briefly.

Will's first pocket yielded a pit from the steak fruit plant and a few bread crumbs. His second contained a flat stone with runic engraving.

"What's that?" Jarl asked.

"It's only an unusual stone I found on the road this morning," Will whined.

"Toss it in the fire," Faf commanded as he removed his tail, stirring the embers into a larger blaze.

The stone sailed through the air. It landed in the center of the small blaze, which immediately went out.

"Oh," Will gasped.

"Isn't it a little dark around here?" Jarl's hand tightened on his sword, but his words sounded confident.

"Yes, I agree," the dragon's measured tones answered Jarl. Faf emitted a pure blue stream of flame directed at the dead ashes. At first nothing seemed to happen, but at last a light formed and sprang into flame, casting a golden glow around them.

"So you can work magic as well, dragon?" An irritated sigh from the darkness followed the rhetorical question.

Faf refused to answer verbally. He flicked the charred calling stone into the darkness with his tail.

"Why do you not join us, dragon? You are a seeker after power, as we are. Join us. We offer all the dark knowledge you wish and unlimited power. Come!"

"Come, come, come," the echoes urged.

In answer, Faf beamed a hot blast of flame into the darkness. For a second both Faf and Jarl were wholly absorbed in peering into the blackness. They saw a faint outline of a cowled figure surrounded by amoeboid blobs of utter darkness.

"Come," the voices tugged at Jarl, but fortified by Wyrd and the moley, he resisted.

Will, however, was unprotected. While the summoning stone could call evil, those truly untouched by evil doings could resist within the protective aura of fire which Wyrd and Faf created. Will had spent too long a time with the brigands trying to survive. Even if he was unwilling, he had participated in following those who did wicked deeds; therefore, he was vulnerable. Before either Faf or Jarl could hold him, he leaped into the darkness and disappeared. His howl of utter despair rang in the air. Jarl was ready to dash forward, but Faf stopped him.

"It is too late already. I'm sorry. I've read of such visitations. I assure you there is nothing you or I can do for him now," the dragon said sadly.

"My—associates—thank you for the donation," purred their shadowy visitor. "And perhaps we shall be victorious the next time. You will have further opportunity to join the shadows."

"Shadowss, shadowss, shadowss." The mockers' voices faded.

The black pall gradually thinned to let the sharp light of the stars shine through. A clean, cold gust of air dissipated the last of the fetid odor.

Faf looked at Jarl. "That's as close to evil as I ever want to get."

Jarl agreed.

"At sunrise I'll have to look at my scales."

"Why?"

"They're probably tarnished. Goodness only knows what pollution those creatures brought with them," the dragon complained. He stirred the fire languidly with his tail. "I'll add a few sticks. This early morning chill is the worst possible thing for a dragon's health."

Jarl welcomed the light and warmth himself. Faf's concern for his health added a touch of normalcy that Jarl needed. He blamed himself for Will's death. Resisting was difficult, and the struggle had exhausted him. He should have given the extra piece of moley to Will. Wyrd at least seemed satisfied. There was no sense of constriction from the bracelet. With this in mind, Jarl fell into a deep sleep.

Faf half closed his eyes and meditated on the nature of the evils so lately encountered.

CHAPTER
Fourteen

*T*HE morning's sunrise pinkened the eastern sky as if to expunge the memory of evil from the minds of the two adventurers. After a short discussion, Faf persuaded Jarl it would only take one extra day to deliver the saddle to the king. Along with it, they could also tell the king what Faf had seen.

"Take the left fork in the road," Faf advised. "If you hurry, you may arrive at the city by noon. Make that pony trot a little. He's getting spoiled. Fat and sassy. If he snorts at me one more time, I'll remove the spell and show him a thing or two," Faf blustered.

"I've taken good care of him. I can get to Mirza faster on horseback than by walking. I'm still not sure this is the right thing to do. Maybe you could go to the king and I could keep on. As fast as you fly—"

"From now on, we're sticking together. Look what happened when I was a little late yesterday." Faf pouted. "Now there's some action starting, you want me safely out of the way."

"I thought you were a pacifist."

Faf snorted.

"Oh, let's go on, then." Jarl kicked the astonished horse into a trot. Faf sailed lazily overhead, keeping a close watch for danger.

The trail led steadily downhill, so Jarl made good time. He clattered over a wooden bridge and passed a rude marker that said "Green Valley." Within minutes he saw signs of human habitation. Neat fields lined the roads. Prosperous farms alternated with smaller holdings. Once Faf saw Jarl safely past the running water, he flew higher and higher, leaving Jarl to his own devices. Faf's infallible magic sense told him every inch of that river was warded with potent spells to protect humans from the machinations of the Shadowlord.

Precisely on the hour of noon the bells in the city rang in joyous cacophony. Jarl dismounted at the castle gate to which friendly citizens directed him.

"And that's why I must see the king," Jarl finished explaining to the portly man who claimed to be the king's seneschal.

"A fascinating tale. We must see that Relnot, the royal magician, hears it." He clapped his hands and a liveried servant arrived.

"Send for Relnot," Jarl's listener commanded.

"Yes, Your Majesty." The servant executed a military about-face and exited the room.

"Your Majesty!" Jarl gasped. Jarl expected a king to look the part. This man dressed richly, but he wore no crown. No courtiers were in evidence, either.

"Sorry, but it simplifies matters if people don't know who I am when they're telling things. I hate formality, and if there's one thing that brings out the awkwardness in people, it's speaking with a king." He smiled kindly at Jarl. "A king is an ordinary man in an extraordinary position. You can't imagine how boring all that yes-Your-Royal-Highness, no-Your-Royal-Highness, yes-sire, no-sire, three-bags-full-sire form of address gets to be. I hope you'll forgive me my little impersonation."

"Of course, sire."

"See? Now you're doing it, too. Ah, well, it was fun while it lasted."

A much-bemedaled man in a uniform hurried through the door. "Tsk, tsk, Your Highness. Up to your little tricks again?"

"Meet my seneschal, Pomfret Pompuss." The king waved his hand carelessly in the direction of the man whose purple pantaloons and yellow velvet jacket warred lustily.

Jarl half bowed in response to the other's gesture. The comfortable atmosphere stiffened. A veneer of court superficiality overlaid each procedure. Jarl saw why the king played truant from formality when he had the chance.

"His Majesty's royal magician, Relnot," a servant intoned.

Jarl turned to watch as a tall, thin man in white robes bordered with cabalistic designs glided into the room. His lined face and silver beard made him look old at first glance. His blue eyes sparkled with intelligence. In one look Jarl judged him trustworthy. The magician's sharp eyes lingered for a second on Wyrd, then passed to the king.

"You called for me, Your Majesty?"

"Who else commands you, Relnot?" Pompuss said.

The king ignored his seneschal. "Jarl, here, has news of Prince Leon. He's the prisoner of the Shadowlord."

"The Shadowlord would like to pass freely over your domain. Kidnapping the prince is his way of encouraging you to join him as an ally." Relnot shook his head.

"Never! Not so long as I am king. He and all those connected with him reek of evil. Even to free my beloved son, I will not betray the trust of the people in this kingdom. What legacy would I leave my boy if I joined the Shadowlord?"

"But—but—" Pomfret Pompuss began.

"I will promise to be neutral, to take no action against him if he frees Leon. Become his ally? Never!" The king threw back his shoulders and placed his hand on his sword.

"Sire, is it wise to be so hasty?" Pompuss interjected.

The king waved him away. Relnot took no notice of his exit, but Jarl was more willing to believe this man was king when he saw the instant obedience he commanded.

Relnot ran his aristocratic hand over his beard. "I will send your message, sire. The Shadowlord has been of interest to me since he first appeared here in Realm. No one knows where he comes from, and he has no friends. My long study of him leads me to believe he will spurn your promise and demand you join him."

"When you first suggested the possibility that Leon is a hostage of the Shadowlord, I thought many days upon what I must do. Now there is proof. There is nothing for it but to become reconciled to the loss of my son." The king's face remained stern and calm, but Jarl saw his right hand clench into a fist as he spoke.

Jarl said, "Is there anything I could to to help?"

Both the king and the magician had almost forgotten Jarl. They turned to him, surprised that he should offer his aid.

"An ordinary person has no chance battling our evil neighbor. His allies destroy every living thing they come upon. They befoul the very air where they pass. I can send no stranger into danger on a fool's errand," the king said.

"Wait, sire," Relnot commanded. "Perhaps Jarl is not an ordinary stranger after all." He pointed to Wyrd. "How came you by that bracelet?"

Prepared for their disbelief, Jarl answered, "It appeared on my wrist after a visit from Rory, the leprechaun."

"Let me see it," Relnot said, holding out his hand for the bracelet.

"I cannot remove it. I have worn it constantly since I received it."

"I have read of an ancient talisman which the heroes of Realm possessed. Supposedly it selects its wearer and remains with him until the need for its aid ceases. Its wearer is the Dragon's Pawn until he masters the talisman's powers for himself."

"That's me, all right," Jarl admitted.

"Then there's some danger to the whole of Realm. The old records tell of an evil demon from otherwhen, defeated by Andronan, the last wearer of Wyrd."

Jarl nodded. "Clearly the Shadowlord is bypassing the normal gates between alternate worlds. His magic is causing the creatures that humans on my planet imagine to become real in Realm."

The magician's eyes flashed. "He swore years ago at the Keepers' Council that he would have vengeance, because they would not allow him to become a Keeper. We have heard little of him until lately. Protected as this kingdom is by my magic, it makes us insulated from his depredations. We have heard terrible tales of his doings. The Keepers were wise to refuse him free passage between worlds."

Jarl told them about Will's death.

The king shook his head. "It did not occur to me they would not go north when I exiled them. You can see why I must refuse your offer of aid. Even wearing a hero's talisman might not save you if the Shadowlord himself decided to harm you."

"Well, at least I can return the prince's saddle to you."

"You have the royal saddle?" Relnot asked.

"It's the one I used to ride here."

"Have it brought to my chambers immediately. Let us see if a little magic can give us further information about the prince."

A servant hurried to get the saddle while the king, Relnot, and Jarl mounted the marble steps to the tower room of the magician.

Relnot's quarters at the top of the main tower were light and airy. Not one cobweb hung from the wooden shelves which held calfhide books. The tops of the tables that curved along one sector of the wall gleamed spotlessly. The embers of a neatly tended fire warmed the room. Jarl looked out the window. The magician had a panoramic view of the southern border of the kingdom. Jarl wondered where Faf was.

"Magic is like anything else," Relnot said into Jarl's ear.

"It's not enough to do a good job occasionally. The real work is seeing to it that things stay in a proper fashion."

He turned at the respectful knock at the door.

"Come in, come in," Relnot said. "Put the saddle on the round table in the center of the room." He approached the table as the servant bowed himself from the room. "Ah, yes. It is the royal saddle."

A shadow passed over the tower, momentarily darkening the room. Relnot whirled, looking for its source. He raised his hand preparatory to hurling a spell at the huge dragon who remained seated on a neighboring tower.

"Wait! That's Faf, my friend," Jarl said.

"A dragon for a friend? You keep strange company," the king muttered irascibly from his spot near the door. It looked suspiciously as if he was planning a little magic of his own—a disappearing act.

"I'm Fafnoddle von Fafnir. It's a pleasure to make your acquaintance," Faf said to Relnot. By stretching, his neck bridged the gap between the towers and his gargantuan head rested on the stone windowsill of Relnot's room. "I've seldom seen so neat a bit of magic as that border ward you have in place."

"You recognize the spell?" The compliment clearly pleased Relnot.

"Oh, yes. I work a little magic myself from time to time."

Fearing the meeting was going to turn into a magical shop-talk session, Jarl interrupted. "This is King Caeryl, Prince Leon's father. The gentleman you're talking to is Relnot."

"Your Majesty," Faf intoned politely, dipping his nose in what passed for a bow with a dragon.

The king smiled graciously. Then he approached the table. "What do you plan to do with it, Relnot?" he asked, indicating the saddle.

"I'll see if it will speak to me when I place my hands upon it," Relnot said. He reached out to lightly touch the saddle.

"Psychometry. I've heard of it," Jarl said quietly, to avoid disturbing the magician.

"Well?" the king asked impatiently. "Is it speaking to you?"

"I see a cave. . . . Mog, the ogre, dwells within. . . . It is dark. . . . The prince and his retainers have made camp. . . . Something evil approaches. . . . There is fighting. . . . The campfire dies. . . . There is no one left alive to tend it . . . the saddle, picked up by Mog and carried to his cave. . . ."

"What of my son?"

"That is all I can see. I also received the impression of a black dragon carrying off a maiden. . . . Can't see how it's connected with Prince Leon, sire."

"The maiden is Mirza, a friend of mine," Jarl interjected.

"I was not certain of her identity. Mirza enjoys changing her shape from one creature to another. It is difficult to recognize her."

"That's Mirza, all right. The black dragon that took her is a creature of the Shadowlord. Faf and I are going to Fellkeep to rescue her."

"You do well to carry moley," the magician said. "Sire, if Jarl Dragon's Pawn is already going to Fellkeep, perhaps he could aid us."

"Well, if he's already decided to risk his life, we would be glad to accept any help he offers." The king smiled at Jarl.

"Jarl, I have a potent spell that weakens me for days. I hesitate to use it unless I know for certain it will bring results. I can have the prince here in this room in a twinkling —but to bring him, I must know exactly where he is. He must also have this in his possession." Relnot reached deep into his robes and removed an ordinary-looking acorn.

"I shall try to see that he gets this. How will you know exactly where he is?" Jarl placed the acorn in his pocket.

"Wyrd will respond if you're willing to expend the power of your talisman in our behalf. From here, it is three days' hard ride."

Faf hissed. "I've been checking the roads. The Shadowlord has made a great many nasty little arrangements for us. Traveling on horseback will be too dangerous, Jarl."

"Then you won't be going to Fellkeep?" The king's face expressed his disappointment.

"I'm going!" Jarl insisted.

"Of course you are," Faf soothed. "As the arrow flies, the journey will only take about a day."

"Are you going to ask Relnot to turn me into an arrow?" Jarl asked, unmollified by Faf's manner.

"Not at all. I'm going to carry you as I did once before."

"But—" Jarl began. He remembered the swooping sensation all too well. If men were meant to fly, they would have scales, he mentally paraphrased an old Earth saying, fitting it to Realm.

"I'm in my prime. I should be able to do it easily. It will mean less fighting and a faster trip to Mirza. It's the one avenue of entry that looks clear. There are suspicious blank spots just over the border on every road, path, and trail that leads out of this kingdom. The Shadowlord means business. Only a master of magic has the power and art to produce so many nothingnesses. Who knows what each may hold?"

"Nothing good, I'll wager," the king said, hoping his attempt at levity would ease the tension he saw Jarl was under.

Relnot and the king were nodding agreement to everything Faf said. Jarl surrendered. "All right, if you say so, I'm game." Sorry about this, he apologized silently to his stomach.

"Stay the night," the king said expansively. "We'll see you both have plenty to eat and a place to sleep." He looked at Faf estimatingly. "How many cattle will we need to slaughter for your meal?"

Faf's wings flew wide, ready to snap together and create a gale of indignation. Jarl recognized the signs. He hurriedly said, "Faf is a vegetarian, sire."

"A vegetarian dragon? How very—"

Faf expected the next word to be *odd* and he raised his head to vent a stream of fire and smoke into the air above the tower. It narrowly missed a pigeon that landed on the windowsill of the other window in the room.

"—er, interesting," the king concluded prudently.

Relnot lost all interest in dinner preparations when the bird landed. He soothed the bird as he untied the small role of paper from its leg. "Sire, this is one of Prince Leon's messenger pigeons." Relnot skimmed the writing and passed the note to the king.

"It's from my son! He's alive." The king straightened as if an invisible millstone had removed itself from his back. "You were right, Relnot. I'm to have three days to remove the magic barrier and welcome an envoy of the Shadowlord's who will bear an alliance treaty."

"Now there's no time to lose." The magician gave the nervous pigeon a last stroke and placed him in a cage. He dropped a cloth over it to blot the sight of Faf from the fluttering bird. "Speed is necessary now. The only way to get Jarl to Fellkeep is by dragonflight. At the end of the three days the Shadowlord will feed the prince's soul to one of his demon allies. If we ever see the prince after that, he will belong to the Shadowlord."

Relnot's words seemed to linger in the air after he spoke them. His listeners understood that his study of the Shadowlord made his gloomy forecast all too probable.

"Faf, are you ready? We could start now and—"

"No, Jarl. It's madness to begin a journey that will bring you from safety during the deepest hours of night when the powers of the Dark are at their zenith. At sunrise, with the Light fully on your side, is the time to begin such a venture."

"Relnot is correct. I also feel a sense of urgency, but we need to begin our journey in the morning," said the dragon.

"I thank you both," the king said quite humbly, considering his rank. "And now I go to order our meal."

"If you need to talk to me, stand below in the courtyard," Faf said. "My neck's getting stiff from all this stretching."

The day waned. Beyond the warded border the many inexplicable shadowy areas deepened to ebon with a darkness that was no mere absence of visual light.

CHAPTER
Fifteen

*T*HE bright yellow ball of the sun lit the sky. It drove the clouds away as Faf carefully clutched Jarl.

"Well, we're off," Faf said joyfully as he cast himself from the top of the tower and hurtled toward the ground with wings outspread.

The king's good-bye still echoed in Jarl's ears. He was happy he had refused breakfast. It proved to be a fortuitous decision. Twenty feet from the ground, Faf caught an updraft and soared into the blue, and Jarl felt rather green. He swallowed. "Faf, was that necessary?"

"What?" Faf banked neatly and flew blind. He curved his head to hear Jarl better.

"That grandstand takeoff," Jarl shouted into the teeth of the wind.

"Oh, that."

"What if that updraft hadn't been there?" Jarl had visions of himself on the bottom of two feet of dragon pâté spread over the courtyard stones under the tower.

"Oh, I practiced that takeoff twice this morning before you arrived. I knew that we'd get airborne. I wouldn't risk splattering a Dragon's Pawn all over the king's courtyard. You know how—"

The huge circle Faf was making dizzied Jarl, so he finished the dragon's statement. "Yeah, I know how violence appalls you. Let's get moving. Flying in circles isn't getting us any closer to Fellkeep."

"I'm not actually flying. This is resting. The thermals are doing all the work. Don't worry."

Jarl felt the dragon's claws clutch his harness through the pad he wore. He looked down at the rapidly passing earth below him, and glanced at the vast bulk of the bronze dragon above him. "Oh, no. I won't," he lied. Then he shot a thought at Wyrd. "I suppose you think this is the only way to travel."

"Yess," drifted through his mind, followed by a chuckle.

Great, Jarl thought to himself. A vegetarian pacifist hypochondriac and the joker of the ophidian set. How could I get so lucky?

A ghostly chuckle brushed his mind in reply. At least Wyrd had a sense of humor. Jarl wondered what had happened to his.

They passed the border without any problems. Faf soared cloudward on a giant thermal, then leveled out, approaching the great Fell Forest with bulletlike speed. Wind stung Jarl's eyes. He didn't see the two birdlike shapes that approached rapidly from the south. Fortunately, Faf did.

"Hmmm. Company," he muttered.

"What?" Jarl shouted.

"Company," Faf roared, making all speed toward a grove of oaks that he could just see on the horizon. "I'll have to put you down for a while."

"Drop me, you mean?" Jarl's eyes widened. Would Wyrd be able to save him?

"I'll land you in those oaks. There's something very strange about those things ahead."

Jarl squinted. "They look like birds to me."

"They're not like any birds I ever saw before. They come

from the south, and I'll bet the Shadowlord sent them. When I meet them, I'd like to be free to maneuver—just in case."

"All right, but you're acting like a little old lady. We're over halfway there because of the tail wind you found, so I guess we can spare the time."

Faf skimmed the tops of the trees as Jarl unloosed the safety loop he had harnessed to the dragon's leg. When Faf opened his claw and dropped him, Jarl floated gently to the biggest tree in the grove. Jarl expected a rough landing, but Faf—or Wyrd—had taken care of him. He arrived as lightly as thistledown.

"Welcome," a friendly voice said behind him.

Jarl carefully held on to some branches near him. He edged his way from the swaying outer portion of the oak to a fork where two branches formed a sturdy crotch. He sat gingerly and looked for the source of the words.

"Here I am!"

Jarl peered toward the sound of the silvery laughter. A lovely woman stood on a bough so slender it moved gently with every passing breeze. The age of the tree he rested in told him the dryad was a mature magical being.

"Hello. I hope you don't mind my being in your tree. I do have a good reason," Jarl told her with a smile.

"I know. I see your friend fighting above us."

Jarl's unique position had temporarily caused him to forget about Faf. Above the forest Faf was quite literally flying for his life. The birdlike shapes in the sky were an enigma to Jarl, until one of them emitted a beam of light that narrowly missed Faf. Faf was doing evasive maneuvers through the air that made his previous stunts look like the movements of a timid field mouse. Jarl's forehead creased. Faf couldn't keep it up forever. He was outmaneuvered at every turn. Beams of light crisscrossed the air. Sooner or later he would make a slight error in judgment. That mistake might well be his last.

Jarl looked at Wyrd. He would have to try to awaken the power he knew lay within his talisman. He began to concentrate.

"No, Dragon's Pawn." A soft hand touched his arm gently. "If you use your power here, you will call the Dark to my tree. I do not wish to see it destroyed. I am responsible for it and the life it shelters, you see."

Her green eyes were strangely luminescent in the dappled light which filtered through the branches. Jarl looked into them. He admitted the wisdom that lay behind her remark. "But I've got to do some—"

"Look!" The pale fingers gestured toward the sky. Three more ominous shapes had joined Faf's first two enemies. Faf belched a cloud of smoke and disappeared behind it. The strange birds clustered, centering their fire upon the cloud. Faf burst through the lower edge of the smoke and headed straight into the midst of his enemies.

An agonized "No!" burst forth from Jarl. Faf acted as if he were a kamikaze pilot. One part of Jarl wanted to cover his eyes. The other part kept him watching, hoping for something—anything—to happen that would save his friend.

There was a strange clap of distant thunder. Faf and the birds disappeared together in an instant.

"Do not grieve. All will be well."

"And how would you know? You've lived by this tree all your life," Jarl said bitterly. Jarl felt as if he had a stone in his chest. His eyes scanned the sky, hoping Faf was still there, somewhere, just waiting until the time was right to swoop down and get Jarl. Slowly the realization came to Jarl that he would never see Faf fly again. He had not known the dragon for long, but the emptiness he experienced was vast, far larger even than the dragon himself. He knew rescuing Mirza would be much more difficult without the aid of his friend. For the first time he felt a personal sense of hatred for the Shadowlord. "How could you possibly understand how I feel?"

"Leafshine is my name, and I do understand. It is true I do not travel, but there are ways of knowing given to our kind."

Jarl regretted his inability to help his friend. He knew he

was incapable of taking an action which the dryad assured him would call the Dark and destroy her tree. Leafshine and her oak were innocent bystanders. Jarl would never forgive himself, never. These black thoughts passed through his mind when Wyrd tightened ominously.

"Just what I need," Jarl muttered. "More bad news."

Leafshine paled to a shadowy pattern among the leaves. Jarl sat still on his perch, nothing moving but his eyes. Where was the danger? In what form was the Dark approaching?

Jarl looked at the dryad and formed a question in his mind, but she gestured for silence and pointed downward.

On the path far below he could see a line of chained prisoners. Guards rode up and down the line urging speed with flailing whips. A man fell, temporarily slowing the group. A rain of blows fell on him and his luckless companions who could not escape the lashes of their captors. Desperately they tugged at him, half dragging, half carrying him as the line began to move at last.

"Be careful, Kurs," one of the bestial guards said.

"I know the way to keep the scum alive," Kurs growled his reply.

"We've been pushing them hard. If one dies before the changing, we'll have to answer to the master."

A look of fear passed over Kurs's face. "No more whipping," he agreed, "but they are moving faster now."

"This will make our quota. We'll get our reward tonight."

"Yeah, women! There's one of them prisoners. . . ." Kurs's voice faded as they followed the staggering line.

The green hand that had been restraining Jarl from action dropped. "I am sorry. The Shadowlord is master of monstrous evil. Many of your kind have passed down this path."

"Women, too?" Jarl asked through clenched teeth.

"And children," was the sad answer that accompanied Leafshine's nod.

"I've got to get to Fellkeep. Are there many of these slave parties on the roads?"

"The number grows daily. The total is unknown. The

raiding parties must now go long distances to find unprotected humans, but there are dozens who search."

"How are these prisoners changed? What is the changing referred to by the slaver?"

"I do not know. Many go into Fellkeep and few come out," Leafshine told Jarl. "There are no oaks around Fellkeep. The ground is swampy. The wyverns have made most of the clear portions of the swamp poisonous so that none can travel there. That way they can better watch the comings and goings of the Shadowlord's servants."

"Is there no safe way to proceed?"

"There is one narrow way through the oak forest made by the Old Ones. With your talisman you may be able to sense it. The old magic guards it well. Evil will not touch him who follows it."

"I'd better get started. There is nothing I can do about my friend, but I can still rescue Mirza." Jarl looked down at the ground far below. Then he started searching for a place to tie the section of rope that had bound him to Faf's leg.

"That won't be necessary," Leafshine said.

"I've got to get down somehow." The oak was large. The spaces between its mighty branches were too wide for Jarl to climb down unassisted.

Leafshine gestured to the other side of the tree. Jarl looked and saw a series of branches sprouting at convenient intervals.

"Will they hold me?" he asked the dryad.

"Of course. I created them for your use."

He tested the first branch. It held, and he began his trip earthward. There was no exact way of telling how far he had come, for the branches disappeared as he finished using them. He didn't bother checking below him. He supposed that the dryad was materializing them under him as he needed them. He reached the ground without incident. Solid earth felt unexpectedly good under his feet.

He jerked as he heard a distant thunderclap. "What was that?"

Leafshine smiled. "It is your friend returning."

"Faf?" A shower of tree leaves answered his question as the dragon arrowed down through the branches to join him on the ground under the giant tree.

"Sorry, Leafshine, I'm wounded and my control isn't all it should be." Some leaves fluttered around Faf as he spoke.

"I understand," the dryad said.

Faf sprawled in exhaustion. Jarl examined the long scorch mark on the dragon's wing.

"Faf, that was a close call. I thought—I thought—"

"I know, Jarl, but aside from my flying's being pretty erratic, the injury is minor."

"What happened up there? It looked as if you and those birds disappeared."

"I just flew home."

"You make it sound so easy. What do you mean you flew home? Your cave is miles from here."

"We dragons have the ability to return home instantaneously from anyplace where we may be. When I got there, the birds weren't with me."

"What do you think happened to them? Did the Shadowlord recall them?"

"I don't really care, Jarl. They disappeared and I, for one, am quite happy to see the last of them. They may look like birds, but magically created weapons is what they are." Faf drew a ragged breath.

Jarl and Leafshine looked at one another. They knew Faf's wound must be serious.

"Leafshine, can Faf stay here with you until he's healed?"

"Yes, if he wishes," she answered.

Faf raised his head proudly. "I'm going with you."

"And I'd like you to come, too, but it just isn't possible. You're already wounded. You can't fly correctly. The only way to reach Fellkeep is to walk—and you know how you hate walking!"

"I won't be able to get airborne for several days. I'll have to walk. At least until I get to the Wyvern Marsh."

"And what will you do there? Swim?"

"I'll get them to help me. My mother was a friend of the wyverns' queen. For old-time friendship, they may cure me with some of the mud from their cavern."

"You'll never be able to walk all that way."

"Perhaps I can help, Noddie." Leafshine patted Faf as if he were a small child.

Too tired to blush, Faf just rolled his eyes and then closed them. Leafshine melted into her tree, but returned in a few seconds carrying a cup-sized acorn full of a dark green liquid.

"Drink this!"

"Do I have to?" The dragon raised his head so it was too high for the dryad to reach.

Leafshine stamped her foot. "Fafnoddle von Fafnir! Stop this nonsense!" She stood directly in front of the dragon as he lowered his head reluctantly. The tip of his red tongue forked out of his mouth slightly. "All the way, now. I don't want to waste any of this," she commanded. The tongue inched out a bit more and she grabbed its tip, pouring the entire dose on it as Faf quickly retracted it.

"See? That wasn't so bad," she soothed as Jarl watched, fascinated. "There's a good dragon," she praised as she kissed him on the snout.

"Bitter stuff," he complained.

"You're feeling better already, aren't you?" she teased.

"Drat it, yes, yes, but—"

The reply reminded Jarl of old Fafnir. Clearly Faf was a scale off the old hide—at least in some ways.

The dryad looked at Jarl. "You'll need some help, too."

"I'm not wounded or exhausted," he assured her hurriedly. He didn't want any part of her dosing.

"Not medicine. Magic." Her lips twitched, but she managed not to laugh.

"Oh," Jarl breathed, well aware of Faf's ill-concealed grin.

Leafshine held out her finger. It swiftly grew into a twig

with one sturdy green leaf at the tip. She broke it off and handed it to Jarl. "Use this to find your way."

"Oh, you mean the Old Ones' path. What am I supposed to do with this?" Jarl looked at the twig. It certainly seemed ordinary enough.

"Simply hold it in front of you. It will activate the spell as you pass. Start to your right," she instructed, fading swiftly from sight before Jarl could thank her.

"Are you ready, Faf?"

"Lead the way," Faf said in a falsely hearty manner. He wasn't very good at hiding his pain, but he tried.

Jarl started to his right. He held the branch in the air. He didn't need to hear Faf's snicker behind him to know he looked odd walking through the woods waving a branch like a fairy wand. He was too glad to have Faf safe to get really annoyed. He was about ready to suggest they find their way to the road and take their chances with the Shadowlord's raiding parties. The woods around them became brighter with a pleasant glow.

A golden avenue almost ten feet wide appeared before them. Following the branch as if it were a dowsing rod, Faf and Jarl trod the Old Ones' highway, safe from the detection of the Shadowlord. They made good time. By nightfall, Faf insisted he could smell the marsh ahead. They camped on a piece of mosaic which held the faded outline of a pentacle within its perimeter.

They ate fruit and bread for their meal. It was the last of the supplies the king sent with them. Faf seemed satisfied, but Jarl entertained a fleeting thought of the old witch's magic bag. A hot meat pasty, a steak sandwich, even a hot dog would have been more filling than bread and fruit.

Jarl watched the moon. He remembered camping trips he took when he was a boy. He felt the quiet peace of the night. This reminded him of other nights sleeping under the stars —except, of course, on former trips he didn't have a dragon curled up around the fire. The heat radiated off Faf's scales. His tail poked the fire if it showed signs of dying down too far. Jarl had a nagging feeling that Mirza needed him. The king had three days to decide about joining the Shadowlord. What might have happened to Mirza in the days since being captured worried him. What did her captor want from her? Jarl didn't know exactly how powerful or important Mirza actually was here in Realm. He did know enough about her to be sure she would never join the forces of the Dark. Were her powers protecting her in spite of her being in the clutches of the Shadowlord? The first time he rescued her she was bound by a magic chain, but she wasn't suffering. She was simply a prisoner. She had not confided in Jarl. How did she come to be a captive? Why was she kept in the desert? What part did the Shadowlord want her to play in his evil schemes? Faf said he could smell the marsh. Fellkeep was close. Jarl knew he had twenty-four hours to get to the prince and rescue Mirza.

He concentrated on Wyrd. He formed a question in his mind.

"Sssleep," a forceful thought came. And Jarl did.

Faf dragon-napped throughout the night. His wound was becoming more painful as time passed. The dryad's restorative gradually wore off. He looked forward to meeting the wyvern queen. Surely when they entered the marsh that was part of their watery domain, they would contact the wyverns. Twice during the night he roused to see the wand and the pentacle blaze with power. He dimly sensed evil within the wood. He thought a question in his best High Dragon, the tongue that dragons used only when conversing among themselves.

His reply came in the same tongue. "Sleep." And Faf did.

The next morning's light found Faf and Jarl following the Old Ones' highroad. Jarl eagerly forged ahead. He wanted to rescue Mirza. Faf was just as impatient to travel, but his reason was the pain from his wound. He always eschewed violence on moral grounds, but now he had an even better reason for his avoidance: violence could hurt. He had no intention of telling Jarl how weak he was becoming. A powerful dragon shouldn't feel like sitting down in the road and crying. He gritted his magnificent teeth and blanked his pain from his mind. He recited basic cantrips and then advanced to more esoteric spells. Right in the middle of a particularly difficult one, he bumped into Jarl, almost forcing him into the slimy pool that lapped the shore on which they stood. Faf and Jarl watched, dismayed, as the oak branch flickered, paled, and died.

CHAPTER
Sixteen

"WELL, that's it, Faf. No more magic in the wand. No more path."

"This is the wyverns' marsh. I know where we are now."

"Looks like a swamp to me, no matter what you call it. Now what do we do? I don't relish wading in that." Jarl poked the withered branch into the murky ooze. A few bubbles popped on the surface. Several feet from the bank the water undulated as if something moved beneath the surface.

"Swamp adder," Faf said, cocking an interested eye at the ripples.

"Poisonous?"

"Not very. A little moley will cure most bites. It only chases things that are smaller than it is anyway."

"That's good news."

"Not exactly" Faf hissed. "Swamp adders have grown to a length of fifty feet."

"Fifty feet!"

"Don't worry. I'm with you," Faf consoled his friend. "Besides, although it's been years since I was last here, I seem to remember a series of pathways." Faf craned his not inconsiderably long neck to the left and the right. "Ah, here it is. A dragon never forgets. The footing here will be tricky. Give me a sprig of your moley. It will ease my pain temporarily and give me strength." Jarl silently passed his friend the herb.

Faf led the way to a half-sunk stone, placed the moley in his mouth, raised his tail over his back, and stepped out. "Just follow me," he advised over his shoulder.

Jarl had always heard that elephants didn't forget. He could see a definite similarity between elephants and dragons. Faf interjected a mental "Humph!" which made Jarl jump. Another glance at the half-sunk stone and he sincerely hoped that on Realm dragons remembered. As Jarl started out, he wondered about how many of his thoughts Faf picked up. Jarl also worried about getting through the swamp before the moley's power to invigorate the dragon ran out. If Faf slipped, being swept into the nearest swamp adder's coils and ending up as a snack was what Jarl envisioned. He hopped carefully after his friend. For Jarl the gaps between stones were large ones, but for the dragon they were small spaces. Jarl was so busy following Faf he didn't even spare a smile at the odd sight Faf made, mincing along from stone to tussock, tussock to stone.

"Are you all right back there?"

"Yeah," Jarl puffed. "I'm fine, but could you go a little slower?" Jarl marveled at the power of the moley. Faf seemed fine.

"This particular piece of the swamp remains alone because there are always some—let us say unpleasant denizens in this part of the marsh."

"Great," Jarl muttered under his breath. "That's me, a hopping hors d'oeuvre for the friendly neighborhood monsters."

"Not such farther. There's a waiting place a short distance ahead."

"Glad to hear it," Jarl answered, more to let Faf know he was still alive and hopping than to carry on the conversation.

When they reached a moss-covered flat ledge some inches above the surrounding muck, Faf swung around to view Jarl's last hop to relative safety. He expelled a short jet of fire at a creeping tendril that writhed toward his friend. It withered from the blast.

Jarl dropped his sword back into his sheath. "Thanks. I'm glad you haven't given up smoking. What do we do now?"

"We wait."

"We don't have time to stand around. We must go on to Fellkeep—"

"It has been long since one of your kind has come to us. What do you and the Man-one desire of the wyverns that you wait upon our Judgment Rock?" The sibilant voice of an unseen listener interrupted Jarl as if the human's comments were unimportant.

"What—" Jarl began.

"Quiet. The success or failure of our mission may rest upon what we say in the next few minutes," Faf warned.

"Speak," the voice commanded.

"I, Fafnoddle von Fafnir, son of Draka of the Flame, claim guest right of Lythyr, your queen."

"What gives you this right, dragon?"

"I do not claim it on distant cousinship, but because of the friendship which my mother shared with Lythyr in the days of her youth before she became your sovereign."

Faf sat like a graven image, awaiting the verdict. Jarl wondered what they would do if the wyverns refused their aid.

"I acknowledge your right."

From the mist that clung to the south side of the rock came a raft poled by two lizard people.

"Come," the disembodied voice invited.

Jarl and Faf boarded the raft, which sank with the addition of their combined weight. Jarl moved to the center when he saw ominous ripples in front of the raft. For once he found Faf's great size a comfort.

The strange craft moved silently through the marsh on the watery byway that was not clear to Jarl. On the north side, at least, the wyverns were impregnable to attack from any ordinary source.

"How far does this swamp spread?" Jarl wondered aloud.

"Several days' journey in all directions except to the south," Faf answered.

The lizard beings said nothing, but steadily propelled the raft forward to a destination known only to them.

"What's to the south—besides Fellkeep, I mean?"

"The Southern Sea and the home caves of the wyverns."

"How do you know so much about them? I thought you said they didn't like males."

"They don't, but my mother used to tell me stories about her dragonettehood. In the old days Lythyr and my mother adventured together."

"Have you met this—Lythyr?" Jarl's human tongue was about six inches too short to give the name the correct pronunciation, but he tried.

"Once when I was just out of the egg, she came to visit. She told my mother I would grow into an unusual dragon." Faf chuckled. "She was correct, but my mother took small comfort from the accuracy of her prediction."

"Are we prisoners or something? Why don't those fellows talk to us?"

"They're male wyverns," Faf explained.

"So what? They could still pass the time of day."

"Wyvern society is matriarchal. One of the reasons wyverns so seldom come into contact with humankind and the other denizens of Realm is they deeply disapprove of our system. The system of allowing the males to be the dominant members of our groups."

"Can't they talk?"

"After a fashion, and then only to wyverns in their clan." Faf smiled at the outraged expression on his companion's face. "It is their way and has been for so long as any can remember. They are as they are."

"That is wisdom indeed, oh fiery one." The words interrupted the conversation.

Faf began to speak to the wyvern who stood on the bank

that loomed out of the mist. "This is Jarl—" He stopped in midspeech.

"Yes. Follow me."

The green body of the humanoid wyvern glistened emerald. Their guide wore no clothing except a thin belt from which hung various implements. Jarl was unable to recognize most of them. He could appreciate the sharpness of the small dagger that hung, unsheathed, at the wyvern's side.

This path reminded Jarl of the Old Ones' road in many ways. Could the Old Ones have been wyvern ancestors? Jarl had received no hint of the shape of the revered legendary Old Ones from the conversations in which they were mentioned. There were so many things in Realm of which he was ignorant. So far he had been fortunate in his mentors.

He wondered how long Faf could keep moving with his wound. Perhaps the Old Ones' way had healing properties like their sanctuaries. The wound looked inflamed to human eyes, but how was one to know with a dragon? Faf's deliberate pace was halting, showing signs of the strain he endured. Jarl marveled at the bravery of his friend. For an ardent pacifist, Faf put up quite a fight when he had to. Jarl expected a scholarly dragon to be persistent and intelligent. Now he realized Faf's courage and stoic endurance of pain. The blood of his lineage made a difference. His father had a son he could be proud to acknowledge when told of this adventure. If they successfully returned after they bearded the Shadowlord in his keep, Jarl amended his thoughts silently.

Their guide passed under the last of the huge vines that snaked across the few trees hardy enough to perch themselves on grassy hummocks and survive. Jarl trailed after at a distance of several feet. His eyes no longer had to adjust to the change in the light. Thus it was that he saw a shadow pass above the wyvern a split second before the creature realized the danger. Jarl's sword sprang to his hand automatically. It sliced the head from the repulsive mottled green and black attacker, spraying its yellow blood liberally. It writhed on the ground as the three watched from a distance.

Finally a last few flops drained it of its remaining pseudo-life and it lay still.

Jarl approached, but the wyvern halted him after the first few steps.

"No, Man-one. Even in death such things are dangerous."

The wyvern gestured to the withered leaves of some plants that blood from the dead attacker had touched.

"What was it?" Jarl asked. He thought it was a good idea to know the name of anything he killed. He marveled at how proficient he was becoming with the sword.

"We call it the Death-that-flies. It is only one of the many reasons for our enmity to the Shadowlord. Such were not seen here until he became Lord of Fellkeep."

The wyvern hurried them through the open spaces and at last turned between two rocks that seemed riven by some giant force. Jarl and Faf passed through the entrance to the wyvern's home cavern.

The smell of the sea air and the brightness of the light gave way to cool darkness as they traveled deeper. The low ceiling made it necessary for Faf to bend his neck to traverse the route. Jarl felt concern for his friend. How much longer could the dragon bear the added strain of a somewhat unnatural position? A draft of warmer air heralded their arrival at a main cavern.

Jarl could see no source of the dim illumination in the vast chamber. Many wyverns passed silently on errands. He received a whispery sensation just out of his comprehension range. The denizens of the cavern were only silent to the human ear. Jarl's mind felt the touch of the wyverns as they greeted their guide. Two wyverns, obviously guards, stopped them when they reached an opening on the other side of the vast hall-like room.

"The queen summoned," their guide explained.

The guards moved aside, giving the party leave to proceed.

"Here is the Man-one you requested, Queen Lythyr."

"Welcome."

The word, spoken in deference to their male state, was

unnecessary. Jarl sensed the ancient wisdom behind the quiet dignity. A slender silver chain hung around her neck. That and the aura of power that emanated from her were the only signs that differentiated the queen from her subjects.

On the chain was a circular crystal disk, rimmed by a thin silver band. Something in the nature of the disk kept Jarl from gazing at it too closely. Yet it was compelling in its beauty, gleaming in the glow which came from the walls of the room itself.

"This one saved my life again," their guide told the ruler.

"So, my daughter, this one rescued you from the korred. I am much indebted to you," she said, turning her huge eyes on Jarl.

"Jarl is Dragon's Pawn," Faf said, as if that explained everything.

"It had been long and long again since Wyrd selected a human as champion. Long-lived though we are, it was in the time of my mother's mother that such happened last."

"Can you help me reach Fellkeep?" Jarl asked. He felt awkward when they talked about him as if he were not present.

"What purpose has the wearer of Wyrd in the lair of Evil?"

"I go to rescue Mirza." Jarl said the words simply, not realizing he had fallen into the diction of the wyvern queen.

"Know you of the evil powers of the Shadowlord? To enter his domain is foolishness indeed unless you are most careful."

"There is great need. Mirza is my . . . friend." Friend wasn't the exact relationship he wanted, but it was the only word that fit. There was no word in his language to express the idea of woman-attracted-to-but-male-has-not-yet-responded.

The queen nodded. "I understand, Man-one. Why ask help from us? Know you that we do not enter into the quarrels among men?"

"This isn't a quarrel exactly," Jarl began.

"Queen Lythyr, the Shadowlord makes war upon us all.

His birdthings attacked me," Faf said, sounding almost indignant at the idea. "The actions of the Shadowlord indicate that he considers anyone not on his side to be either his enemy or his prey."

"To our recent sorrow, we know. Six of my warrior maidens died, and still the korred captured Seabreeze. Your saving Seabreeze allowed us warning of the evil planned for our race."

"Does he want to force you to become his allies?" Faf asked.

"Seabreeze discovered that the Shadowlord plans to go far upstream to the source of the mighty river that forms this marsh and block it."

"Then the marsh will dry. . . ." Jarl thought aloud.

"Yes, our natural protection would vanish. Our magic workers are too few to guard our borders successfully on four sides. Evil will flow against us from every direction."

"Won't the Keepers aid you?" Faf asked quietly.

"Our calls have gone unanswered. It is many days' journey to the north. The way is long and dangerous after we pass King Caeryl's land."

"His kingdom, too, is in danger of being sucked into the power of the Shadowlord," Faf said gloomily.

"What mean you, fiery one?"

"Prince Leon is now a prisoner in the castle of Fellkeep. Jarl here has a magic talisman he needs to deliver to the prince if he can. If Jarl fails, King Caeryl must become a vassal to the Shadowlord or lose his son forever."

"May I see the talisman?"

Jarl dropped the acorn into the three-fingered hand of the queen.

"Ah, it is a transportation spell that Relnot intends. His border magic is excellent, but this will not be effective within the confines of Fellkeep. The Shadowlord would be instantly alert to any good magic within the walls of the castle."

"Then it is hopeless?" asked a disappointed Jarl. Did he now have two people to rescue?

"Not worthless if you can get the prince here to Judgment Rock. It was a place of power to the Old Ones. Enough yet remains to animate a spell for Good."

"Do you make a practice of rescuing the innocent, Man-one?" Seabreeze's question held a tinge of amusement.

"Well, not until lately," Jarl said honestly. "Wyrd is a good influence on me."

"As Dragon's Pawn, will you carry word of our circumstances to the Keepers?" the queen asked as she returned the acorn to Jarl.

Faf focused his half-closed eyes on the queen. "Didn't you and my mother venture into Fellkeep during the years when it was empty?"

"You have not outgrown your habit of questioning, fiery one," the queen began. "So you know the tales of your mother's deeds. Many times we searched where wiser heads would have forbidden us entry had they known. Perhaps it was part of the great design that we should seek knowledge which seemed to have no usefulness save that it was perilous to gather."

"Did you find anything that might help me gain entrance to Fellkeep?" At any other time Jarl would have enjoyed listening to the wyvern's tales, but now the urgency of reaching Mirza took precedence over all else.

"It is many years since the way had travelers. I can draw a map, but whether it would serve you as it served us remains hidden."

"Mother, can you not use your scry stone to look?" Seabreeze suggested hesitantly.

"What you ask may be dangerous, but with proper precautions—perhaps."

"The Man-one aided me. . . ." Seabreeze's reminder trailed into silence.

"Very well. I shall try." The queen passed through a low doorway, beckoning for them to follow.

Jarl ducked to enter the small room where Lythyr seated herself on a throne, submerging the disk on her neck in a circular pool. Scenes passed over the surface of the water.

Fafnoddle, unable to enter because of his size, satisfied himself by peering from the doorway.

Lythyr's voice spoke in the minds of her watchers. "Two will search the ancient passages. . . . One returns, the other travels onward. . . . A door opens. . . . Within the room lies . . ."

Jarl! Is that you? I sense the power of the Light. Who is it? Mirza's thought reached them clearly. She was mind-sending through the wyvern's disk.

"She is indeed One of Power," Lythyr whispered. "Answer quickly, Man-one. To hold power within the circle is difficult."

Jarl looked at the blurred image in the submerged disk. "How can I find you within the Keep?" He hurled his thought with all the force he possessed.

Mirza winced. Jarl was becoming adept at mindtalk and didn't realize he need not shout mentally to make himself heard. "I'm within the south tower. The evil here insulates me from Realmgate."

"Hurry!" hissed Lythyr. "I sense the Shadowlord. He has begun tracing the link!"

"Jarl, come quickly! I've found out—"

"Is she all right?" Jarl said. "What happened?" He looked into the swirling mists of the disk.

"I do not think your mate suffered any physical damage when the Shadowlord destroyed the link," the queen told Jarl gently. "Sometimes the stone tells more than present things. Within the stone, time is of no consequence. Perhaps my visions were of incidents yet to occur."

"Could you see Mirza?"

"For me, she was shrouded by mist, battling some evil I can only sense. The danger to her is of the Dark. It is well you hurried to her aid, Man-one. I fear the Shadowlord knows you come. The time grows short." Lythyr turned from Jarl to Fafnoddle. "Fiery one, you are in great pain. Why did you not tell us of your wound?"

"It is only a small scratch—"

"Do males ever admit the truth? Turn and go to the other

side of the main cavern, bender-of-truth," Lythyr said, shaking her head at Faf's folly. She pointed. "There you will find a pool of heal mud, one of the wonders of the ancient dwellers that still serves the Light."

Faf withdrew his head, allowing them to exit the room that held the submerged throne. They watched him stagger to the heal mud. They heard him grumble, "It's a great deal of fuss over nothing." He sank into the mud. Only his head remained on the bank. His great eyelids closed in a blissful expression. "Very comfortable," he managed before falling asleep.

"He rests. That is good," Seabreeze said.

"In a day or two he will recover his full strength," Lythyr added indulgently.

Jarl knew the queen had a soft-scaled place for the child of her old friend. "Poor Faf. He wanted to go with me to Fellkeep."

"He will sleep until healed. When he wakes, he must feed. Then we will see. We must have many fish prepared."

"Not fish, Your Majesty." Jarl explained. "Faf's a vegetarian. He eats mushrooms, fruits, nuts, and berries." Jarl enumerated the things he had seen the dragon eat.

"That simplifies matters. There are many edibles which grow in the marsh if one knows how to look. Your friend may eat his fill when he wakes."

"Will you not share a meal with us, Man-one?" Seabreeze asked.

"I can't wait to begin my trip to Fellkeep." Jarl excused himself.

"Some little time has passed in the outside world. Now the Dark rules. It's better to begin our journey tomorrow," Seabreeze told Jarl.

"Our journey? You can't go with me! It's too dangerous for a—" He searched for a word. If he said female he'd probably get lynched. "Wyvern." He felt a chuckle from his bracelet. Clearly Wyrd understood what was happening although he chose not to play a part in events.

"I, too, can use the disk—even when it's worn by my

mother," the wyvern explained. "The two figures she saw were you and I."

"But—"

"The disk sees truth, Man-one. I will be your guide."

"Far be it from me to resist both magic and female logic." Jarl snorted.

The wyverns nodded, accepting his words as a simple statement of fact.

Seabreeze looked at Lythyr, who stood silent during the conversation between her daughter and Jarl. "After dinner, we will study the map my mother has made for us."

"But I will start my journey to Fellkeep as soon as I have seen the map," Jarl insisted.

Lythyr's three-fingered hand lightly touched the device at her neck as she looked at Seabreeze. A silent message passed between them.

"It shall be as you say, Man-one. We shall assist you on your way. Tomorrow I shall join you, and I shall be your guide," said Seabreeze.

And womanlike, the wyvern had the last word.

CHAPTER
Seventeen

*J*ARL stood on the bank and watched the raft which had brought him to shore disappear in the evening mists over the wyverns' swamp. Somehow the darkness of night seemed deeper here on the bank so near to Fellkeep. Jarl walked carefully, looking for the large tree that the wyverns had told him about. It would give him some protection from the Death-that-flies and the other weird creatures that infested the area the Shadowlord controlled. Jarl's confidence in Wyrd's powers had amused the wyverns, but Jarl felt he couldn't wait. Tomorrow was the third day of the three granted by King Caeryl. Jarl felt he needed to get to Fellkeep and find the prince as soon as possible. The wyverns had told him where he would find an entrance, and he expected to be there long before Seabreeze caught up to him.

Looming ahead of him, he saw the huge tree, covered with moss that almost touched the ground. It made a darker blot in the darkness that seems to clutch him with palpable fingers. Jarl took a deep breath and entered. Inside, the darkness was less dense. Clearly the evil appearance of the tree was a clever disguise meant to ward off evil. There the wyverns could rest safely right under the nose of the Shadow-lord—if he had a nose, Jarl thought grimly. Everything depended on what he could achieve the next day. He was honor bound to try to rescue Prince Leon. As soon as he delivered the boy to the wyverns for transportation to Judgment Rock, he would try to rescue Mirza. No, he amended to himself. I *will* rescue Mirza.

Jarl reached into his pocket and brought out the fire stone the wyverns had given him. It looked like an ordinary piece of coal to Jarl. If the wyverns said it would start a fire at his command, he was ready to believe it. Too much evidence had piled up to prove magic existed here on Realm. At home placing an unlit piece of common coal upon the ground and telling it to light mentally would have earned Jarl free room and board at a local funny farm. Here, the coal lit a cheery blaze out of nothing.

Jarl sat and absentmindedly rubbed Wyrd. He felt a little lonesome. The bracelet sent no sense of communication into Jarl's mind. It was as if the bracelet were exactly what it pretended to be: an odd piece of jewelry. Jarl wondered if Wyrd feared the Shadowlord. Or could it be that the dragon was merely saving his vast powers for the rescue attempt the next morning? Jarl had almost dozed off when he saw the hanging moss at the edge of the tree-created clearing begin to move. His hand clutched his sword. Had Seabreeze changed her mind? Just like a woman. She had promised to join him later. How late was later to a wyvern? Jarl had the impression she had stayed to finish off some magical mumbo jumbo, wyvern style. He knew it was nowhere near morning. Wyrd remained relaxed on Jarl's wrist, so he knew whoever came was a friend. He sat, alert, waiting.

A human hand brushed the hanging moss aside. A dark-haired man entered the open space. He wore a black belt over a dark outfit. His clothing marked him as a martial arts master of some kind.

The stranger smiled at Jarl and gestured to the small fire. "May I join you?" he asked.

Jarl glanced at his bracelet. Wyrd had not tightened;

therefore, this man, whoever he was, must be a friend. "All right."

"I suppose you wonder what a decent human being is doing so close to Fellkeep," the stranger began conversationally.

"And?" Jarl replied

"Sent here by some mutual acquaintances, you might say," replied the stranger.

"Mutual acquaintances?" Jarl repeated. "Who?"

"One of them is a little old lady," the stranger began.

"Say no more." Jarl smiled. "Is she as enigmatic with you as she is with me?"

"I don't know if I'd choose that word exactly. Since most of what she says must be nonsense, you could say she didn't come across as much of an explainer."

"Yeah. I know just how you feel," Jarl said, accepting the man without reservation for the first time.

The man covered his mouth to hide a yawn. "If you don't mind, tomorrow is time enough to talk. Let's catch a little shut-eye, okay?"

Jarl noticed the use of the term shut-eye. "You're from Earth, too, aren't you?"

The man nodded. "Got it in one," he murmured, settling down on the other side of the small blaze.

Jarl smiled to himself. Well, he thought silently, even if Wyrd is strangely silent tonight, I've still got friends pulling for me. A martial arts expert would make a fine ally, if he would join Jarl. And why else would the old wise woman send him if not to help? Cheered, Jarl fell asleep.

A shadow moving across the dappled sunlight woke Jarl from his sleep. Jarl started to stand and then realized he was trussed like a Thanksgiving turkey. His hands were tied behind him. The stranger was minus his black belt, so Jarl knew what restrained him. "Traitor," he hissed, sounding more like Wyrd than he knew.

"No, not traitor," the man said. "Ally."

"Is that how a friend behaves on Realm?" Jarl pulled at his bonds futilely.

"If I could figure out how anything in this damn place works, I wouldn't be here. I am the Shadowlord's enemy, not yours."

"So you tie me up so near his keep that he could send a little old lady to drag me in and succeed?" Jarl's lips thinned mockingly.

"Can't you just take my word?" The question seemed anguished.

"Seeing is believing. Just take off these bonds if you're so friendly, and then I'll believe you."

"It's necessary that you stay tied for a while. You'll work your way free eventually."

"Liar." Jarl spat the word angrily.

"I can prove myself the Shadowlord's enemy," the stranger said sadly. He reached up with his gloved hand and pulled the rubber mask from his face.

Jarl stared in horror. The warty green visage which stared at him contained human eyes, but the dripping fluid which seeped from the creature's face radiated a sickening green glow.

"The Shadowlord did this to me. I was to be the hero and rescue this crazy place from the Shadowlord. I brought modern weapons and all my tactical skills to the battle."

"Then why did they need me? How could you lose?" Jarl asked, trying to settle his stomach by looking into the creature's eyes and ignoring the horror of his face.

"I lost because I can't believe in magic. The Shadowlord asked me to join him. I still think I'd have to be nuts to start taking orders from some charlatan in a hooded robe. He looks like some monk out of the Middle Ages. He must have some mental powers, but he can't be a magician because there aren't any such things!" He pounded his clenched fist into his other hand.

"How can you doubt that magic works here? There are too many strange events for logic to explain away. I didn't believe at first myself, but after meeting dragons, and a unicorn, and the old witch—" Jarl shook his head. "I know I sound crazy, but magic does exist, and on Realm magic works."

"I didn't believe in magic when I came and I still don't."

"Then how do you explain what has happened to you?"

"It's some kind of germ warfare. It must be."

Jarl felt sorry for the creature. Not being able to accept the reality of Realm made him even more vulnerable to the powers of magic. The poor guy had never had a chance. Jarl thought of the many times magic—or magical beings—had saved him.

The creature was pulling a second mask out of his small pack. Jarl watched as the creature pulled it on. The creature pulled out a bracelet in the shape of a dragon and put it on his arm. "Now I'm ready," he said grimly.

"Ready for what? Halloween? Let me go and we can team up. I have to enter the keep and free—"

"No, don't tell me. It's better if I don't know. In case the Shadowlord tries to pick my brain, there won't be any information there that will help him."

"Wait!" Jarl called softly. "Where are you going? What are you going to do?"

"I'm going to leave you tied, for starters, and then, like the hero I'm pretending to be, I'm going to keep an appointment."

"An appointment?" Jarl mentally cursed his tendency to repeat parts of a statement when he didn't understand. He thought he sounded like an idiot when he did it.

"The Dragon's Pawn must die," the creature said calmly. "My condition is not correctable—or so the old woman says. Once the green grue gets over your head, nobody can do anything. I choose not to live my life as a mutant or whatever the Shadowlord has made me into with his strange drugs or rays. So the Dragon's Pawn shall die in battle, taking as many of the enemy with him as he can." The Jarl mask smiled down at the tied man. "Wish me luck, buddy. Once the Shadowlord thinks you're gone, you should have an easy time thwarting him." With a wave of his hand, the Jarl impostor disappeared through the moss.

Jarl lay on the ground, struggling silently with his bonds. In the distance he heard the noise of battle, but he couldn't get free. "Wyrd!" Jarl thought. "Why don't you help me?"

Wyrd gripped his arm tightly but made no reply.

"You must know all about that poor guy. I don't even know his name," Jarl muttered through clenched teeth.

Wyrd remained inanimate.

"And I trusted you! What's this lesson supposed to teach me?" Don't even trust your allies on Realm?"

The sounds of battle stopped abruptly.

Jarl sighed. "That's it. Scratch one human."

The tree moss swayed as a body forced itself into the open space beneath the moss.

"What the—"

"I told you I would be your guide, Man-one," Seabreeze said. "I mourn our loss."

"Our loss? Yeah, our loss. My loss, you mean. Why didn't you help that poor guy?"

"Because we wyverns are magical creatures—and he did not believe in magic. Many allies he had if he could only have believed in our powers. He destroyed himself by refusing the aid of the magical beings that were his friends," she concluded sadly.

"Now we go to rescue our friends." She folded the black belt and offered it to Jarl. "Perhaps you would like this," she added as she turned and left the shelter of the tree, knowing Jarl would follow.

Jarl didn't want to remember the trip to Fellkeep. The wyvern quickly deserted solid ground for more marsh. Jarl felt safer within its walls than he did passing through the marsh on foot and on the wyvern's craft. That morning he saw more ripples than before. He watched the giant black and gold reptiles slide like animated branches from half-sunk tree limbs. He prudently kept his hand on his sword the whole time because of their waterly coming and going. He wasn't certain if the adders were so active because it was breakfast time, the end of their night's hunting, or because his giant companion had intimidated them the previous day. He knew that feeling the hard rock of the shore under his feet was a distinct relief.

Brush and boulders screened the opening to the passages. Only someone looking for the entrance and knowing its probable location could find it. Jarl's skin tingled as they passed within the confines of the castle.

"It's raw power," Seabreeze said. "The Shadowlord draws it from other worlds regardless of what he does to the energy balance. It may well be that some sun is being depleted to feed his insatiable machines. If the gate he forged here collapses, my people and our home will disappear in a burst of ravening power that may well split this world. Do you now see why my kind shun men?"

"All men are not like the Shadowlord," Jarl protested.

"Where you come from all men are peaceable and rational?" The wyvern cast him a sly look.

Jarl did the best he could without actually lying. He ignored the question.

"Follow," she said. "Past this point, only necessary talking lest we stir trouble best left alone."

"Agreed," Jarl answered. He acted as yes-man for the wyvern, and he didn't like the idea much. It didn't fit his picture of a hero.

"Indeed," she added, having the last word as usual, "when one enters the mouth of the mercat, one does not prod its tongue."

Their way led forward into the bowels of the keep. The walls showed no breakages once past the entrance. The dry walls glowed with the form of light Jarl recognized as a hallmark of the Old Ones' construction. A barrier of stone blocked their path. He stopped, but Seabreeze kept walking. She faded into the barrier and disappeared.

Jarl gulped and followed. Anything a wyvern could do, he could do, too. After a cool sensation, the darkness was total.

"Ssss," Seabreeze whispered her caution as she opened the pouch on her belt and took out what seemed to be a live coal. She dropped it on the unlit torch she carried. It responded with a warming light. Again she led the way.

Now the air cooled. The light flickered, illuminating half-visible scratches on the wall a good six feet from the floor. Small scurrying noises told them they were not alone in the passages. Seabreeze never faltered as she led them past openings that were the beginnings of other corridors. The torch glow was strong. Against the wall Jarl saw a misshaped skull. Tiny scurriers had carried off the smaller bones of the creature years ago. The larger bones remained as mute witness to one adventurer who had entered and found death.

Jarl and Seabreeze ascended a series of steps. He was certain the curved walls meant they were within the tower stones themselves, but he saw no signs of any openings. Were there no windows in Fellkeep? Or were they cleverly hidden under the treads of the stairs they climbed?

"We are near the one you seek." A three-fingered hand pointed ahead.

"Is there an entrance marked on the map?"

"There are many ways to tower rooms from this passage. We must use care that we do not enter a place where Evil waits. It is possible that Relnot tuned the acorn you bear to the presence of the prince. If this is so, we can tell when we are near him." The whisper of the wyvern was as soft as her name.

Jarl took the acorn from his pocket. Seabreeze touched it briefly and nodded. He felt a flicker of life within the magician's token.

"I sense the Powers of the Dark within."

Within where? Jarl thought. He could see no differences in the stones which formed the walls of the passageway.

"I use the deep sight of my people. To me, there are doorways. We have passed many such, but their contents were not meant for us. Now I sense a young manling who may be the one you promised to aid."

Jarl willingly gave the acorn into her hand. When she

raised it to the wall and traced a path against the stones, it began to glow greenly.

"The one you seek is within," Seabreeze said with certainty. She traced patterns which glimmered in the air. A door-shaped crack appeared in the stone. Jarl bent his head and passed into the room.

A flaxen-haired boy sat on a rough cot pushed against a bleak wall. His eyes rounded in wonder as Jarl beckoned to him. The boy's head raised proudly at Jarl's gesture. His resemblance to King Caeryl was plain.

"Who are you?" he asked with a great deal of dignity for so young a person.

"A friend. Your father wants you to come with me." Jarl smiled as the prince bounced off the cot.

The prince didn't look behind him as he slipped easily through the narrow door. "Hello," he said courteously to the wyvern. Behind them the door closed silently.

"So, young Man-one, it may be that you are a worthy successor to your father." She handed him the acorn. "This from Relnot. Used properly, it will take you home. It may not be safe to use it yet."

"Isn't my father all right?" the boy asked anxiously.

"I did not mean to alarm you. I spoke of future happenings. You are brave for so small a human."

"I'm as tall as you are. I'm quite normal for my age," Prince Leon assured her seriously.

"Come, then, Evil-slayer. We have no time to waste," Seabreeze told the boy.

"Wait!" Jarl hissed, sounding like Faf. "What about Mirza? I won't leave without her," Jarl said.

"My sight tells me the young one and I are to leave. Before nightfall, he will be at the Rock of Judgment. It will amplify Relnot's spell and carry the prince home. You must continue your quest alone." With these words, she handed Jarl the almost consumed torch. "Good-bye, Man-one." From her pouch she took a silver circlet which glowed when she placed it on her head. She motioned to the boy; they descended the stairs.

CHAPTER
Eighteen

J ARL deplored the rapidity of her exit. She hadn't even told him if the trick for finding the doors would work with Wyrd as the activator. A slight tightening on his arm reassured him.

"Hurry," Wyrd's thoughts echoed in Jarl's mind. "There still lurk in these secret ways creatures we are as well not to meet."

"Agreed," Jarl answered mentally. "And now that Leon is on his way to safety, there's always the possibility that someone will check and find he's missing." Adrenaline flowed through Jarl. He was preternaturally alert. He and Wyrd were on their own again.

Jarl stepped upward, stair by stair, until Wyrd signaled the place of Mirza's confinement. Jarl held his arm next to the wall and somehow he knew the correct movements to make with the bracelet. The pattern he traced was not exactly like the wyvern's, but it produced the same result. The solid wall shifted silently. Jarl mentally applauded the architects of the Old Ones. They certainly knew how to build. Not for the first time Jarl considered what might have happened to so talented a race. They mastered everything they set their abilities to do. What would cause such a race to disappear from Realm?

The shaft of bright light that lit the stones before him showed the layer of dust that had accumulated since anyone had opened the door. Jarl cautiously stepped into the light, and Mirza almost knocked him down, running into his arms.

"Jarl!" she cried.

Despite the danger of their position, Jarl was gratified by the exuberant reception he received. Could Mirza have grown more beautiful during their separation? Their long-delayed embrace was everything to Jarl imagined—and more. Facing the Shadowlord would be a small price to pay to regain Mirza's company. He held her tightly for long seconds, wishing he never had to release her.

Mirza recovered her composure too rapidly to suit Jarl. She shook her head and gently pushed herself away from him. "Do you know a way out?"

"Yes. It's the same way I got in." Jarl grinned. Wyrd tightened on his arm. "Come," Jarl urged, drawing Mirza to the narrow opening.

"No!" a cool voice said from behind them as the opening disappeared in a puff of sulfurous black smoke.

"It's the Shadowlord," Mirza thought to Jarl before they turned to face their enemy together.

"How foolishly brave you've been, Dragon's Pawn."

Jarl stared at the cowled figure that stood before him. Although the setting sun lit the room, a curious haziness existed under the hood where the face of the Shadowlord should have been. Mirza and Jarl stood together before the naked evil of the wizard.

"I thought you were dead—more punishment for those demons who reported you killed. I also did not know that a human could master the power of the talisman so quickly." He peered at their clasped hands. "Or can it be that you gallantly came to the rescue of the fair damsel without mastery of your only weapon?"

"I have my weapon," Jarl started to reply.

"Silence! In Fellkeep there is little that I would use against you that so common a weapon as a sword could destroy."

Jarl looked at it. Common was the last thing he would say about it, but to his surprise it no longer glistened with gems. A plain metal guard protruded from its sheath. No wonder his enemy made light of it! "Perhaps," he said quietly.

"You have caused me considerable annoyance. The prince escaped because of your meddling. I am not yet ready to attack Relnot, so the kingdom will remain independent—for now."

"Good," Jarl said, certain another of Wyrd's scales had turned to gold.

"I will remove those puny border wards when I am ready. You are quite resourceful for a mortal. Because of your potential, I will make you a generous offer."

Jarl said nothing. Mirza clasped his hand wordlessly.

"Aiding the enemy, my dear? In the fullness of time, you, too, will join me."

His remarks rang in Jarl's ears. The words were freighted with menace. He knew Mirza would never willingly aid Evil.

The Shadowlord turned slightly to focus on Jarl. "I offer you the opportunity to join me. I will give you the rulership of Earth."

"What's the catch?" Jarl asked. Perhaps this offer would give him a clue to the Shadowlord's plan.

"There would be certain little tasks given to you—and of course, some minor contributions to our cause."

"Minor! He means letting earthlings become slaves!" Mirza burst in hotly.

The Shadowlord ignored her words. "What is your answer—Pawn?" Jarl's title sounded like an insult coming from the mouth of the wizard.

Jarl wanted to return to Earth, but now that he heard the offer, he knew rather than take it he would remain in exile forever. Jarl gave his answer deliberately. "No."

"They named you well. You are a pawn of the Keepers in a vast game you do not understand. Why should you care for the citizens of alternate earths? If you join my cause—you can protect the majority of the citizens on your world. Isn't Earth one of those places with democracy? Isn't the majority most important?"

The insidious logic of the Shadowlord washed over Jarl. In a strange way, the Shadowlord was right. By joining, Jarl could partially mitigate the evil magic of the empire the wizard would create. Jarl thought about the denizens of Realm. These creatures—no! These people were real. Some of them were his friends. He could not allow them to perish without trying to save them. The Shadowlord was not the type to do favors for anyone. Wyrd must be a lot more powerful than he thought for the wizard to offer power as he had.

"No," Jarl repeated.

"Stubborn, too? Even the powers of the Light must use flawed tools." The Shadowlord laughed. "I will give you until tomorrow to reconsider. If I do not like your final choice, both you and your companion shall know the force of my wrath." The wizard delivered this threat in pleasant tones which underscored his power.

Jarl welcomed a respite. "I will reconsider your offer only if you leave Mirza with me."

"So bold? You are a sparrow bargaining with a hawk, but I will grant your request. Those who follow me get all they desire—within reason." The Shadowlord glided close to Mirza. "Perhaps you will use your charm to encourage him to make a wise decision. You might wish to offer yourself as an object lesson on the folly of noncompliance."

Jarl watched, astounded, as Mirza turned pale. The Shadowlord laughed wickedly. Then he literally winked out as a puff of air extinguishes a candle flame. Nothing of him remained in the room except a faint scent of brimstone which a breeze from the tower window soon dissipated.

"Mirza, are you all right?" Her pallor concerned Jarl. What hold did the Dark have over her? Or was it just his imagination? Most of the women he knew would have had a screaming fit after a scene with a person like the Shadowlord. They needed to escape. Jarl supposed it was a forlorn hope, but he walked over to where the door to freedom had so lately closed. He raised his bracelet. Jarl waited for the surge of knowledge that would tell him how to move his arm to activate the mechanism—or magic—that would open the door for the second time that day. Nothing happened!

Mirza smiled ruefully at him. "Did you actually think our enemy is so inexperienced as to leave a way open to our powers? If that were so, I would have returned to you long since."

"Then you've made no progress in discovering a way to escape?"

"I've tried every kid of magic I ever learned, but all of my spells failed. I can't even change my shape to fly away. My best efforts were the moments of mental contact with you."

"So at least one thing does work." Jarl pondered. "What happened to the black dragon that brought you here?"

"You mean Ebony?"

"Ah, you know his name?"

"Not his—her," Mirza corrected.

"So Ebony is a female dragon. . . ." Jarl imagined a scenario in which Faf recovered, wooed the dragon, and managed an airlift out of Fellkeep. He shook his head. He must be getting desperate. A scenario like the one he envisioned wouldn't even make a good plot for a grade-Z movie.

"She is ensorcelled by the silver chain about her neck. So long as she wears it she is bound to do the bidding of the wizard. She has no choice in what she does."

"Do you talk to her mentally?"

"Oh, yes. Sometimes she flies to that tower over there." Mirza drew Jarl to the one window in the tower room. Looking out, he could see another tower, twin to the one they were in, across the paved courtyard which was many feet below. He gazed down with interest. From this height it was difficult to make out details, but there were groups of nasty-looking creatures passing through the courtyard on various errands. Some of them reminded him of nightmares he'd had as a child. The others were worse.

"They are truly horrible, are they not, poor creatures."

"You pity them when they propose the destruction of your world?"

"Of course I do. Recruited from many places, dependent on the powers of the Dark for their daily food. No chance to return to their own worlds, they are worthy of compassion. Some of them are demons, but many are mere shells, kept alive only by black magic. Others found themselves displaced from their homes in Realm and elsewhere."

"Well, you're more charitable than I am." Jarl slipped an arm around Mirza's shoulders to take the sting from his words. "I only want to find a way to get us out of here. Does your dragon friend fly up here to talk to you?"

"She perches on the top of that tower and then we mind-talk."

"Doesn't anyone have the power to hear your conversations?"

"Mindlink is rather rare between species. Sometimes there is an affinity between beings. I have such a one with Ebony. Perhaps it's because I have flown as a dragon."

Jarl's eyebrows shot up.

"Only when the moon is full," Mirza teased.

Somehow her effort at humor relaxed Jarl. "Can you call her now?"

"Perhaps."

"Well, call!"

"Why?"

"Trust a woman," Jarl muttered. "Look, Mirza, the only avenue we have open is your telepathic power. Wyrd refuses to respond to me. Perhaps we can use the dragon as a messenger."

"Oh. And have you acquired an army that will come at your call?"

"Not exactly, but I may just have a dragon or two up my sleeve. So call!"

"Very well," Mirza replied, a puzzled look on her face.

Jarl couldn't hear a thing. "Are you trying?" he asked.

"Yes," she snapped. "How can I carry on a conversation if you keep interrupting?"

"You're talking to the dragon now?" Jarl cast an injured look at his bracelet. Wyrd lay inert on his wrist. Why wasn't he helping? Was the bracelet saving power until they really needed it? Or was the Shadowlord's magic stronger?

Jarl started thinking—hard. How was he going to free the black dragon from the silver bind-chain? He looked out the window. Silhouetted against the gray dusk of the evening was the twin tower. As he watched, a great shadow glided in and perched on it. The whole scene looked like a cutout from a child's Halloween card. Far in the background the globe of the moon inched over the horizon. The view was oddly beautiful, if menacing. Far below, shrieks, bellows, and some unclassifiable noises, best left unidentified, drifted upward to the tower room.

"Feeding time at the zoo," Jarl said, wondering if he and Mirza would get a meal. He decided they would not be able to eat it for fear of drugs—or something worse.

Mirza gave him an inquiring glance, but he shook his head, indicating he had not really meant the comment for her ears.

"Jarl, Ebony is willing to help—if she can. She will try to fly a message, but if the Shadowlord finds out, he may kill her." Mirza frowned, worried about her new friend.

Jarl eyed the top of the window. It was tall. A plan began to form in his mind. "Ask your friend to fly over and sit on this tower. Then I want her to lower her neck through the window." Jarl hoped Ebony's neck was as long as Faf's.

Across the courtyard, Ebony opened her wings. An updraft floated her from the tower. She guided herself to where Mirza and Jarl waited.

"Is there always an updraft near these tall towers?"

Mirza nodded.

"Well, that explains why so many of the old castles had towers. They're really takeoff sites for dragons."

"Everybody knows that," Mirza snorted, reminding him of the brown mare's shape she liked to wear.

"In Realm, maybe. On Earth towers were used for defense."

The winged form settled over them, blocking out the moonlight. Shortly, a huge nose and one plate-sized eye appeared outside the window.

"Ebony wants to know what you expect her to do."

"Wait until I climb on the sill. I need to get closer to the chain on her neck." Jarl put his hand on the side of the opening, jumped up, and landed, surefooted.

Mirza gasped. A slight miscalculation and he would have fallen into the courtyard. She watched as he looked at the silver links which were clasped around the neck of the dragon much as a pretty girl might wear a necklace. The silver was beautiful against the iridescent black scales.

"May I touch it?" Jarl asked. Without his association with Fafnoddle, voluntarily approaching anything with a mouth of teeth the size of the dragon's would have been the last activity on his list of things to do.

"Yes," Ebony replied mentally, moving her neck closer to ease Jarl's exploration. In the stress of the moment none of them realized the oddity of Jarl's being able to hear the dragon speak.

"There are no breaks in any of the links. I can't find a single weak spot."

"Naturally not. It was forged by magic power," Mirza reminded him.

"The chain's not tight. Perhaps I can cut it off with my sword—if it's retained any of its magic with its change in outward appearance." Jarl drew the sword, held the chain as far as possible from the dragon's body, and brought the sharp edge down directly on the metal. Ebony's eyes were closed, but she bravely held steady. At the moment of impact, a high keening sound assaulted their ears. Mirza put her hands over hers. Jarl gripped the window's edge tightly as vertigo assailed him. Ebony herself blinked her watering eyes.

"I'm sorry," Jarl apologized.

"Do not be sad. At least you tried to release me." The dragon's tones were grave and showed her resignation to her fate.

"I'm not ready to quit yet. I haven't tried Wyrd."

"Do you think it's safe to activate Wyrd again while we are here in the citadel of the Shadowlord?" Mirza touched the bracelet with gentle fingertips.

"If that noise didn't bring a guard, probably nothing will. We'll never know till we've tried." Jarl looked at Wyrd. He received no sign that the circled dragon was anything more than an unusual piece of jewelry. Jarl held the bracelet close to the chain, commanding with all his mental force, "BREAK!" A bolt of energy sparked across the gap, and the chain disappeared.

"Free at last," the dragon hissed happily.

"Wyrd broke the spell," Mirza said, smiling.

"Thanks, Wyrd," Jarl told his bracelet. He received no reply, but Jarl noticed another scale had turned to gold.

"I am yours to command, my lady," Ebony said to Mirza.

"Then listen to Jarl's plan," Mirza urged, certain he would have one.

"I'd like you to fly to Judgment Rock in Wyvern Marsh. Do you know where that is?"

"It is a landmark fliers know well, the only bare area in the marsh."

Jarl almost sighed with relief. He hadn't the slightest idea of how to direct anyone to find the rock. Perhaps their luck had turned. "Someone will communicate with you if you land there. Ask them to send Faf back here with you."

"What will this—Faf do?" the dragon asked.

"Faf is a dragon like you. He has carried me in the past. If you can carry Mirza on your back, he can carry me. We can mount from this window."

"Do you mean Fafnir? He's too old," Mirza said.

"No, his son, Fafnoddle."

"What changed him? I haven't seen him for years, but he was always a peaceful creature."

"Some birdthings burned him in a fight."

Mirza looked surprised at the news but said, "Perhaps he'll be unable to carry you."

"If he can't, Ebony will take you to safety at least. I'll wait here alone. I'll still have my sword, and perhaps if things get bad enough, Wyrd will help me." Jarl forced a smile to his face, trying to cheer Mirza.

"I won't leave without you."

"Don't be stubborn. It's not ladylike," Jarl teased. "Anyway, I bet you'll find a ready Faf—wounds healed or not. You'll see."

"I shall fly to the rock. Tomorrow, just at sun's rising, we will come," Ebony promised.

"We'll be waiting," Jarl said.

"Be careful. May the Light protect you," Mirza wished.

The giant head disappeared from the window. Jarl and Mirza watched as the saurian sailed away, a black silhouette of hope against the waxing light of the full moon.

Jarl sat on the crude cot with Mirza nestled close to him. No words were needed between them. The kindly eye of the night looked down; Jarl was amply rewarded for his heroism.

CHAPTER
Nineteen

*T*HE long night paled in the east. The evil inhabitants of Fellkeep slept while two mighty dragons flew above. When Ebony landed on Mirza's tower, Faf did the same on the other. Seeing the inquiring eye of Ebony at the window, Jarl woke Mirza.

"It's time to go," he said softly.

"I won't leave—"

"Yes, you will, and so will I. Faf's across the courtyard on the other tower. There's no time to waste. So far our luck has been phenomenal. Let's get moving before our cowled friend reappears."

Jarl helped Mirza onto the window ledge. The wyvern queen must have used her magic disk to see the need for a safety harness. The harness and a rope were attached to Ebony. It was the work of moments to secure Mirza to the rope the dragons held. Ebony slowly drew her to the tower top.

As soon as Ebony took off, flying slowly to the north, Faf arrived. His great head snaked down to the window.

"Hurry, Jarl!" We have little time. The spell thins."

"What spell?" Jarl asked as he climbed the rope Faf held for him.

"The one Wyrd and the wyverns have woven for you two this night. It was some kind of false-seeming. The Shadowlord thinks Ebony still wears her collar and that you two are sound asleep." Faf checked Jarl's readiness, held out his wings to receive an updraft, and sailed into the relative safety of the sky.

Faf flew as well as he ever had. The two dragons arrowed north for the border of King Caeryl's land. Once past that magic line of power, they would be safe. The dragons seemed tireless. They soared on the air currents like hawks, and like hawks they watched. Not for prey, but for the enemies they knew searched for them.

As they traveled, Mirza and Jarl spoke to each other telepathically.

"Mirza, can you tell what's happening behind us?"

"You should link with Wyrd to get that information."

"Won't it distract him if he's doing something? Faf said the wyverns and Wyrd cast a spell to help us escape."

"Don't concentrate hard. Merely look at Wyrd and allow your mind to drift. Perhaps you can become an onlooker because of your proximity to him. It shouldn't disturb him to have you see his handiwork."

"I don't understand his ability to cast spells with the wyverns. I get the impression they didn't think much of humankind and that they wanted to remain neutral."

"The Shadowlord provoked them. He would not leave anyone alone. He boasted of the things he's accomplished, like his isolating them from contact with those at Realmgate. Then there's his plan to dry up the wyverns' ancestral marsh before attacking them. He wants to be the only remaining entity with magic powers of any consequence. The wyverns are extremely powerful if the ancient tales are true," Mirza told Jarl.

"Why do they accept Wyrd so easily?"

"In the legends of the time when Wyrd appeared here, the first wearer of the bracelet was a wyvern."

"Oh, so wyvern males do get to be heroic!" Jarl said before he thought.

"The Dragon's Pawn was a female priestess-warrior," Mirza told him with an undertone of feminine satisfaction she did not try to hide.

"Does the legend say anything more about Wyrd?"

"A fragment of an old tale says Wyrd was once mighty, but he misused his powers and punishment followed."

"What did he do?"

"We have lost that part of the story. It may be somewhere in the Chronicles of Realm in the library at Realmgate, but I've never seen it," Mirza said.

"Well, I suppose it's not important—except to Wyrd—after all this time."

Jarl's curiosity led him to focus on Wyrd and try to daydream. Gradually the blowing winds and the fast-moving earth below him faded from his consciousness. There was a lack of light and a sense of the Dark. He felt raw emotions. Anger. Dread. At Fellkeep the Shadowlord was trying to remedy their escape. Fearful workers hurried to loose the birdthings. A vision of the tower room showed Jarl a place bare of everything. It looked as if a giant fist had obliterated all the material articles in the room, which still echoed with the anger of the sorcerer. The Shadowlord didn't like being thwarted. He believed the magical seeming that had been insinuated, ever so carefully, into the tower room during the long night while Jarl and Mirza awaited the return of the dragons. Jarl felt a sense of satisfaction that could only have come from the wyvern Queen Lythyr.

"Yes," echoed in Jarl's mind. "Now we prepare to face the wrath of the Shadowlord." And abruptly Jarl was high in the sunlit air, flying north to escape the Shadowlord's power.

Jarl told Mirza what he had experienced. "I just hope we haven't been the cause of the Shadowlord's attacking the wyverns."

"Remember he was already using his dark powers to plan their destruction," Mirza said. "His agents captured Seabreeze. If you had not rescued her, she might well be in his power now. Any inconvenience we caused is outweighed by that."

"You may be right. At any rate, Queen Lythyr is enjoying her retaliation against the Shadowlord."

"She is surprisingly bloodthirsty," Faf added his thought to the conversation.

"How so?" Jarl asked.

"I was there to see the beginning of the preparations her people are making to defend themselves, and they plan some extremely violent surprises. If the Shadowlord thinks he will have an easy conquest because the wyverns have always been peaceful, he has made a major error in judgment." Faf chuckled.

"What's so funny?"

"The marsh holds many of Realm's nastier creatures. When Evil enters that marsh, it may well find itself in the position of the fisherman who sits on one of his own lures."

"Are you tired?" Jarl asked, remembering Faf's wound.

"No, but I'm worried about Ebony," Faf answered. "She's never carried anything so far before."

"What about when she stole Mirza?"

"Oh, the Shadowlord used some machine to transport her to Fellkeep instantly. They were only airborne for a few minutes."

"How did you find out about that?"

"You don't think you and Mirza are the only ones who can talk together mind to mind, do you?"

"Oh," Jarl said rather lamely, chagrined to find he hadn't thought of a telepathic link between the two dragons.

"Actually, all dragons prefer to mindspeak. We sometimes speak aloud for humans because it disturbs most of you to converse dragon-fashion. You're a refreshing change from the average human."

"Perhaps Wyrd had something to do with my acceptance. I always thought of myself as quite ordinary. When you talk to a bracelet—and it answers—well, let's just say it's an experience that changes one's way of thinking."

"You've done nobly," Faf complimented. "Coming from a world which has largely rejected magic for technology..."

Jarl got the feeling that Faf stopped talking to save his pride. Perhaps science was wrong in refusing to believe in magic. He couldn't imagine Earth if magic became a normal occurrence. And telepathy... what if people could know what their friends actually thought of them?

Wyrd tightened around Jarl's wrist. "Faf, something has disturbed Wyrd. Do you see any danger?"

The dragon obligingly turned his head to look around. "Your talisman is correct. Those birdthings that kill with light beams trail us."

"Relnot's border spell should protect us," Mirza said.

"Will you have to set us down to fight or can we beat them to the border?" Jarl twisted in his harness. The bird-things were gaining.

"Fight? With what? You must save Wyrd for special occasions, but I rather think I can help us now."

Faf clearly held mindspeech with Ebony, who let Mirza tune in to the conversation. Mirza looked at Jarl.

"What do you suggest I do?" she asked.

"How am I supposed to know? I'm not sure what your powers are. Can you turn birdthings into butterflies?"

Mirza shook her head. "No. Because they are Dark-forged, I couldn't. Have you another suggestion?"

"Could you turn them into jet planes?" Jarl asked, forgetting Mirza wouldn't know what a jet was.

"What's a jet plane?" she asked.

"Never mind. I don't have time to explain. Where are they now?" Jarl struggled to turn. It was difficult because Faf and Ebony were no longer gliding, but actively flying, which created a fierce wind.

"Behind us and closing in," Faf thought grimly.

"Can you conjure a—a large storm just behind us? One with plenty of lightning bolts." Jarl suggested to Mirza.

Jarl could see Mirza's lips moving. One hand sketched a strange pattern that etched a design on the wind. Behind them, thunder boomed. White fluffy clouds clumped together, turned gray, darkened, and hung, green-black, in the air. Faf and Ebony circled so Mirza could complete her spell as they watched.

"That's some storm," Jarl commented admiringly.

"Storm magic is one thing I'm not very good at. I did conjure a brief shower once, but I had a headache for days afterward. I'm impressed," Faf told Mirza.

They heard the roar of the wind behind them. The strange storm advanced on the attacking birds. The birdthings did not emerge from the clouds which shrouded them.

"That did it!" Jarl shouted into the wind.

"I hope so. It took a great deal of energy. How far is it to the border of the kingdom?" Mirza asked, closing her eyes.

"Only a few minutes' flying time," Faf answered.

"That's just as well. Carrying me is tiring for Ebony."

"Yes, but I'm using every thermal I find to help me, and I will take you as far as necessary." The quiet thought entered the minds of Faf, Mirza, and Jarl.

"Soon we cross Relnot's magic protection spell. Then we can rest," Faf told her.

"We should travel directly to the castle. Mirza isn't in any shape for camping out, even overnight," Jarl said.

Mirza turned a frightened face toward him. "Why do you say that? Have I not been with you before?"

"I just meant being a prisoner and all, it would be nice to be coddled a bit." Had he offended her? He only wanted her to be comfortable. Her face seemed so white. Perhaps she only seemed frail in comparison to the huge dragon who carried her.

"Thank you," she told him softly. "It will be good to be clean and to sleep in a warm bed."

"We can fly the added distance easily," Ebony and Faf assured her.

"Are you certain, Faf?" Jarl asked. "Those burns you had were bad ones."

"That wyvern mud bath cured me completely. When I awoke, I found that you went without me. That disturbed me."

"I couldn't wait. I only had three days. Prince Leon needed rescuing and I wanted Mirza out of there. We reached them through some almost forgotten tunnels that the Old Ones made. The wyverns knew of them. You couldn't have passed through them."

"I know."

"You knew about the tunnels?" The statement surprised Jarl.

"No, but I watched all that happened to you through Lythyr's crystal disk. There was great rejoicing when Seabreeze returned with the prince. As soon as they were safely on the rock, the prince used the acorn and disappeared. The wyvern queen said the spell was a success and he was home with his father."

"I'm glad to hear that. Fellkeep is no place for anyone who is decent, let along a youngster."

"Look, Jarl. Isn't that the castle ahead?"

"That's it. I can't understand why the major city is near the southern border. I'd rather have my capital as far as possible from Fellkeep."

"When building the city, there were cordial relations between the keep and the castle. When the old wizard who lived there died, it stood empty for a long time. One day when the Shadowlord is overthrown, the wyverns may want peaceful humans at Fellkeep and may resume trade. The Meander River wanders over much of the landscape. It eventually drains into the sea near Fellkeep. It made a natural highway for traders." Mirza finished Jarl's brief history lesson.

Jarl looked down at the river below. "We're over the border now, but I don't see much traffic."

"No," Ebony answered him. "When I began wearing the collar of Darkness, I harassed the shipping. Finally the few people who lived in the region once governed by the Keep fled. The Shadowlord forced me to do other—things." The pause in Ebony's explanation showed how much she regretted serving the Shadowlord.

Her listeners wisely refrained from asking for more details. Ebony's unhappiness was clear.

When they reached the castle, there was not enough room for both dragons to land on Relnot's tower, so they elected to settle on a wide, clear area that was the field for jousting contests and fairs. Jarl and Mirza removed the harnesses from the dragons. Jarl carried them over his shoulder.

"Ebony and I will be leaving now. We'll return to this spot in two days to fly you to Realmgate."

"You're not staying?" Jarl had become fond of Faf. He would miss him.

"I've been away from my cave for too long. Ebony will come with me for a visit."

Wasn't that a twinkle in Faf's eyes? Jarl looked at the black dragon for confirmation. She lowered her head almost coyly.

"Thank you both. Be careful. Being north of Relnot's magic barrier seems to be some protection, but I know it's not perfect. Jarl and I will see you in two days." Mirza waved as the dragons beat their mighty wings and sailed into the sky.

"What was the matter with Ebony? She seemed a little— weird," Jarl said. He guessed he still had a lot to learn about dragons.

"Silly! You can't see romance when it's right over your nose." Mirza gave him an indulgent smile.

"You mean—" Jarl looked at Mirza wide-eyed.

"Of course," she answered complacently. "And now, if you're ready, our ride to the castle is coming."

CHAPTER
Twenty

J ARL turned as a magnificent coach, pure white with gilded wheels, approached. "Welcome!" the king's familiar voice said. Relnot and the prince were with him.

The coach had barely stopped when the king hopped out. "Come, come," he said, motioning for them to enter the coach. "Leon told us everything. We've been expecting you." He stood aside courteously as he helped Mirza in. Then he motioned for Jarl to precede him. "Don't stand on ceremony, Jarl. You're a hero to everyone in the kingdom. That's why I came for you in this behemoth. It's a blasted nuisance, but on occasions of state, it's tradition to use it."

"Your Majesty is very kind," Mirza said, every inch a lady.

"Have to be, have to be. Jarl here saved my boy. I know your grandmother, too. I'd not want her to think I'd slighted her favorite granddaughter."

"Only granddaughter, you mean," Mirza teased gently, responding to the real warmth of the king's personality.

"How is your grandmother?" the king asked.

Jarl wondered about Mirza's family. What kind of weird

relatives would she have? If he and Mirza ever got any time to themselves, he decided he would have to ask a few questions. Was the old wise woman related to Mirza? If she was Mirza's grandmother, that would explain why she was so helpful. Jarl wished he had more answers and fewer questions. Mirza and the king seemed to know each other well, judging from their conversation. He listened as Mirza answered the king. "Hale and hearty, busy as ever."

The coach bowled swiftly into the city where cheering crowds lined the streets. The king waved to the populace. Under cover of the excitement, Relnot said quietly to Mirza, "Are you in need of help?"

She glanced at him quickly before replying, "Later, please."

Short as the exchange had been, Jarl heard it, but decided it was not the time to ask for further information. At the palace they separated.

"You must have time to refresh yourselves before dinner," the king decreed.

Jarl was glad of a chance to wash. One of the things he missed most from Earth was the modern plumbing. The steaming tub of water the servants carried into his room would never replace a hot shower. Still, it was a far cry from the cold washes he had been taking daily as the terrain allowed.

For the first time he dressed in the clothing of Realm. From the large selection at his disposal, he chose a soft brown leather jerkin and matching breeches. Since the servant looked scandalized by the color he selected, he added a brown velvet cape with dragons embroidered in thread of gold. His high boots glistened with polish. While the colors were much quieter than those of the other courtiers he had seen, Jarl felt comfortable in his choice. At least he wouldn't disgrace his host with his clothes.

He followed a servant to the royal banqueting hall, which resembled a scene from a medieval tapestry. The large T-shaped table at one end of the hall stood burdened with food. Servers scurried about, bringing more as he watched.

Rushes were strewn on the floor. Jarl hoped the tapers which lighted the room would not fall and ignite the substitute for carpeting. Small groups of courtiers stood talking. They waited for the king, Jarl was certain. As he stood silent and alone, Mirza joined him. Her golden dress glittered, as did the ornaments she wore in her hair.

"You are very beautiful, my lady," Jarl said, bowing over her hand.

She smiled. "I feel dressed like a queen. I wouldn't care for it all the time, but for tonight it's pleasant." All signs of tiredness had disappeared. She tucked her arm in his and began walking toward the table.

The king entered from the far door. He spoke briefly to a servant who approached them.

"His Majesty awaits your company at the table."

"Honored," Jarl said before he and Mirza joined the king.

During the meal Jarl watched the other guests. Their clothing was so brightly colored that he began to understand why the servant had looked shocked by his somber color selection. From his place at the king's right hand, Jarl was able to see everyone except Mirza and Relnot, who both sat on the king's left. He did notice that Mirza and the magician spoke together. He wondered what she found so interesting in the conversation and then decided that it was probably an interest in magic. Mirza looked like a young woman. He reminded himself that she was the granddaughter of a witch. Did that make her a witch, too? What of her mother and father? She had to be older than she looked or they wouldn't let her wander around shaped like a fennec. Everyone knew her. Most referred to her as "my lady." Did that mean her father was a king or lord or something? Jarl made a mental note to ask her when they were alone sometime.

It was late the next morning before Jarl awoke. No sooner had he stirred than a servant tapped on his door. Later, suitably dressed for the day, he went to find Mirza. She was not in the room assigned to her, but her maid said she had gone to see Relnot.

Jarl finally found the steps leading to the tower. When he

stood outside the heavy oaken door, he thought he heard the sound of sobs, but upon his knocking, they stopped. Relnot himself opened the door.

"Good morning," Jarl said.

"Come in," Relnot answered with a quiet smile. His measured invitation did not match his visitor's cheery words.

"Is something the matter?"

"No, Jarl," Mirza answered, but her eyes were suspiciously bright.

"My lady," Relnot began.

"Relnot and I were investigating an interesting piece of spell work together," she told Jarl.

Relnot spoiled his agreement by shaking his head. Jarl caught the gesture out of the corner of his eye.

"Have you eaten yet?" Mirza asked, ignoring Relnot entirely.

"I wanted to see you first."

"Let's descend and find our meal together," she suggested. "Do you want to come with us, Relnot?" she asked courteously.

"I have some work to attend to before this afternoon's conference with the king. So, thank you, no."

Jarl and Mirza found their way to the breakfast table with the help of Prince Leon, busy enjoying a few days of freedom from his tutor. His bright chatter livened the atmosphere as Jarl finished a large breakfast. Mirza ate very little, he noticed.

"And when I am older, I shall have one of the stallions for my very own," he heard the prince telling Mirza.

"So you like horses?" Jarl asked, unsure how to speak to a royal child.

"This kingdom raises the best horses in Realm," Mirza explained. "'To ride a southern horse' is a proverb here."

"It means to have the very best," the prince added, gratified to be able to tell a grown-up something.

"Oh," Jarl said, rather less than brilliantly.

"Would you like to see the horses?" The boy was eager to show them, so Mirza and Jarl followed him to the stables.

An army of servants—far more than were in use in the castle, an amused Jarl noted—cared for the horses. No burrs were visible in silken manes and tails. The liquid eyes of the animals watched the visitors, and several nickered as if they knew the prince. One golden stallion especially caught Jarl's attention.

"You have a good knowledge of horses," the prince said, sounding just like his father. "Oromon is the best horse we own. My father has trained him as a battle stallion in case we ever have to go to war," he said seriously. Leon unconsciously aped the stance and manner of his father. "Here, you can feed him today, if you're not afraid." The boy offered a carrot to Jarl.

"Please remember that I need to conserve my strength," Wyrd's voice hissed through Jarl's mind.

"I didn't call on you for anything."

"I can't very well sleep if you are going to do foolhardy things every time I close my eyes. That brute of a horse has large teeth. You'd better be sure he doesn't decide to bite the hand that feeds him. You won't be able to hold a sword with half your fingers missing."

"Don't be such a worry-Wyrd," Jarl teased. "This time I know what I'm doing."

"I hope so. Don't call unless you're in real need, and I'll take a short nap."

"Agreed," Jarl thought. The whole mental exchange had taken place with such rapidity that the prince was still waiting for Jarl's answer.

"All right," Jarl agreed, unaware that all work stopped while the stable boys watched him feed Oromon. He held out his hand, saying, "Here, boy." The horse bowed his golden neck graciously and accepted the offering. "Good fellow," Jarl said as he stroked Oromon. The horse munched contentedly.

The grooms made small sounds of amazement among themselves. The prince exclaimed, "You fed him!" and then quieted. He knew he should not raise his voice around the excitable thoroughbreds.

"Sure. Why not? Doesn't he like carrots?"

A groom bowed low before Jarl. "Oromon is the king's mount. He is very particular about the people he allows near him, yet he accepted you."

"Well, perhaps today is my lucky day," Jarl answered off-handedly, not impressed by his performance.

"I must tell my father that Oromon accepts you. Perhaps the stallion knows you are a hero. Horses are very wise."

"He's a fine animal. Perhaps he senses my admiration for him," Jarl answered aloud. Mentally he wondered if his bracelet had anything to do with his affinities for the inhabitants of Realm.

"You do have a way with horses," Mirza said as they walked back to the castle.

"Oh, I've had some practice riding fiery mounts. One of them in particular was very headstrong, but I could tame her." He flashed a mental image of Mirza in the brown mare's shape to her.

Mirza tossed her head and snorted. He laughed at her equine gesture.

By the time they reached the castle, Prince Leon, who had run ahead, had already told his father about Jarl's feeding Oromon. "—And Oromon liked him, Father."

"Oromon is a very wise animal, my son. I will consider his opinion of Jarl when making my decision."

"What decision, Father?"

"Matters of state, Leon. Today you may join us for a meeting of the Council. Then you shall know." He ruffled his son's hair, noting how tall he had grown. It was time he learned more of how to govern the kingdom.

Jarl thought the council hall was a bit austere. Battle armor hung on the high gray walls. A long U-shaped table dominated the room. A plain gold throne filled the open end of the figure. The king, who sat on the throne, wore navy-blue robes of state and a golden circlet rode upon his brow. Jarl knew the king well enough to guess he didn't enjoy the trappings of his office. King Caeryl's grave visage set the mood for the meeting.

Pompuss sat on the king's right hand. Beside him sat the prince. Jarl and Mirza sat beside Relnot, close to the king.

The king raised his hand, and the low murmur of voices ceased. "We gather today to discuss a matter of importance to the kingdom," he began.

Heads nodded in agreement. All knew the subject of this meeting.

"The Shadowlord abducted Prince Leon and ordered me to join his cause."

A few gasps of surprise and lifted eyebrows greeted this announcement. This fact was news to some of the Council.

"Jarl, the Dragon's Pawn, whom you met last night, rescued the prince with the aid of Relnot's talisman and the wyvern Queen Lythyr." The king looked steadily at his advisors. They were attentive to his words. "Now we must choose: war or peace?"

Pompuss, resplendent in green, spoke in an excited voice. "This means war! How dare this upstart wizard detain a royal personage!"

"War is a very serious undertaking. Can we not just make use of Relnot's magical defenses and remain inside the kingdom?" The thin man in gray who spoke rubbed his black beard in agitation.

"How stand our defenses, Relnot?" a third asked, leaning his stout body over the table until his buttons threatened to pop.

Relnot answered after the king signaled him to do so. "For now, the defenses hold." A collective sigh of relief came from the advisors. Relnot raised his hand in admonition. "I must warn you that the power of the Shadowlord, once a minor aggravation, is waxing stronger every day. There are vast amounts of energy being channeled into his projects. Eventually he will be able to overcome my best magical efforts unless we stop him or keep him busy elsewhere."

The advisors sat stunned by this news. "What then shall we do? Begin war immediately before he is too powerful to stop?" The black-bearded man spoke for all of them.

"It is already too late for that. We have two choices open

to us," the king said. "We can close our borders with Rel- not's most powerful spell and hope the Shadowlord ignores us, or we can ally our kingdom with his enemies."

"Who are they?" Pompuss asked, so absorbed in the in- formation he forgot to act injured because he didn't know about the Shadowlord's enemies beforehand.

"Jarl, can you tell us of the conditions outside of our kingdom? Since Relnot created the border ward, few of our people have left to travel in the outside world."

"I have recently been both north and south of here," Jarl began. "The Shadowlord has enough power to command the evil tribe of korred to do his bidding. He has enslaved a number of peace-loving creatures, one of which, a black dragon named Ebony, freed of his bondage, helped us escape."

"A black dragon, you say? We have been raided by a vicious dragon who disrupted our shipping and trading," a red-faced man said.

"Ebony had no choice in what she did. While she wore the collar of the Shadowlord, she was his slave, forced to do his bidding by an evil spell," Mirza explained. "Many crea- tures from many lands form his forces."

"Why should we care? Evil creatures cannot cross our border now," another said.

"If a dragon can be enslaved," Relnot answered, "a man most certainly could be ensorcelled."

Jarl added, "He is calling creatures from another world to do his bidding. There are metal men, flying machines that use rays of light to maim and kill, and other monsters, such as a flying thing called Death-that-flies by the wyverns." Jarl ignored the whispering around him and went doggedly on with his information. "I have been under the walls of Fell- keep, and it vibrates with a strange power. The Shadowlord calls more and more evils to the keep. When he is ready, he will attack any on Realm who do not offer him absolute fealty."

Silence fell on the group as they considered his words. Only a few advisors looked disbelieving.

"This is true," Mirza spoke quietly. Her words dropped into the pool of silence around the table. "During my imprisonment in the tower at Fellkeep, I learned the Shadowlord means to attack Realmgate itself." Ripples of disbelief touched each listener.

Jarl could see this news astounded the Council. Their surprise made him realize how important the gate and the Keepers must be to this society. Attacking them seemed to be sacrilege to the men seated at the table.

"I will carry a warning to Andronan, the Elder Keeper. The hosts of the Shadowlord will march before the summer ends," Mirza concluded solemnly.

The king studied the faces of his councillors. "Will we abjure the neutrality we maintained during the reign of my father and go to war?"

The answer was obvious.

"Tomorrow Jarl and Mirza go north to Realmgate. They will carry my message to the Keepers that we will send what help we can. Pompuss, raise and equip the kingdom. By the next new moon, our army must march to Realmgate!"

CHAPTER
Twenty-One

J ARL and Mirza stood waiting on the field where the dragons agreed to meet them.

"I hoped they would join us before it was too late. Many of the races of Realm have pledged to support the Keepers in their fight to keep Realm free. If the Shadowlord gains control of Realmgate, he may pass between worlds unhindered."

"How could anyone who knows the Shadowlord ignore him? Thinking he could force King Caeryl to join him and deliberately alienating the wyverns may be the very mistakes that win the battle for us." Jarl told her soberly.

Two specks appeared in the sky. Ebony and Faf produced an amazing aerial performance before landing.

"Don't they look happy?" Mirza commented as she and Jarl watched.

"I don't see what for," Jarl said. "Here we are planning a war effort, and two of our best weapons are acting like a couple of teenage show-offs."

"Well, dragons don't take honeymoons, and some celebration is in order," Mirza said, defending them.

"Honeymoon!"

"Yes! This event will please Fafnir. He's worried about the family name dying out, and now, given enough time, he'll be a granddragon."

Jarl stared at her. "How did you know about all this?"

"Any woman could tell. You men just don't have enough romance in your souls." Mirza scolded him gently. Her face saddened momentarily, then brightened. "I'm very happy for them."

"Do we say congratulations or anything?" Jarl wondered out loud.

"I doubt it. Even I don't know all the dragon protocol. Faf marches to a different drummer anyway. In the great library at Realmgate University there is a set of fifty volumes containing the dragon etiquette. Thick ones," she added when Jarl looked as if he was having trouble believing her.

They had asked to leave quietly. Only Relnot, the king, and Prince Leon stood waving at the edge of the field when the dragons took off bearing Mirza and Jarl. Gradually the neat fields below gave way to forest, then to wild land. Finally Mirza announced they had passed the northern border, guarded like the others by Relnot's magic. Jarl touched Wyrd, appreciative of his watchdog qualities.

"All is well," Wyrd whispered in Jarl's mind. Then he perversely refused to answer any of Jarl's questions. It was almost as if Wyrd did not reside in the bracelet at all times. When Jarl came to consider it, this odd thought was no more unbelievable than wearing a talking metal talisman. Just so long as Wyrd was there when Jarl needed a warning...

"Where are we now?" Jarl asked Faf after they had flown for several hours.

"Over Feraland. The Old Ones ruled here, the legends say. Then one day they just—left, disappeared," Faf said.

"Doesn't anyone know where they went or why?"

"No being now living, Jarl," Mirza chimed in on Faf's history lesson.

"My great-great-grandmother said an old legend told of their desire to change and be something they were not. The

Old Ones couldn't reach their objective so long as they stayed on Realm," Ebony said.

"I never heard that. I spent a great deal of time studying the Old Ones when I was a student. None of my teachers mentioned that information. In fact, none of the books in the library carried that tale," Mirza said.

"My family handed the information down," said Ebony. "One of my ancestors was a special friend to the Old Ones. There are as many dragons interested in history as magic. We live long lives and see how most thing work out in the end."

"Feraland looks like wild country to me. I hope King Caeryl can keep the promise he made the wyvern messenger," Jarl said.

"We left before they settled everything, but I'm sure Seabreeze and her companions will come to a satisfactory arrangement with the king. Together they will see that the Meander flows, unblocked and in full spate, to keep Wyvern Marsh as wet as it has always been," Mirza said.

"Oh, but it wasn't always wet," Ebony said, matching her glide perfectly to Faf's.

"I know. Don't tell me." Jarl grinned. "The information was part of an old family story."

Faf fixed one enormous eye on Jarl. If Ebony had shown any sign of being upset by Jarl's teasing, Faf would intercede.

Jarl made a mental note not to tease Faf's dragonlady—or wife, or mate, or whatever one called the female half of a pair of dragons. If he got the chance, he planned to find out how long dragons lived.

That night they made camp deep in Feraland. The tall trees fought for a ray of sun. Because of the many trees, Faf and Ebony had difficulty finding a place large enough for them both to land. When they spotted a clearing, they settled into it gratefully. It had been a long day. Jarl and Mirza were stiff from their time in harness. They hobbled around, getting their land legs. The earth seemed strangely still after the constant movement of the wind, the dips and glides of the dragons, and the updrafts which carried human and dragon into the clean blue sky.

Faf watched amusedly for some time and then asked, "Do you think you'll be all right if Ebony and I go for a short flight?"

"Yes," Jarl answered, and Mirza smiled her agreement. Both couples would enjoy a little privacy. Ebony rose first, with Faf flying after her in a gigantic game of aerial tag. They were much more agile without riders, Jarl noted.

"They're like two children," Mirza said.

"Better them than me. How anyone would want to fly after the day we've put in, I don't know."

"Remember the air is their natural home. It's wonderful to fly lightly without an unnatural weight," she added thoughtfully.

"Watch out who you're calling an unnatural weight," Jarl warned her mock-seriously. He enjoyed being alone with Mirza.

"Night will come early here. If we plan to have a fire, someone must search out branches."

"Someone hears and will obey, m'lady," Jarl told her.

He gathered a sizable number of suitable dead branches quickly. The trees were so thick there was little or no undergrowth. The deadwood was easy to find lying on the bare ground.

When Jarl dumped the first load in the clearing, he stopped a moment to ask a question. "Are there dryads in these woods?"

"Can't you tell?" Mirza counterquestioned. "If dryads rule over a forest, it is a living thing, filled with the sounds and sights of life. Birds fly between the branches and roost in nests. Squirrels frolic from tree to tree. Ground creatures like rabbits and badgers make holes at the foot of trees, and owls inhabit openings in large trunks. This forest is dead."

"I hadn't actually thought about it before, but if I compare this forest to the one near Fellkeep, I can tell there is a difference. It's as if it's waiting for something. It's an eerie sensation, but we should be safe. Wyrd hasn't tightened at all."

"Most people feel uncomfortable in Feraland, so it is sparsely settled. This used to be one of the main areas for the Old Ones. Some say Feraland waits for their return."

Jarl cleared a space for the fire and placed some sticks ready for the match he didn't have. He supposed they would have to wait for Faf or Ebony to start their fire. "They've had a pretty long wait, if you ask me. Even long-lived creatures like the dragons have never seen an Old One. What did they look like?"

"Old ballads say they were surpassing fair with moonbeams woven in their hair and sunlight in their hearts."

"Sounds a little uncomfortable to me. Using that description, it would be hard to recognize one," Jarl said.

"The Old Ones were teachers. They shared their magic gladly. At one time the humans on Realm could do almost as much as the Old Ones themselves. To be in contact with them . . . changed people. The foolish became sensible; the intelligent became wise." Mirza looked wistful.

"Too bad they're gone. We could do with a little of their magic. Just think what it would mean if the old places were reactivated with their former magic powers." Jarl didn't like the look on Mirza's face. She seemed sad. He was just about to talk to her about whatever was bothering her when she spoke.

"It would lighten Realm with joy. And speaking about light, we have very little of it left. I suggest that we both gather as much wood as we can in the next few minutes. Long before the sun actually sets, we will be in darkness because of the thickness and height of these trees."

The two of them gathered a few more armfuls of wood. Jarl and Mirza sat on their cloak-blankets. Each was more sumptuous than the one Jarl had purchased from Trader Krom. The king had spared no expense in outfitting their party. He wished they didn't have to sit in the gloom waiting for the dragons to return to light the fire. Just then Mirza started the blaze with a negligent gesture.

"Boy, it surely does beat rubbing two sticks together," Jarl said, warming his hands in the cheery flames.

"Bring me a food pack so I can prepare a meal," Mirza commanded Jarl with a smile.

"I'll do that, Mirza, if you can set a magic border around this place like Relnot did around the kingdom."

"It is small magic to hide two people. I will make us unnoticeable."

"Why not make us invisible?" Jarl asked.

"That takes more power. With this glamourie we shall be unnoticed by anything that might pass or fly over. It is much easier and just as effective. Tomorrow may bring a need for my strongest magic, and I want to have a reserve."

"How will Faf and Ebony find us?"

"I don't expect to see either of them until tomorrow. They like to be alone together, too, you know."

"That makes good sense. Besides, Wyrd will be watching." Jarl opened the pouch containing the food. "Hmm. Bread, cheese, a flask of cider, and fruit. It looks as if Faf chose the food."

"I didn't know what the conditions would be. If we were unable to light a fire, I wanted us to be able to eat something decent," Mirza explained.

"Well, I'm so hungry anything would taste good," Jarl said before biting into his bread and cheese.

After eating, he prepared the fire so it would burn as long as possible. Then he and Mirza wrapped themselves in their cloak-blankets. He wasn't sleepy and would have been glad to talk. However, Mirza breathed deeply almost as soon as she stretched on the ground, so he was quiet. Being the prisoner of the Shadowlord was an ordeal to weaken even a hardy soul. Moreover, flying north via dragon express was not a particularly refreshing way to spend a day, either.

Jarl awakened to the snapping and crackling of a brisk fire. Early dawn tinted the sky above, and the earth smelled as if it were invigorated from the cool night breezes.

"Time to get up, sleepy one. I've already found a stream

through the trees. Go splash a little water on your face and you'll get alert fast," Mirza promised him.

He watched for a moment. From somewhere she produced a small pan into which she was sprinkling herbs. The resulting tea smelled delicious. The idea of breakfast galvanized Jarl into action.

The small spring that fed the stream bubbled clean and cold from between two rocks. Jarl was shaking the water from his hair when he heard the sound of swords clashing. Wyrd had tightened, but his hands were so cold he hadn't noticed.

He arrived at the clearing on the run. Mirza was slashing valiantly at two men, but Jarl could see she was tiring. His sword leaped to his hand. The first cut severed one robber's head. The second was unnecessary, for when the remaining robber saw an armed man instead of a woman before him, he fled into the trees. Jarl started after him, but stopped when he noticed Mirza's white face.

"Are you all right?" he asked, kneeling beside her.

"Yes," she told him gamely, looking down at the damp patch that was forming on the breeches she had chosen to wear, saying earlier they were more comfortable for traveling.

"No, you're not. Let's get those breeches off so I can assess the damage."

"No," she said. She turned even paler as Jarl watched. "I'm all right. I tell you," she insisted.

"Little liar," Jarl chided gently. "No more nonsense now. Let me see the wound."

"No!" This time she sounded mule stubborn. She clutched the breeches to her possessively.

"Mirza, the stain is getting larger and larger. At this rate you'll faint from lack of blood, and then I'll take off those pants and care for your wound. Wouldn't it make good sense to let me help you before that happens?"

"Oh, Jarl, no," she moaned.

"Don't be shy of me. I've seen you in next to nothing, and you've never been like this. Remember the night you wore that green dress you insisted I bring from Mog's treasure hoard?"

A small smile was his only answer, but it told him she would allow him to help her.

She slipped out of the boots that covered her feet. Jarl schooled his face to show no shock, for human feet were not in those boots. Instead he saw hideous splayed paws—or were they hoofs? Jarl had never seen anything like them.

When she removed her clothing, he saw the full extent of her deformity. From the waist down she was a monster. What happened? That night in the glade when he first saw her she had human feet.

Mirza must have read some of what Jarl was feeling from the look on his face. "Now you know," she told him flatly.

"Now I know what?" he repeated.

"What a monster I'm becoming!" she flared through her tears.

Jarl ignored her words and began to bind her wound with a piece of cloth he found in their provision bag. "How did this happen?" he asked gently.

She didn't pretend to misunderstand. "It's a spell of the Shadowlord," she admitted tiredly. "When I refused to join him, he said some words I've never heard before and he laughed. Every day it creeps higher on my body. When it reaches my face, it will be permanent and impossible for anyone—even the Shadowlord—to remove."

"Is there nothing that can be done?"

"That's what Relnot and I were checking the morning you came to his tower. Relnot thinks that the heal spring north of Realmgate may be able to cure me."

"We'll go straight there," Jarl announced. "Where is it?"

"I'm afraid not," Mirza countered in her quiet voice. "The rate of the transformation has increased now that I'm away from Fellkeep. Even on dragonback we cannot travel fast enough to reach the magic spring before it's too late." Her brave smile almost broke Jarl's heart.

A shadow swept over them, followed by another. Jarl half drew his sword, then replaced it. The dragons had returned.

"Faf!" Jarl shouted as his friend landed in the clearing, "Can you fly any faster than you have been?"

"We're not that late," Faf answered. Then he looked around carefully, noting the headless human corpse. "What happened here?" A gout of steam showed his concern.

"We were attacked, but Mirza fought them off."

Faf and Ebony saw from the cutaway portion of Mirza's clothing the unnatural green and gray color of her warty hide.

"No, Jarl, Ebony and I can't fly any faster," Faf replied slowly, trying to understand what his air speed had to do with Mirza's affliction.

"This—stuff—is creeping upward each day," Jarl explained, putting his arm around Mirza's shoulder. "We have to reach the heal spring north of Realmgate before she's totally changed. The spell may be reversible until then."

Faf looked at Ebony, who nodded. "If you and Mirza are willing to take a little risk, we can travel faster."

"How?" Jarl asked practically.

"Both Faf and I have discovered we have a new talent."

"Talent?" Jarl and Mirza chorused.

"What Ebony means is that we can think of where we want to go when we're airborne, and then somehow we're there instantaneously."

Mirza shook her head. Evidently the unauthorized gate of the Shadowlord was awaking strange new powers in the beings of real magic. She explained her theory to Jarl.

"Well, dragons have always been somewhat of a mystery. Multidimensional transport seems pretty farfetched, but on Realm anything can happen. If Faf and Ebony can fly to places they can visualize, we'd better make use of their newfound ability. The Shadowlord has not only opened the gate to the Earth monsters he's recruiting. Somehow other attributes have slipped through, too. That's why you can fly in this new manner," he told the dragons.

"It's true that no dragon we ever heard of ever flew like this," said Ebony, accepting her new ability easily.

"I'm not altogether sure we can carry a passenger while we do it," Faf said.

"I'm willing to try it, if Ebony will carry me," Mirza said with a look of hope on her face that cheered Jarl.

"Let's pack up. Ebony carried Mirza before. Both of you should be able to take us with you."

Jarl helped Mirza get ready. He fastened the last buckle on her harness and kissed her quickly. "Don't worry. This is bound to work," he assured her, hiding his doubts.

"You can kiss me after what I've become?" Mirza said in wonder.

"I've liked you as a fennec, admired you as a unicorn, and been in tight spots with you in a horse's shape. The form you wear doesn't change my feelings for you," Jarl told her stoutly. The shine in her eyes repaid him handsomely for his avowal. "I'm always yours, m'lady," he said, giving her hand a squeeze.

As soon as Jarl was in the harness, Faf joined Ebony in the air. They flew north for a little distance and then separated.

"We'll see you in Realmgate," Jarl sent a final thought winging to Mirza and Ebony.

"Agreed."

BLACK. COLD. LIGHT.

CHAPTER
Twenty-Two

JARL looked down. "I guess it was a failure," he told Faf in disappointed tones.

"Look ahead on the left," Faf advised.

A series of iridescent towers and domes filled the skyline in the distance. It was Realmgate, the citadel of the Keepers.

"Where are Ebony and Mirza?"

"Behind us." Far chuckled. "You can't let females get too far ahead."

"You're right. If they did, we'd never catch up."

Faf wheeled in a giant circle so Jarl could see Ebony and Mirza coming. They swooped by and Faf rose on a giant thermal to glide close behind them.

"Where are you going to land?" Jarl asked.

"Outside the wall," Faf answered.

"Ebony and I are flying into the hills to the spring first," Mirza said.

"Shall we come with you?" Jark asked.

"No need. Just show the gatekeepers your talisman, and they'll tell you where to go."

When Mirza finished speaking, Ebony flew on and Faf started down.

"Are you sure we shouldn't go with them?" Jarl asked.

"The healing spring was originally the shrine of a goddess. Women have always gone there. Males are only tolerated. I've never actually been there myself, but I remember my mother talking about it."

"Is there any place on Realm your mother didn't see?" Jarl asked, really curious.

"She only admitted to four thousand years, but even if she was that old, that's enough time to visit a great many places.

"What did your father do when your mother traveled?"

"She hadn't chosen him yet. He was busy pillaging around on his own, to hear him tell it. With daring parents like mine, you can understand what a disappointment I always was to them."

"Your father will be proud when you tell him about your adventures."

"After Mirza visits the spring. I want Ebony to meet him."

"That's a good idea. Give him my thanks for suggesting we be partners."

"After we see my father, we'll return," Faf promised, landing softly on a grassy meadow outside the Realmgate's walls.

Jarl loosened his harness and shouldered it and his pack. "Are you coming with me?"

"I'll scout around a little. I haven't been here since I was a youngster. Things change in a few hundred years, you know."

Jarl waved, then turned toward the city where he hoped to get answers to some of the questions he had. The high walls of gray rock were imposing. The heaviness of the architecture reminded him of ancient Egypt. The walls looked as if the Old Ones built the citadel.

He trudged down the stretch of road that led to Realmgate. Several farmers with carts preceded him, and a merchant's caravan passed him. He stepped off the road to allow the dust of the horses to settle before continuing.

"What's happened to that fine mare you rode when last I saw you?" a hearty voice inquired.

It was Krom, the master trader. Jarl recognized his portly form at first glance. Thrown over his shoulder was his dark brown travel coat. Jarl noticed he wore a sword.

"She's changed a bit since you last saw her," Jarl joked in his turn. The twinkle in Krom's eyes when he asked his question told Jarl the trader knew Jarl's mount had been a were-horse.

"Were you and your horse—" he chuckled, "—being carried by those two dragons I saw fly by earlier?"

Jarl grinned. "That was Mirza and I."

"I take it you've given up riding and become a certified walker," Krom said, looking down from the back of the gray gelding he rode.

"Well, it's a change from flying, I'll admit, but now I have no horse and the gates are near, so I suppose I'll survive."

"If you should be in the market for another horse, I have two fine ones for sale. One is a perfect mount for a lady," Krom added as an afterthought.

"Where will you be staying, Master Krom?" Jarl saw Krom raise his eyebrows at the question. "In case I should decide to buy a horse or two."

A laugh escaped from Krom. "My caravan will be north of the city. Ask anyone for me and they will tell you."

"Can you recommend an inn where I can get rooms?"

"There's no place that will board two dragons," Krom warned. "Even in so cosmopolitan a city as Realmgate, they have their little idiosyncrasies, and harboring dragons inside the town is one of them."

"Faf and Ebony will take a holiday while we're here. I need a place for Mirza and myself."

"Since you have a lady with you, you'll want better accommodations than many of the inns in town offer. I'd try the Unicorn and the Dragon, if I were you."

Jarl raised his hand to wipe the dust from his face. Wyrd's scales caught the light of the sun and reflected it.

The trader gave a small gasp of recognition. "Is that not a talisman?" he asked, pointing to the bracelet.

"Yes, that's Wyrd."

"Then you're the Dragon's Pawn, the hero who is to help Realm in this age!" he said excitedly. "That explains your sword and your ability to kill Mog."

"I'm afraid so," Jarl said ruefully.

"You will have no need to find an inn. As Dragon's Pawn, Andronan will find rooms at the university for you."

"Who's Andronan?"

"The main purpose of Realmgate is the keeping of the gate between the worlds. The university trains the Keepers, and Andronan is the Elder Keeper."

"How do I find the university?"

"It's the largest building in the city. See the triple spires that reach the heavens?"

"I can't imagine how they were built so tall."

"Magic."

"Don't tell me. The Old Ones?" Jarl guessed.

"This gate is the only operational one remaining on Realm, and for that reason it is precious. Only the will of a master wizard can harness the energies needed to open a gate."

"One person could do all this?" Jarl's tone expressed his disbelief while his eyes swept the triple spires in awed appreciation of their iridescent beauty.

"One Old One," Krom corrected. "Today the art of gate creation is beyond our knowledge. No one now living knows the secret. Considering how dangerous a gate can be, it is well that Realm only has this one."

"What's dangerous about a gate?"

"Sometimes strange things appear in the center of the triangle formed by the spires. Then the Keepers must establish communication or send it back to whence it came, if it is bestial and had only stumbled on a gate in its own world."

"You know quite a lot about gate-keeping," Jarl observed.

"Keepers do not always stay here in the citadel. Sometimes they journey far. On such a trip they may well need allies and friends. I have known many Keepers."

Judging from the reception he got, this hardly counted as a first trip for Krom. The watchman waved Jarl and the trader through respectfully. The people in the streets went about their business, and Jarl noticed that many greeted Krom. Krom stopped before an oaken gate set in a marble wall. It opened before he knocked.

"Welcome, master," a young man in a brown cassock greeted Krom.

"Here is one Andronan will be glad to meet," Krom said quietly. With a friendly nod, he gestured to Jarl to enter. "This is Tieron, who will take you to the Elder Keeper. I'll see you later."

Jarl followed his guide. Outside the oaken door the cobbled street had been rough under Jarl's feet. Within the walls of the university, a marble mosaic composed of intricate designs paved the courtyard. It reminded Jarl of the other pavements of the Old Ones. Flowers, bushes, and trees bearing apples, cherries, pears, and oranges graced the neatly kept walk. Strange fruits and blooms in a myriad of colors swayed gently in the breeze that ameliorated the heat of day. A bush covered with blue roses scented the area.

"I see you appreciate our garden," Tieron said.

"It's unusual to see so many different plants growing together in one place."

"Here under the influence of the gate, we are able to grow species from a thousand worlds. When we Keepers become sojourners on the planet we adopt as our own, we search out the best to add to the garden. Each planet with a gate has only one plant here. Only old Earth had more than one specimen in the garden."

Jarl felt like a country bumpkin as he gawked at the sights. The fruits were of every hue and shape; the flowers called for attention by scent and color. "Where are you taking me?" he asked at last, when Tieron showed no signs of pausing.

"We've been expecting you for some time. Andronan wants to see you."

"Tell me about him," Jarl said.

"He is the Elder Keeper," Tieron answered, as if that was all the identification needed.

"What does he want with me?"

"I do not know. You have learned much as Dragon's Pawn. Perhaps it is time for you to take the final steps to becoming Dragon's Knight. My appointed task is to bring you to him." Tieron entered a low door and led Jarl up a long flight of stairs. They stopped outside a small room. "This will be yours. You may leave your pack here."

Jarl felt lighter when he put his pack in a corner of the room. "Er—" He stopped, not sure what to say.

"Yes?" Tieron inquired politely.

"I have a friend with me. She'll need a room, too."

"The Lady Mirza?"

"You know her?"

"Indeed I do. She is often here at Realmgate. Her room awaits, always prepared for any time she chooses to use it."

"Fine. Then I'm ready to see Andronan."

The hall they trod was light, although windows were few. The walls themselves seemed insubstantial, subtly shifting in some way that Jarl could sense but not see, even though he stared.

"In here," Tieron said.

Jarl crossed the threshold of the doorway to a small closet-like area. To his astonishment, they began to rise in the air. His stomach gave a queasy rumble.

"This is a gravity well." Tieron smiled. "I didn't think to warn you. Many of the artifacts of the Old Ones affect humans in odd ways."

"I should have known." Jarl found floating upward with no support an unusual experience. They passed openings that led to other floors, but no passengers joined them.

Tieron said in a low voice, "We get off at the next level." He took Jarl's arm and pulled him over the doorsill onto solid floor. Jarl almost stumbled.

"Sorry," he said.

"Do not worry. The first time anyone exits a gravity well is somewhat awkward. You'll probably not have any trouble the next time. My first exit was without help. I fell flat on the floor. Most upsetting," Tieron said solemnly.

Jarl couldn't help smiling. Tieron's words and actions were those of a much older man and sat oddly on the young guide's shoulders.

A few short steps brought them to another door. Tieron knocked discreetly. The door opened silently, showing them a monastic room furnished with a bed, a table, and a chair.

"Come in, Tieron," the aged occupant of the room commanded quietly.

"Yes, sir."

"I see you have brought the Dragon's Pawn. Thank you. You may leave," he said kindly, for Tieron's awe was palpable. Tieron bowed and left, closing the door behind him. Andronan looked at Jarl and said, "So you are Jarl Koenig, Dragon's Pawn."

"Yes, sir." Jarl found himself answering respectfully, understanding the guide's actions better now that he was under the bright gaze of the old man's deep purple eyes.

"I am Andronan. I serve Realmgate as Elder Keeper."

"I've heard the name before," Jarl said.

"More years ago than I care to count, I, too, was Dragon's Pawn."

Jarl heard Wyrd speak. "Greetings, Andronan."

"Ah, Wyrd. You, at least, have not changed."

"If all goes well, I am nearing the end of my—servitude."

Andronan smiled. "You have done well in choosing your companion."

Wyrd made no reply. His talisman gave Andronan the silent treatment, which surprised Jarl. The old man, however, seemed not to notice that his last statement went unremarked.

"The Shadowlord waxes while the magic of the Old Ones wanes. The coming battle between Light and Dark here on

Realm will be a decisive one. We shall need your willing help. Do you give it freely?"

"I do," Jarl said, feeling that some ceremony had occurred. "After the battle, will I be able to return to my own home?"

"In that battle you shall be Dragon's Knight. As Knight, you may pass unhindered to any location in the alternate universes that the gate serves."

"When do I change from Pawn to Knight? In the battle?"

"You shall be a full-fledged Knight before you face the Shadowlord. Only as Knight will you be able to withstand the tests of battle."

"What do I have to do to become Knight?"

"Your eagerness gladdens me, Jarl. Soon I shall have word of the activities of the Shadowlord. I feel the time of battle approaches on swift feet. In these days that yet remain before the testing, you will study here in the university."

"Do I learn battle tactics?"

"You might call it that, but the easiest word for it is magic."

"You mean I'm going to become a magician?" Jarl's mind jumped to the incongruous picture of himself pulling rabbits out of a hat.

"No," Andronan said, looking deeply into Jarl's eyes.

In Jarl's mind the rabbits turned to dragons in midhop and flew away into the air. "I didn't think that!" Jarl said.

"No," Andronan assured him, "but the power to make others see the visions you create is one of the weapons you may well face in the coming war."

"And I'll learn to do that to others?"

"You will have many abilities that you do not now envision. To withstand a magical assault, you must know how to wage one yourself. To have the power to do a thing, however, does not mean you must use that power—except in defense or extremity. As the Champion of the Gate, or Dragon's Knight, you must master the magic of Realm. Even if it is a poor remnant of the glorious wizardry which existed before the Old Ones vanished."

"I should like to know more of them."

Andronan looked pleased at Jarl's interest. "The library will be open to you. Wyrd will make it possible for you to read the Old Ones' tongue and any other language you may find in the books that are here."

At this point the door opened and Mirza rushed into the room, crossing it rapidly. "I'm back, Grandfather," she said to Andronan, while a startled Jarl watched her kiss the old mage. "You look tired. Why are you standing?" She pulled up the chair, and he sat, shaking his head. With a flick of her hand, a stool materialized. She sat, arranging her skirts carefully.

"And what of our guest?" Andronan reminded her. "He has no chair."

"Oh, he can make one for himself," she said.

"I can?" Jarl asked.

"Of course, silly. Just concentrate on the spot where you want a chair to appear. Think of the type of chair you want, and Wyrd will help you form one," she said patiently, as if she were teaching a child.

"Okay. Here goes," Jarl said, following her instructions carefully. If she thought he could, he would. He pictured the overstuffed chair he had in his den, complete with a handle that put up a footrest. The air shimmered, then with a dull pop the chair appeared. Jarl sat.

"Very good!" Mirza clapped.

"I have never seen a chair like that," Andronan said as Jarl pulled the handle that raised the footrest.

"They're very popular where I come from," Jarl said.

"You need Grandmother back to take care of you." Mirza fussed gently at Andronan. "Sometimes I wish she wasn't so powerful. Neither of you can be enjoying her guarding the whole southern border," Mirza muttered.

Andronan turned to Mirza. He ignored her outburst. "And what have you been up to since your last visit?"

"I've been making friends with Jarl and helping him get here," she said, making it sound very unexciting.

"Good. I'm glad to hear your madcap ways have not got you into any difficulty."

She squeezed his frail hand gently. "I've been very good. You've nothing to worry about at all."

"Then shall we forget about your being a prisoner of the Shadowlord—twice?" he said roguishly.

"Oh, Grandfather, don't be so fussy. Everything was quite all right. Jarl came to the rescue both times." She looked at her rescuer and added, "He's very good at heroing."

"And you're a minx, just like your mother and grandmother."

"Have you heard anything from Mother and Father?" she asked.

"They are off Realm on an assignment. Perhaps you can visit them when this is all over."

"You're becoming too tired. I'll take Jarl with me and start him on his basic lessons."

"Very well. I shall see you both later."

"You will rest, won't you?" Mirza said.

"Go along, and we'll see," he half promised.

Mirza took Jarl's hand, and like two children they left the room together. As they closed the door, they heard the sound of the lever on the chair raising the footrest.

"So that's the way of it," Andronan muttered to the empty room after they were gone. "Just like her mother. . . ."

CHAPTER
Twenty-Three

"**W**ELL?**"** Jarl asked as they floated gently downward in the Old Ones' version of an elevator.

"Well, what?" Mirza countered.

"Are you all right? I mean, did the heal spring break the spell?"

Her eyes met his seriously as she gave him a sad smile. "No."

"What do you mean, no!"

"The Shadowlord's spell is more powerful than the residual magic of the goddess. All over Realm the old power is fading. There are no Old Ones to revitalize the magic, and the Shadowlord must be the single most potent magic worker on this world."

"What do we have to do to cure you?"

"I don't know," Mirza sounded resigned.

Jarl couldn't understand her calm. Perhaps her ability to shape-shift had made her more tolerant of strange forms. If she turned into a warty gray-green monster, surely it would bother her. He tried to ignore how much the idea worried him.

"But—but you know all about magic. Surely there must be something we can do! Maybe Andronan would know..."

"He's old. He won't allow himself to die until he's seen Realm in safe hands. He limits his magic to the gate and its uses. It can't aid me in this. I cannot burden him with my problems."

"Not my—our," Jarl told her, placing his hand in hers when she reached for it.

"Our problem," she amended, pulling him onto another level.

"You're certain there's nothing you or anyone here on Realm can do?"

"I'm certain."

"Then I have an idea that may work," Jarl said.

"What is it?" Mirza's grip on Jarl's hand tightened. Becoming a monster bothered her more than she was willing to admit to Jarl.

Jarl had forgotten how lovely she could look when she felt excited. "Well, perhaps since the dragons only have to visualize a place to fly there instantaneously, perhaps if they visualized a time as well as a place, then they could take a rider back in time itself."

"How would that help me?"

"If a dragon envisions a place in the past, the dragon may be about to fly to that place and that time. The Old Ones existed in the past. Surely they could break the spell if Ebony can time travel."

"I'll ask Ebony if she'll try."

"Is she still around? I thought she and Faf were going to visit Fafnir."

"She's found a comfortable cave in the mountains. She and Faf weren't leaving to see Fafnir until tomorrow. If I mindcall, I'm sure she'll come."

"I'm not certain I want you to take the risk. It may be that on Realm dragons can only fly from place to place instead of from time to time. Perhaps Ebony isn't strong enough, or—"

"Don't be silly. She's coming now. She'll meet us at the north gate," Mirza called over her shoulder, running down the corridor.

"Wait for me." Jarl dashed after her, watching her long auburn hair flow behind her as she sped into the street.

Jarl marveled that no one in the city stopped him. Everyone knew Mirza. She called greetings as she hurried by, with Jarl following her as closely as he could. She was amazingly fleet of foot (perhaps because she understood the movements of animals). He stopped twice to make apologies, but she never bumped anyone.

The gatekeeper smiled indulgently as they flew by him. It occurred to Jarl that the people they met must think he and she were lovers. The fatuous look on the gatekeeper's face confirmed Jarl's suspicion.

On an open space on a small hillock outside the city gates, Faf and Ebony perched like two overgrown canaries. The dragons had the advantage of being able to fly straight to the meeting place instead of dodging through winding city streets filled with half the population of Realmgate.

"Are you ready?" Ebony asked when Jarl and Mirza drew close and stopped to rest.

"Oh, yes. Can we go now?" Mirza asked, advancing to stand beside her friend.

"Wait a minute," Jarl and Faf roared in unison.

"We've got to discuss this first," Jarl said.

"Where exactly are you and Ebony going?" Faf asked Mirza.

Mirza was almost incoherent because of her excitement. "Not where! When!"

"Not so fast," Jarl cautioned.

"Haste is imperative," put in Ebony. "Show him," she commanded Mirza.

"I don't want to—"

"Show me what?" Jarl asked belligerently. Things were moving too fast for him.

"Oh, Ebony, I hoped he wouldn't ever have to see." And under Jarl's scrutiny, she opened the top of her dress a fraction. A few inches from her neck a scaly green patina marred the whiteness of her skin.

Jarl's protest died a sudden death. Wordlessly he gathered Mirza close in his arms.

"You're right. There is no time to lose," Faf said. "I'll fly you into the past."

"I'm afraid not, Faf. There should be a special bond between rider and dragon. There is a better chance of that between Ebony and Mirza."

Mirza withdrew from Jarl's arms and stood next to Ebony. Without further speech, Ebony seized Mirza in her claws and rose into the air. Faf and Jarl were unprepared for their departure. The dragoness barely cleared the ground before she and her burden vanished.

A chill wind enveloped Jarl and the remaining dragon. "Goodb—" echoed in Jarl's mind amid a sensation of otherwhereness.

"They're gone," Jarl said flatly.

"We can follow," Faf hissed as he always did when he was genuinely disturbed.

"Where? Or rather, when? Mirza didn't tell us where—or when—she intended Ebony to take her. Did Ebony tell you?"

"No, and there are too many places and times for us to be able to check."

"Were you linked to Ebony when they disappeared?"

"I had a sense of total blackness and cold, but nothing else." Faf's huge wings beat the air in frustration.

Jarl braced himself until Faf settled down again on the ground. "What are you going to do now?"

Faf shrugged his wings in an almost human gesture. "I'm not sure."

"Will you return to the cave Ebony found?"

"I'll nip back to my own cave and check my plants, work on a few spells, and wait."

"How can I get in touch with you so you'll know if they return?"

"Not if, Jarl. When. You don't know Ebony as I do. She's a very determined dragoness. If she sets her mind on going back in time, she'll arrive. We've talked about the Old Ones. In her family they remember many stories of which I knew nothing—and I am something of a historian. She, perhaps better than any living being that now exists, can visualize Realm as it was in the time of the Old Ones."

"I'm happy to hear it, but I can't help worrying. You still didn't tell me how to reach you," Jarl added as an after-thought.

"Every day at noon I'll return here for an hour. If Mirza and Ebony return, I'll be here."

"Very well, take care. If the Shadowlord figures out who helped Mirza and me to escape, he may want to gain revenge," Jarl warned.

Faf's next words proved how much adventuring had changed him. "I have a well-protected cave. One advantage of flying this new way instead of the regular way is instantaneous transportation. At Realmgate it should be safe enough —until his army attacks," Faf said.

Jarl watched silently as Faf rose into the air, flapped his wings once, and disappeared. Now the long wait for news began. Jarl trudged to the city. His enthusiasm for learning had dimmed. He scuffed his feet occasionally as he walked and took no note of the brightly hued garments of the populace. He started when someone placed a hand on his arm.

"Jarl, what happened out there?" Krom asked.

"Mirza and Ebony are seeking aid for a spell the Shadowlord cast over Mirza when she was his prisoner."

"Who has the power to lift an enchantment of that strength?"

"The Old Ones."

"The last Old One disappeared from Realm ten thousand springs ago!"

"That's when they've gone," Jarl said.

"When they have gone? Don't you mean 'where'?"

Krom's bushy eyebrows twitched while he struggled to understand.

"No. When. Ebony and Faf have discovered they have some abilities they didn't have before the Shadowlord began opening his version of a gate to admit the fantasy creatures from my world to Realm."

"They can fly into time itself?" The ends of Krom's mustache quivered with interest as he heard Jarl's information.

"Yes. In addition, they can fly instantly from one place to another in some kind of shortcut through—" Jarl groped for words, "—somewhere."

"By the Bright Ones! That's wonderful news. Their ability will be of great help to us in battle."

"Yes. I'd be feeling optimistic myself except for one thing."

Krom looked at Jarl expectantly, his inquiry written on his face.

"I'm not sure whether Ebony has the ability to fly back in time, Krom."

"Then where are they? I saw them disappear as I was searching for you."

"That's a good question. I only wish I knew the answer."

"When will you know for certain?"

"They set no time for their return. If they fly into the past, if they find the Old Ones, and if the Old Ones can cure Mirza, then they will return."

"What you need is something to take your mind from this while you wait for news. No amount of worry will help, you know."

Jarl shrugged. "What do you suggest?"

"Some study about the powers of Wyrd, for one thing."

"How do you know about that?" Not for the first time Jarl felt as if everyone on Realm knew more about his business than he did.

"Andronan is my master," Krom said simply.

"I should have known. Are you some kind of Keeper, too?"

"You might say that." Krom's eyes twinkled. "Let us return to the university," he suggested, taking Jarl's arm just in time to pull him out of the way as a cart rumbled by.

"Agreed. Perhaps if I can command Wyrd's full power, Faf and I can search for Mirza."

'If she and her dragon find themselves trapped in a time corridor, there is no hurry."

"What's a time corridor?"

"One of the old books mentions something of the sort. . . ."

"What are we waiting for, then? Come, show me where the book is," Jarl commanded, glad to have something he could do besides wait.

Krom hid his smile as best he could and accompanied Jarl through the streets of Realmgate, hoping to get him interested in his studies through the old manuscripts. The trader tossed a coin to a passing street vendor to pay for the two fruits he selected, then strode after his young friend to share his purchase.

Two weeks passed as Jarl immersed himself in learning all he could. His spare time rushed by. While he spent time perusing the old books, his main task was mastering his bracelet and the power he could summon with its aid. Every day at noon he strolled outside the city to meet Faf, who never failed to come, bringing steak fruit or some other proof of his horticultural prowess. The cook at the university appreciated the additional provender. So much so that a steak-plant seedling reached to the sky out in the garden.

Jarl sat by an open window facing into the garden when a messenger brought word that Andronan wanted to see him at once. Jarl closed the dusty tome respectfully and returned it to the old librarian, who could find any book at will, using some system known only to antiquarian librarians. The man seemed as ancient as his volumes. Jarl believed he probably had read them all. The librarian was old enough. The rules for finding books in the library made little sense to Jarl. He was not the only student who found it easier to ask for help rather than search the shelves himself.

"Thank you, Librisald," Jarl said, handing the book to the librarian carefully.

"You are most welcome, Jarl. I have noticed with satisfaction your joy in the old histories of Realm. So few appreciate them, you see," he added sadly, pushing his long eyebrows out of one eye. His gnarled fingers touched a binding fondly.

"They're very interesting, but now I am summoned by Andronan." Jarl bowed his head in leave-taking as did all the other students who used the library. Everyone treated the old librarian with great respect.

Jarl located the gravity well with ease and walked out onto seeming nothingness with confidence. His rise was faster, for he found that by standing in the exact center one could almost double the speed of ascent.

Andronan's door was ajar, and yielded to him before he knocked. Within he saw a wyvern, Master Krom, and the Elder Keeper himself.

"Welcome, Man-one," the wyvern said, identifying herself as Seabreeze by her tone of voice and way of addressing Jarl.

"Good day to you all." Jarl smiled and turned to his host. "Andronan, is there something you wanted of me?"

"Yes, but Krom will tell you much you need to know." Andronan sat in the chair Jarl had created, but he motioned Jarl to another chair which faced them all.

Krom began without wasting any time. "The Shadowlord is massing an army on his northern border. Seabreeze brought us word. Relnot's magical powers have sealed the borders of King Caeryl's kingdom to all. The result is to protect the citizens and to force our enemies to detour, giving us several days' delay in the arrival at Realmgate. By tomorrow a regiment of the king's best fighting men will be at our gates. The wyverns will hinder the Black Legion to give us more time to set up our defenses."

In the middle of his report, Krom started pacing as if he could not bear inaction, but he stopped, glanced at

Andronan, and sat abruptly. "I'm sorry," he apologized to the older man.

"Years ago when I was assistant to the Elder Keeper, I also had difficulty in showing composure at all times," Andronan told Krom.

When the Elder Keeper finished speaking, Jarl asked, "What do you want with me?"

"You will lead our army in battle."

"What army?" Jarl had spent long hours at his studies and was unaware of the large force that mustered during the days and nights of study.

"Each kingdom of Realm has sent a number of men. King Caeryl himself has sent a thousand," Krom said.

"The wyverns have sent three mistresses," Seabreeze said.

"Mistresses?" The word puzzled Jarl.

"You would call them adepts or workers of magic," Andronan told Jarl in serious tones, although his eyes twinkled at Jarl's mistake.

"If you'll excuse me, it's almost noon. I'll need to speak to Faf when he comes. Then I want to see some of the troops I'll be leading and talk to their captains," Jarl said with sudden decision. He had never been a battle commander before, but he was a good chess player. He would not surrender Realmgate to the Shadowlord without putting up the best fight he was able to produce. The Dragon's Pawn now had the knowledge to become the Dragon's Knight.

"Correct," a sibilant voice hissed in Jarl's mind.

"Give my flying cousin my regards, Man-one," Seabreeze said.

"I will," Jarl promised.

"You'll find the troops massed on the plain north of the city. I shall see you there this afternoon, I trust." Krom nodded shortly.

"Krom, I begin to have hope of victory," Andronan said as Jarl strode from the room, an excited gleam in his eyes.

CHAPTER
Twenty-Four

*T*HE icy lightlessness swirled around Mirza and Ebony.

The dragon's thought penetrated her companion's wonderment. "Picture with me the healing spring," Ebony urged. "See the day when the Green Lady presided over a newly created mere."

Mirza joined her thoughts to the dragon's. Ebony had a clear visualization of the spring area, complete with rose garden massed alongside a temple that was in ruins in their time. In a dim corner of her mind Mirza realized that this was a seeing passed down from mother to daughter for generations to insure the memory of the glory of the past. Then, with a wrench of the senses, they were there, a part of the scene they had envisioned together.

"We did it!" Mirza said jubilantly, enjoying the panoramic view that spread below them.

"Of course we did," Ebony replied with the saurian equivalent of a chuckle. "Was there any real doubt in your mind? Once you gave me the idea, I realized I could do it. So long as we can see the place and the time to which we go, I can take us anywhere and anywhen you choose." The quiet confidence of Ebony was cheering.

"Do you think the Old Ones or the Green Lady will be able to cure this?" Mirza's hand crept to her throat and withdrew hastily as her fingers touched rough scales.

"In the old stories I learned as a dragonette, there were miraculous healings—believe in a cure."

Ebony swooped in a vast circle, searching for a smooth spot in which to land her rider. The courtyard behind the temple was small, but of adequate size to land if the flyer were careful and competent. Ebony alighted swiftly, releasing her claw grip of Mirza at the precise moment to let her stand upright on the pavement. Mirza staggered and would have fallen but for an assist from the dragon's tail which curled gently about her waist, giving her time to regain her balance.

"All in one piece?" Ebony asked.

"Yes, thank you. Do you—" Mirza began and then stopped abruptly as she saw a tall, willowy form approaching. The Green Lady, legendary goddess of the pool, drew nearer. In the faded murals on the interior walls which were still standing in Mirza's time, artists had faithfully depicted the attributes of the goddess. No artist, however skillful, could do justice to the serenity of the wise green eyes of the Green Lady. The color reminded Mirza of every spring she had ever seen. Also brought to her heart was the first real rays of certainty that her plight was curable. Without her volition, Mirza's hand opened the top of her robe, exposing the scabrous ugliness to the view of those calm orbs which saw into her very soul.

"Come, daughter," a leaf-cool voice commanded softly. "You have almost left it too late. There is little time to waste."

"Don't you want to know—"

"Later, child, later. Now you need the water's power, pure and good. Bright Ones can work through the waters here," she continued, leading Mirza in the direction of the shimmering basin.

On the bank Mirza quickly divested herself of her clothes and slipped into the water, feeling it close over her fevered body with a caress of returning normalcy. The Green Lady entered the water, which seemed not to wet her robes. Her slender hand reached out in benediction and touched Mirza's head, indicating she should submerge herself completely. When Mirza regained her breath, the lady touched her head a second and then a third time. Her serene face lit with gladness. Mirza knew the lady had freed her from the spell.

The lady returned to shore. She waved her hands in an intricate movement that caused the very air to become visible. In her hands she held a robe of the finest cloth. The iridescence of the material resembled the pale color in the buildings of the Old Ones in present-day Realmgate.

"Oh, is that for me?" Mirza said when the Green Lady offered it to her.

"Woven from the dreams of the Bright Ones is this robe, and therefore it can be anything its wearer wishes."

Mirza was not able to imagine wishing it to be anything else than what it was. It clung to her body lovingly. In it she had the fragile beauty of a butterfly.

"Come. There is much for you to learn in your allotted span here with us. Only a most powerful being could so twist a spell of the Bright Ones to produce the enchantment that brought you here." The Green Lady's voice chimed against the slight breeze and interwove itself with a nearby bird's song.

Mirza marveled at the manner in which the lady blended into the natural beauties of the landscape. All of the harsh destruction which the years would wreak on the site had not yet happened. There was a springtime freshness evident in every flower and blade of grass. The shapes of the blooms were subtly different, and the colors had a vibrancy of hue that had not survived into Mirza's time.

"Can you tell me who the Bright Ones are? I always thought it was another way of referring to your people."

"Ah, no, my daughter. The Bright Ones are the stars themselves, more mighty far than we. In their infancy they had physical bodies as do we, but now they are pure thought. We are their inheritors as you are our heirs."

"Do you serve them, then?"

"In a way. It has long been our task to guard the gates, those lines of communication made possible by the will of the Bright Ones. We may, if it is needful, pass between the children of the Bright Ones."

"Then the children of the Bright Ones are suns!"

"Just so," the Green Lady answered.

"How wonderful that you are able to open and close the gates."

"It is both our blessing and our curse. Some of us are even now using our power to enslave and toy with the fortunes of the simpler beings that inhabit the worlds which circle the suns."

"Why don't you stop the evil ones?"

"Because it is not in our nature to kill, only to heal and help."

"We are much in need of your powers in my time. There is in Realm an evil one who serves the Dark—the Shadowlord," Mirza explained simply.

"I have seen your coming and the future of Realm in the face of the moon. I am to teach you to strengthen the gate magic, now weakening for lack of understanding."

"We have the university at Realmgate, where all the old books are. Some of us study all our lives to keep the gates."

"Does it not take at least three of you in your time to open the door between the worlds?" The lady's smile took most of the sting from her words.

"Yes." Mirza looked down at the ground, and then she raised her chin defiantly. "We do serve the gate," she said proudly.

"You keep the gates. Pleased are we with the Keepers."

"Why did the Old Ones leave Realm? Surely you could have stayed to keep the gates if it was your wish."

"In my vision I see the natural abilities of the human race twisted, dwarfed, and stunted because of the powers that we used, meaning only to help them. Soon I must tell our

Council. They will agree that we must move from Realm so that your race may grow and prosper."

"But—" Mirza began in denial.

The Green Lady raised a finger for silence. "It is time for us to move to another existence in another reality."

Mirza frowned, trying to understand.

"Those of us who elect to obey the Council will become . . ." She searched for words which would have meaning for her curious listener, ". . . things of the spirit, totally free of our material bodies, free to wander not only from one world to the next, but also free to move in the spaces between universes and in the stream of time itself."

Mirza's silence showed her degree of incomprehension.

"It is of no matter. Those of us who most helped the creatures of this world will not vanish without preparing a gradual withdrawal of our gifts. I was the healer. This spring will cure physical ills and give peace to twisted minds for many years after I have gone."

"You look sad. I am sorry," Mirza said.

"There is no need, daughter. For us, the millennia we have enjoyed physically were a type of childhood. It is no easier for an Old One to become mature than it is for your kind," she said with a wry smile. "Since you have come all this time, I must teach you some of the magical skills you will need to set your universe aright. The forces of the Light must triumph over the forces of the Dark this time."

They walked to the center of the rose garden where Mirza smelled a lavender blossom with delight. She flushed guiltily. "I forgot. Where is Ebony?"

"I mindcalled some of her ancestresses to offer her hospitality while we are together. You would not want her to lose the opportunity to learn more legends for her vast store of knowledge."

"Do you know everything?" Mirza burst out, awed by the revelations of the lady.

"I am the Green Lady. I weave the web of life for many. The thoughts of all things living I can see," she sighed.

"Because that is my curse, I dwell far from most of those you call the Old Ones."

"Curse? It would be wonderful to have your ability!"

"You speak as a child. Would you want every evil idea that hatches in the dark reaches of the minds of those around you to be your burden? You would know every lie, every greed, every perversion of the good that existed. Those who were not perfect in their thinking would shun you. Do not wish for such an ability."

Mirza felt the rebuke keenly, but she said nothing, for she knew she had wished foolishly. How could the lady teach anyone as thoughtless as she?

"Do not take on such a burden, daughter. Your judgment of yourself is too harsh. I will teach you many things that can only enhance your natural abilities and help to make you a force for good."

Mirza basked in the ray of the Green Lady's smile. Threaded amid her excitement was the humble desire to be worthy of the lady's teachings.

"Let us enter the temple and begin," the Green Lady said, drifting over the ground like mist. She entered a small door outlined by a cascade of roses red as blood.

Mirza wished Jarl could know she was free of the Shadowlord's spell, but she dared not return until she learned all the Green Lady wished to teach her. The scent of the roses clung to her dress as she entered the door in her turn.

Jarl wearily dismounted from Oromon, the magnificent war stallion that was the gift of King Caeryl. "Give him a good rubdown, will you?" he said. He waited for the freckle-faced groom's acknowledgment of his order before adding, "Add an extra measure of oats. He deserves them." Jarl stroked the velvety nose that nudged his chest. "Yes, boy, rest well. Tomorrow night the moon will be a silver sickle in the sky. In the waning of the Light, the powers of the Dark will rise and do battle."

"Are—are we ready, sir?" the groom asked timidly,

which surprised Jarl because as a normal thing every freckle on the boy's face danced with mischief.

Jarl smiled at him grimly. "As ready as anyone can be for a Lord of Shadows," he said as his hand gripped the groom's shoulder in a reassuring contact. "If each of us does his part, we shall make a good fight."

He watched as Oromon tamely followed the groom to his stall. Realmgate bulged at the seams. Each building housed some of Jarl's army. The citizens regarded it as an honor to host the Legion of Light within their walls. Remembering how people in his world felt about quartering soldiery, Jarl couldn't help but appreciate the hospitality bestowed on his soldiers. He realized that most of the fighting men would revert to being simple citizens themselves after the battle.

In his room he stepped into the marble tub already prepared for him. He was seldom alone and had less time than that for reflection, but as always his thoughts went to Mirza. She and Ebony, gone for weeks. Would they return? There was no way of knowing until Faf was free to begin their agreed search in otherwhere—or otherwhen, he amended his thoughts.

Faf roosted in an empty tower above the university. He kept the old librarian rummaging through long-undisturbed stacks of tomes for books to delight his taste for ancient history. If Librisald liked Jarl, he positively doted on the dragon. The elderly man and the saurian spent many interesting hours researching and sharing their finds. The more obscure the item was, the more pleasure it gave them to find it.

One piece of research made them aware that Wyrd was more of an amplifier of power than a source. For that reason, the person who wore the bracelet had to understand the basic tenets of magic. Under the direction of the Dragon's Knight, Wyrd could lend strength to the power of other, more magically talented people. Jarl blessed Lythyr for sending the three mistresses. He couldn't tell them apart. When they united to accomplish a task, they evinced all the paranormal abilities known on Jarl's world plus a few he had not known existed. Magic seemed to consist of an ability to turn probabilities into realities.

Jarl enjoyed the new room he had been assigned by Andronan. It shielded him from the common coming and going of the myriad of people that overflowed the main building and filled the town. He was a light sleeper and found the responsibility thrust upon him caused him to awaken at a hint of noise, of difference, of change. He didn't understand how he almost slept through his first meeting with the Dark Forces. Now the slightest tightening of Wyrd would bring him to his feet, alert and ready for whatever came.

He padded to the bed, where a clean tunic and breeches rested as if put there by invisible hands. Tieron, his servant, was as awed of Jarl as he was of Andronan. He appeared instantly at Jarl's call, but otherwise he served silently and unobtrusively. Jarl fastened his belt around his waist and pulled on his boots. He was ready to go down for his evening meal.

Wyrd tightened on his arm.

"Well, this is it," Jarl said aloud. "And a day early, too!"

"Not so. Mirza returns." Wyrd's words hissed in Jarl's mind.

"When? I mean, where?" Jarl asked, striding down the hall and jumping into the gravity well that would take him to the lower floor.

"At the place where you left her," Wyrd answered.

Jarl paused to say to a student, "Send word to Faf in the tower. The Lady Mirza has returned!"

Too preoccupied to notice the shadows that gathered in dark pools in relatively protected places, he raced out of the university and through the streets of the city. He nodded and waved briefly to citizens he knew. They stood talking in small groups after he passed them on his way to the north gate.

Scouts' reports from the west told of vast windstorms over Gran Desierto. The sun was shrouded by the amount of flying sand in the air. It reposed, blood-red, on the top of the low range of mountains to the west. Jarl judged the sun would set in two hours. He increased his pace. He wanted Mirza and Ebony inside the walls of the university before nightfall.

A heat haze rose from the bare rocks which formed a portion of the northern plain. Wyrd clasped his wrist firmly, as if to remind him of the nearness of the dark. Occasionally Jarl's peripheral vision caught hints of filmy shapes. One resembled a giant lizard, but not exactly. Another vision was an amorphous blob, an animated mouth, complete with yard-long fangs. If the massing horrors took part in the attack on Realmgate, the mistresses from Wyvern Marsh would have enough to slay. Even their bloodthirsty instincts for revenge would be sated, Jarl thought as he jogged onward.

In the distance, silhoueted on the ruby disk of the sun, the gigantic black form of a dragon appeared in a wink. It increased in size as Jarl watched. A shadow passed overhead. Jarl drew his battle sword. He reluctantly turned his eyes from Ebony to face the new danger, only to relax with a sigh. In was Faf, who settled beside him and hissed a greeting that was almost unintelligible. Jarl observed that in moments of great emotion, Faf's precise human mindspeech became more reptilian.

Where was Mirza? She had left clutched in the talons of the dragoness. Now he could not see her. Had something gone wrong? "Faf! Can you see Mirza?"

Faf gazed at him with one plate-sized orb. "She is safe."

"I can't see her!"

"Wait and you will," Faf advised. "Why not try mind-talk?"

Jarl called mentally, then looked at Faf. "You see—"

"We're coming. Don't be so impatient," Mirza's thought reached out to silence Jarl.

"Welcome home," Faf said as Ebony made a two-talon landing beside the watchers.

"I'm hungry," Ebony said as Mirza slid from her seat between her wings. When she rode, Ebony's neck hid her.

Jarl gathered Mirza in his arms. Faf showed his joy by blowing a series of ecstatic smoke rings into the air.

"You weren't really worried about us, were you?" Ebony said. She was astounded at their relief. "I wouldn't put Mirza in danger. I knew I could do it," Ebony told them modestly. Only Faf seemed to hear her, so she gently nudged Jarl in the back, almost knocking him down.

"Hmmm? Oh, yes, of course," he said. His mind was on other things than conversation.

"There was no danger," Ebony repeated.

The words registered this time. "Well, I'm glad to have you both back safely."

"If the reports we've been getting are correct, there will be danger in plenty as soon as it gets dark tonight," Faf said grimly.

"You're right. We'd better get these two inside the gates." Jarl kept his arm around Mirza as they talked.

"Can't we go to our cave in the hills?" Ebony asked.

"Not tonight. Realmgate is the focus of the Dark Legions. The mistresses from Wyvern Marsh have seen a host of evil slowly closing in on the city," Jarl answered.

Faf snorted a jet of fire. "Let them come. We're ready to fight."

"Weren't you a pacifist when we left?" Mirza looked puzzled by Faf's warlike air.

"Still am," he averred. "However, if you had been here and heard about the kinds of outrages the Dark Legions have perpetrated on anyone unlucky enough to fall into their power—well!" He emphasized his point with a three-yard burst of pure blue flame.

"What about the wounded?"

"Come with me. You can see the casualties that survived to shelter with us," Jarl told Mirza. "We've hauled barrels of the healing water. That cures some of the minor wounds, but others are beyond the water's power." His clenched teeth told her how badly hurt the worst cases were.

"Show me the water. There is something I can do to increase its strength," Mirza said, walking rapidly toward the north gate and safety.

"I'll see you in the tower after dinner," Jarl called to the two dragons that rose in the air behind them and quickly passed above them.

CHAPTER
Twenty-Five

A N icy blast scudded black clouds toward the half
disk of the sun that was still visible above the
mountain peaks. As Jarl and Mirza entered the
gates, the huge portals closed silently behind them. They
turned to watch the clouds occlude the sun as the preterna-
tural twilight closed over Realmgate.

"We'll not have long now before their first attack, sir," the
gatekeeper said, hefting his war ax in his hand.

"Send word at the first sign of attack."

"Yes, Sir Jarl!"

Mirza covered her mouth with her hand. "Sir Jarl?" She
giggled.

"I've asked them to call me plain Jarl, but I seem stuck
with the title."

"Don't worry," she told him mock seriously. "I'll call you
Plain Jarl if it will make you happy."

"I'll call you plain minx," he said, giving her a hug as he
guided her through the almost deserted streets.

"Where is everybody?"

"We thought it best if the women and children remain

indoors. Some women are tending the sick in the refectory at the university. The men are waiting in their assigned places. We're ready to repulse an attack."

"It sure does feel warm," Mirza commented, lifting her long hair from her neck.

"You're right. Every night until tonight it's been cold. Now it's warm." As Jarl spoke, the heat increased. "Get inside," he said, shoving her gently through the outer gate to the university. "This is part of the attack. I recognize it," he finished bitterly.

"But what is it?"

"It's a fire storm. If the wyvern mistresses and Andronan can't extinguish it or shift it or something, we'll all be very dead shortly." He turned his back on her abruptly, running toward the south gate. He knew it would only be a matter of time until every combustible thing burst into flame spontaneously. Sometimes he almost regretted the amount of knowledge he gained from reading those books that Librisald gave him to study.

"My Lord Jarl," a sweating guardsman said. "Look!"

Jarl didn't need the pointed finger to show him the direction of the bright ball of flame that raced toward the walls. It expanded from its white-hot core to a gigantic size as they watched. Despite their bravery, the heat overcame some men. Jarl felt nauseated himself. His armor was hot to the touch.

"All right, Wyrd. Now what?" he asked.

Wyrd glowed with a phosphorescent light that spread downward onto the iridescent walls that surrounded Realmgate. A cool breeze sprang up and rushed to meet the blazing air. From the walls themselves a vapor misted, smelling of fresh spring rain, diluting the scent of charred wood. Before the eyes of the startled defenders, a huge whirlpool of disturbed air formed. Thunder boomed and lightning cracked. The walls emitted a soft, white vapourous moistness that spread a protective layer over the entire city.

The storm raged in a pyrotechnical display that was a thousand times the equivalent of any fireworks Jarl had ever seen. When the heavy rain began to fall, he managed a weak question. "Wyrd, did you do all that?" He expected no answer to his rhetorical question, but this time his talisman was almost garrulous.

"The Old Ones built the city. Thought you that unrealmly science could breach its walls? The walls themselves were their own defender. Now the Shadowlord must wage war fairly and in the proper manner." There was a smug complacency to Wyrd's mental message that chilled Jarl. Who but an alien creature would think that wars were fought according to some etiquette?

After Jarl checked the guard posts along the walls, he was certain the attack was over—at least for a time. The hard rain pelted the ground, splattered wetly, and filled the streets with water, then ran along the ancient cobblestones and exited the city via great conduits. Gradually it slackened to a fine mist which stopped after a final wisp over the city. Jarl saw the faint gray line in the east that presaged the dawn. He believed the light brought safety, but in that assumption he was incorrect. Almost within minutes of the sun's rising, the heat combined with the watery mist that saved Realmgate to form a heavy blanket of humidity. The heat and humidity made every breath an effort. The heat brought with it a feeling of despair. Jarl didn't see how anyone could fight well under the conditions that prevailed in the city. His only hope was that the Shadowlord's forces would suffer as well. He forced a smile at the tired defenders he saw as he headed for the refectory at the university.

"You were magnificent!" Mirza told him excitedly as he snatched a hurried bite of food.

"I was?" Jarl mumbled between mouthfuls.

"The way you held Wyrd and he called the stones of the walls to save us. . . ." Her voice died when she saw the look on his face.

"Where were you during the attack that could give you such a vantage point?"

"Up in the tower with Faf and Ebony."

"In the tower! You little—muttonhead! What do you

think I shoved you into the university for? I thought you'd have the sense to stay with Andronan. Why in the name of the Bright Ones did he ever let you go into that tower?"

A ghostly chuckle echoed in his mind. Faf's precise mental message was succinct. "Do you think any being could stop her if she decided to do something?"

Jarl paused. "You're right," he thought in the dragon's direction.

"We wouldn't let anything happen to her," Ebony explained in mindspeech. "Besides, she is a powerful magic user herself."

It wasn't the first mental communication Jarl received from the dragoness, but it surprised him that he recognized her so easily. Magic and mindspeech were psi abilities he was coming to take for granted.

"And just what could you do against a menace like that fire storm?" he said aloud. He wanted to give his message maximum clarity, and hearing the words helped him to focus his thought.

The dragoness's answer made his mind feel as if it had just received a sharp tap. "I would have flown her to another time or place."

"And taken the top of the tower with you, I suppose?" Jarl lasered a thought upward in exasperation.

"Oh, I didn't think of that."

Jarl felt the mental anger of Faf building. Therefore he said, "Well, you should. It would upset Mirza if you destroyed the university. I do appreciate your care of her."

"I would much prefer it if you three would stop talking about me as if I were a wayward child," interrupted Mirza.

Jarl eyed the curves the iridescent dress outlined so faithfully. "Wayward, I agree with you one hundred percent. Now, as to the child part—"

"Men!" Mirza snorted in exact imitation of Ebony.

A messenger rushed into the room, bowed respectfully to Mirza, and said, "Sir Jarl, strange visions are appearing outside the walls."

Bidding Mirza a quick good-bye, Jarl hurried after the

messenger. He joined a group of men on the wall. Strange shapes swirled from a ground-hugging miasma that seeped into the air. It smelled like stagnant pond water. The men watched silently. They knew that if the nightmare shapes materialized inside the walls, they would have to fight them in hand-to-hand combat.

"They are demons from another world," Mirza said in Jarl's ear.

"You get inside someplace," he commanded as he slipped his arm around her waist for a quick hug.

"Don't be silly. If these demons are materializing from the Earth, they may be capable of appearing anywhere inside the walls as well as outside. Where do you suggest I go?" she asked sweetly.

Jarl knew when she used the saccharine, submissive style of speaking she was most stubborn. "Well, at least you could stay near Ebony," he growled.

"I shall go help the wyverns," Mirza announced. "I know when I'm not wanted." She pulled free of Jarl's encircling arms and descended to ground level so rapidly she disappeared into the unnatural darkness as if by magic.

"Jarl, trying to keep the Lady Mirza out of danger is a hopeless task," Krom said as he stepped up beside the younger man on the walls.

"Can't she see—those things out there are becoming more solid by the minute and they'll rush us," said Jarl. "I've better things to do than worry over her hurt feelings."

"I've known her since she was born. She doesn't hold a grudge—usually," Krom added an admonitory condition to his comforting words.

The sun poured from the sky, sucking the water from every puddle and adding to the humidity as a mass of unbelievable horrors became carnate before Realmgate. The demons came in many colors, all evoking sensations of discomfort when Jarl tried to look at them closely. None of the shades were normal. They hurt human eyes when they forced themselves to look at them. They called forth the basest feelings men were capable of experiencing. As soon as human minds registered their unnaturalness, they shifted into something worse. Some resembled the paintings of Hieronymus Bosch. Some were composed of portions of animals that seemed vaguely familiar. Some resembled Jarl's choicest nightmares, and others bore no likeness to anything describable. No matter what the form, sullenness and total enmity radiated from each. Wyrd grew steadily tighter until Jarl gasped, "All right. I'm alert. If you keep tightening, I'll be a one-handed fighter. My fingers are cold as it is." Wyrd relaxed in response to Jarl's complaint.

Hopping, skittering, crawling, scuttling, the nightmare attackers came at the walls. The rain of arrows from the defenders did only slight damage, and few of the demons were stopped by the barrage. Jarl moved to the ladder that descended near the south gate where the major attack massed. He drew his sword and felt the strange life that pulsed within, eager to slay. Then the first of the shapes touched the walls of Realmgate. Howls of pain and terror rose from the demons. They melted away like ice upon a warm hearth.

"Wyrd," Jarl began.

"It is the wyverns and Mirza. They have powered an ancient defense built into the walls. Mirza must have learned of it when she went back in time," Wyrd answered before Jarl had voiced his question.

The cheers of the defenders rose over the mewling caterwauling of the demon horde. Jarl knew the battle was far from over, however, for Wyrd had not loosened his firm grip on Jarl's wrist. Jarl turned to speak to his men and looked behind him for the first time. The demons who had disappeared from before the walls of Realmgate had rematerialized inside the walls, behind the row of resolute defenders.

"Don't desert your posts," Jarl cried. "Pass the word. Work in pairs." Jarl sent a messenger to inform Andronan of the latest calamity. He summoned the few reserves that remained, men he had allowed to rest. While his losses were not as great as the Shadowlord's, there had been a steady attrition as the wounded had disappeared into the university for care. Jarl felt the heavy sense of doom that hung over the battle sites. He forced himself to advance on the demons who attacked the defenders far inside the walls. They outnumbered Jarl's forces. When the next wave attacked from the outside, Jarl knew they also would breach the walls. What he needed was a new weapon. Where was he to find one? His forces stretched thinly around the walls. He didn't have an inexhaustible source of manpower, or demonpower, he thought sourly.

"Drive them over here, to the square in front of the tower," Faf mentally commanded. "They are creatures of the dark, and they can't stand against fire!"

Jarl commanded his men, "Light the torches that line the walls. Use them to drive the demons!"

Every spare man—and some that weren't—began driving the demons before Faf and Ebony. They spouted long gouts of flame which effectively dispersed the demons. Jarl and the other sweating defenders stood victorious. But they were so enervated by the heat and the humidity, they could only turn and slog grimly back to their posts on the walls of Realmgate.

"Count off by threes. Excuse every third man for a break to drink and cool off," Jarl shouted.

Jarl's command sobered the ebullient spirits of the battle-weary men who had yet to face the minions of the Shadowlord at close quarters.

"What is he likely to send against us next?" Jarl asked Krom, noticing the sun flickered, then resumed shining, but not as brightly. The day darkened much as it does before a major storm when heavy clouds cover the sun. Only now there was not a cloud in the sky. Jarl worried. How dark could it get? There was still light enough to see by, but he preferred the full light of the sun. What damage was being done to the sun by the Shadowlord's illegal gate? Jarl hadn't studied enough to know all the details, but he knew there were limits beyond which it could be fatal to steal energy from a sun.

"Otherworld science failed, as did otherworld demons.

Now he will use the creatures he has created in his laboratories."

Krom's estimate of the situation proved to be correct. The last of the demons disappeared in a red haze. In their place marched regiments of human beings.

"Are there so many renegades who would desert humanity?" Jarl asked bitterly, thinking of the men who would die at his command.

Before Krom could answer, the men on the walls began crying out, "That's my neighbor who disappeared two years ago," "There's my brother," "I see my sister's child, killed in a battle with the Dark Ones. . . ." The voices carried anger, pity, and grief. Jarl understood the Shadowlord's plan. His men would face the forms of those they knew or loved. "Don't panic, men," Jarl called. "Those who approach are only shells, the outer husks of those whom you knew. They have been reanimated by the Shadowlord's necromancy."

Mutterings greeted Jarl's announcement, but each man kept to his post.

The human forms ran the short distance to the walls and began hoisting the scaling ladders which they carried. A giant of a man hacked at the oaken gate, uttering bestial roars.

"That's Hugh, the blacksmith. He's the strongest man in King Caeryl's kingdom," a youth said with awe in his voice.

"Aye, that he was," his grizzled companion agreed.

The very wall itself reverberated to the powerful blows being rained upon it. With an earsplitting sound, the gate which had protected this section of the city for years gave way. Jarl came down from the walls and faced the blacksmith, unconscious of his rapid descent.

The sword in Jarl's hand glowed with the heat of battle. It parried the thrusts of the immense Hugh, who did not seem physically hindered by being a living dead man. Jarl's sword flashed, gashing great wounds in the pale flesh of the Shadowlord's creation, who fought on bloodlessly. All around Jarl the battle raged. In a daring move, Jarl ducked under the arms of his enemy and beheaded the one-time blacksmith. He paused a fraction of a second and almost lost his arm when the giant fought on, minus his head. Unable to see, the monster cut a wide swath with his weapon. Jarl dismembered the body piece by piece. Not until Jarl hacked the legs and arms from the torso did the body give a final twitch and melt away into an oily black spot. It exuded the foul stench of corruption. The day seemed to lighten fractionally as the evil creatures died, Jarl noted. He hoped it wasn't just wishful thinking.

Jarl led the soldiers sent by King Caeryl. Although the group was only half its original size, they burst through the gates in the walls of the city in the forefront of the group that attacked the Black Legion. The solid thud of the gates behind them reminded them there would be no turning back until the battle ended. The defenders of Realmgate had learned that dismembering the enemy brought an end to their unnatural lives. They fought the not-men who had once been their friends and loved ones grimly, with a sense of purpose. As Krom remarked to Jarl later, "Each man felt he was allowing those he fought to obtain a clean death at last, so that they might rest in peace."

The vast number of living dead dissolved before the eyes of the war-weary defenders. Only a few pockets of resistance remained, and they were widely scattered.

Jarl allowed his fingers to loosen on the hilt of his sword. He was bone tired. Looking at his men, he realized how exhausted they were. He was just about to order the gates reopened when he noticed the faint shimmer that always preceded the arrival of more of the Shadowlord's hellish allies. The sun itself paled. What now? Jarl thought to himself wearily. He watched in disbelief as characters from man's vast array of fiction began to appear on the battlefield and engage his weary men.

Over half of his men were gone. Hundreds of new allies of the Shadowlord kept appearing before him. "Faf," he called mentally. "Can you and Ebony help?"

"Sorry, Jarl. We're all flamed out from the last wave."

For the first time Jarl considered the possibility of actually losing to the Shadowlord. His sword arm ached. How could the rest of his men keep fighting? They didn't have magic swords to help them." Wyrd," he called in desperation.

"Wait, Knight."

"Knight?" Jarl clenched his teeth. Now was no time for a battlefield promotion. They were about to lose the war! Jarl hacked grimly, lopping off the limbs of the indescribable creature that faced him, hoping each stroke could be his last.

Behind him he heard the great gates of Realmgate swing open. He didn't have the time to turn around and look to see who was joining his side. There couldn't be many, that was for sure.

A huge wolf, easily three times Faf's size, had materialized on Jarl's left along with a laughing man with fire-red hair. Jarl recognized them both: Fenris the Wolf of the World's End and Loki, the Trickster, from Norse mythology. They wreaked havoc among Jarl's thinly spread troops. Jarl began to work his way toward them when two huge men passed him, running easily. Jarl did not recognize them at first. When he did, he shouted for joy. The one-handed warrior was Tyr, the legendary enemy of Fenris. The other man was Prometheus, from Greek mythology, long the friend of man as Loki had long been man's enemy.

"How did this happen?" Jarl said aloud.

"Andronan and I worked together," Wyrd hissed happily in Jarl's ears. "If the Shadowlord could bring evil creatures, why could we not summon good ones?" Jarl sensed the satisfied tones of his bracelet. He glanced at it and could have sworn it wore a smirk.

He picked up his sword to join the battle once more.

"Rest now, Dragon's Knight," Wyrd commanded. "We may have need of your talents later."

So Jarl watched the miraculous battle unfold. Arrows thunked into the carcasses of strange beasts. The Lincoln-green of the archers told him Robin Hood's band was on his side. The one-eyed Egyptian who battled another must be Horus and his legendary enemy, Set, the Egyptian god of evil. Jarl didn't see any modern characters from fiction that had come to the aid of Realm's defenders. "Need sscience to fight," hissed Wyrd. Jarl guessed the two huge men with the curly black hair and hooked noses were Gilgamesh and En-kidu from Babylonian mythology. They were superb fighters, and Jarl admired their technique. Two ogres who were even uglier than Mog struggled with a giant blue ox and another man who was even larger. Jarl recognized Paul Bunyan as the giant ax flashed, lopping limbs. Paul's laughter boomed across the battlefield.

As Jarl scanned the battlefield, Wyrd tightened. Jarl felt the cold chill of danger behind him. He swung around, sword ready to strike. The Shadowlord stood, enigmatic as ever. His hooded robe hid any humanity the Shadowlord might claim. The long-nailed fingers started to move in an intricate pattern, forming a black hieroglyph which hung in the air as if it were written on paper.

Jarl stood, mesmerized by the magic of the Shadowlord. Time slowed and the Shadowlord's actions commanded all of Jarl's attention. His muscles locked into rigidity. He strove to wield the sword, but his body was immobile. Only his mind raced, desperately searching for an answer.

A gray mist enclosed Jarl and the Shadowlord. The sun became a red ember as the Shadowlord tried to destroy Jarl.

Jarl realized he couldn't defeat the Shadowlord alone. "Wyrd!" he mindcalled.

"Strike!" Wyrd commanded in a voice loud as thunder, which blew through the strange symbols, leaving tattered rags of black. They faded even as Jarl's sword glistened and hummed its way directly through the body of the Shadow-lord. The mist disappeared abruptly and the Shadowlord himself paled and blew away on the wind.

Jarl watched dumbly, unable to believe he had defeated his enemy. He looked back at the battlefield, but he could see no trace of his adversary. It was too easy. Was the Shad-owlord destroyed? Jarl wasn't sure. Where was he? Wyrd did not respond to Jarl's repeated questioning, so Jarl as-sumed his talisman was searching for the elusive wizard. In the distance he heard the booming laughter of Paul Bunyan as his giant ax destroyed another evil creature.

This laughter seemed to be the actual turning point in the battle. The enemies of Realm were gradually winking out, recalled by the Shadowlord, who must have realized he was losing.

"Jarl!" Mirza called, running through the gate. "Come! The Shadowlord is escaping!"

Until their meeting, Jarl had seen no cowled figure on the field. He decided the Shadowlord must have retreated to Fellkeep, the nexus of his power. His birdthings were destroyed by Faf before he flamed out, but shadow magic could have enabled him to see through the eyes of any of his creatures. Mirza's knowledge resulted from wyvern magic, he was sure.

Ebony and Faf were already aloft as Mirza said, "The Shadowlord has withdrawn all his power from his creatures and allies. He is using it to force another gate at Fellkeep."

Faf swooped, clutching Jarl unceremoniously in his talons. At the same instant, Ebony snatched Mirza, who seemed better prepared for Ebony's actions. Great wings beat the air.

The two dragons rose above Realmgate and disappeared.

"There is no time to lose," Mirza mindspoke grimly into the black otherness in which they traveled. "If he forces a gate, he will escape."

Jarl felt a queasy stab of vertigo as Faf dropped from the air above Fellkeep, but Mirza warned, "Back! It's too late!"

As Faf and Ebony wheeled away and upward, a coruscating light blazed below them.

"It's the unchanneled power of the sun the Shadowlord harnessed. Help me close his gate or all of Realm perishes!"

Jarl received a psychic picture of a vast yawning maw, incandescent with raw fusion. Mirza veiled the light with a green shield that flickered insubstantially. Jarl concentrated on reinforcing her command of the shield, picturing a solid, nonpermeable substance. As his mental eyes "saw" the shield, his physical vision fixed itself on Wyrd, calling on the store of magic to which the dragon bracelet was the key. The green orbs of the dragon grew. A lambent coolness bathed the mental projection that Mirza and Jarl shared. A slight tremor passed through Jarl's body. Almost at the end of his endurance, he wondered how Mirza was able to continue. Her chalk-white face was masklike with concentration. Then when Jarl could stand the tension no longer, the linkage they shared snapped just as a solid green shield extinguished the last escaping gleams of raw force.

Mirza turned her pale face toward him. "The gate closed. It can never be reopened." Then she smiled wearily. "Look at your bracelet. All the scales have turned to gold!"

During the excitement of sealing the gate, Jarl had forgotten where he was. The tight grasp of Faf reminded him that he and Mirza were hundreds of feet in the air, firmly clutched in the talons of two dragons. The dragons had circled the scene of the action while the gate sealing took place.

"How about returning to Realmgate—if we're finished here?"

"Have you the power, my friends?" Mirza asked.

A mental snort from Ebony was the answer.

Jarl had one moment to glance down at the blasted, smoking ruins which covered the top of the cliff with rubble. Then they were otherwhere. The black nothingness was a welcome relief after the raw power they had battled. Then they were above the city. They landed gently on the clock tower of the university. A great cheer rose from the populace when they recognized Jarl and Mirza.

EPILOGUE

THE cool hall of the university, once so strange to Jarl now seemed like home. Mirza's color returned to normal as they rode the gravity well to Andronan's room.

"Hail, Dragon's Knight," Andronan and Krom intoned together as Jarl entered the room.

"We sealed the minigate the Shadowlord created, Grandfather," Mirza announced.

"That was only a minigate?" Jarl gasped.

Krom and Andronan smiled at Jarl's flash of naiveté. Mirza grasped his hand firmly and nodded.

"We owe you a great deal of thanks. You both have done a very brave thing," Krom spoke quietly.

"The Shadowlord got away," Jarl said.

"To face the unharnessed power of a gate, even with the help of Wyrd, takes courage."

"We didn't have a lot of choice." Jarl grinned, giving Mirza's hand a squeeze.

"Faf and Ebony would have taken you otherwise. Ha

you chosen, you and Mirza could have escaped Realm and left us to our fate," Andronan said as he laid an approving hand over their clasped fingers.

"What would have happened if we hadn't been able to close the gate?" Jarl asked, feeling curiosity now that he had time to think.

"The gate would have absorbed Realm, and the sun would have died," Andronan said.

"How can a sun die?" scoffed Jarl.

"We do not understand exactly, but whatever sun was powering the gate would have disappeared from its logical place in all the universes. We do not know where such suns go," Andronan told them.

"You have done well," Krom told Jarl seriously from his seat near the window. Faint sounds of revelry came through the opening, reminding Jarl of the people below.

"How are my men?"

"All who have survived are well or are being tended by the wyverns. Mirza revitalized the spring of healing during the battle. The water saved many lives. The cures it now fosters are miraculous."

Andronan looked from Jarl to Mirza. "And now it is time for your reward, Dragon's Knight," he said.

"Reward?" Jarl repeated.

"Was not your greatest wish to return home?"

"Well, yes, at one time, but—"

"Earth needs you. The Shadowlord will not rest or know satisfaction until he masters the universes. The Keepers on all planets will watch. Now that we no longer need face evil here on Realm, we will be free to train many of our young as Keepers. For now, however, we are woefully short of watchers."

"What do you have to do to be a Keeper?" Jarl asked, knowing he was going to volunteer to watch over Earth before he heard what he must do to qualify. There was no way the scientific community could counter the magic of the Shadowlord, should he decide to invade. After all, people will not fight something they don't believe in—or in this case, something they believe doesn't exist.

"You need to understand the gate system," Krom said.

Jarl nodded yes, vigorously. Part of his study time had taught him gate lore.

"And you need a partner," Andronan added slyly.

"Oh." Jarl's face fell. He didn't think Faf would leave Ebony to go with him.

"Let us go to the gate area. With three of us, we can open the gate and send you home. We will send someone—suitable." Andronan's eyes twinkled. "When we can."

The gravity well moved them down slowly, probably because all four of them were in it at the same time. Jarl wanted to stay on Realm, but he realized it would be impossible to let Earth be unprotected. How long would the Shadowlord take to recoup his losses? Where would he appear next?

The gate covered a huge, flat area behind the main tower which housed the clock. Faf and Ebony perched on the tower's crenellated edge, much like a pair of giant economy-sized lovebirds. Jarl suspected they had been mentally eavesdropping, but he didn't care. Faf was one of the reasons why he would miss Realm.

"I learned much in my adventures with you." Faf's words echoed in Jarl's head as he took the place Andronan indicated near the center of the golden star which marked the portal.

"I'll miss you," Jarl thought back. "And you, too, Ebony," he added.

"I owe you thanks," Ebony spoke in his mind. "Without your removal of that cursed necklace, Faf would still be in his cave alone."

Jarl caught a flash of Faf's horror at the thought. "Goodbye, you two," he spoke to them mentally for the last time. "Good-bye, Andronan, Krom." He bent his head toward each man briefly. Then Jarl turned to Mirza. "I'll miss you, too."

"For goodness' sake, why?"

"Well, you'll not be a very easy person to—forget," Jarl ended weakly. "You'll be here, and I'll be on Earth, and—" He stopped because Rory and the witch materialized next to Andronan.

"Hello, Grandmother," Mirza said calmly.

"I thought it was time for good-byes, so I picked up Rory—"

"Without so much as a by-your-leave, as usual," the feisty leprechaun spluttered.

"Didn't you want to come?" the old woman asked him teasingly.

Rory's face flamed another shade brighter, but he ignored her and said to Jarl, "You be careful. Don't let that bracelet get you into any trouble." Rory offered his hand to Jarl along with the advice.

"I'll be careful," Jarl promised.

The students and faculty of the university had gradually gathered. Now they called their good-byes. Jarl felt angry. They were all smiling, except for Rory, whose grin literally went from ear to ear. Probably they would be glad to see the last of him, Jarl thought sourly to himself.

"Well," he added lamely, trying to be a good sport to the end, "good-bye, Mirza."

"You don't think I'm letting you go alone, do you?" Mirza said, standing beside him, her face lit with the iridescent glow the star was beginning to cast. "Come on." She laughed, pulling him into the center of the star and through the gate.

"But—" Jarl began.

"No audience," Mirza assured him gaily.

"No audience?" Belatedly Jarl realized they stood under the old oak tree near his cabin.

She pulled down his head, snuggled close, and warned, "You'd better make this worth my while."

"Always happy to oblige you, my lady. I expect we'll

have a little peace around here to get to know one another better."

"Much better," Mirza whispered in agreement.

On Jarl's wrist the golden Wyrd relaxed his awareness of the pair and prepared to wait until he was summoned. One eye closed in a gentle wink, and his tiny gilded tongue curled into a dragon's version of a smile.